Thomas Stevens

Through Russia on a Mustang

Thomas Stevens

Through Russia on a Mustang

ISBN/EAN: 9783743422278

Manufactured in Europe, USA, Canada, Australia, Japa

Cover: Foto ©Andreas Hilbeck / pixelio.de

Manufactured and distributed by brebook publishing software (www.brebook.com)

Thomas Stevens

Through Russia on a Mustang

THROUGH RUSSIA

ON A

MUSTANG

BY

THOMAS STEVENS

AUTHOR OF "AROUND THE WORLD ON A BICYCLE," "SCOUTING FOR
STANLEY IN EAST AFRICA," ETC.

With Illustrations from Photographs by the Author

NEW YORK

CASSELL PUBLISHING COMPANY

104 & 106 FOURTH AVENUE

The story of a ride from Moscow to the Black Sea, made by the author last summer (1890) for the New York *World*, to report on the condition, manners, customs, etc., of the people of European Russia.   The ride (about 1100 English miles through the heart of Russia) was made on a " Wild America " mustang, bought from the Carver-Whitney show (like Buffalo Bill's), that happened to be exhibiting in Moscow at the time.

T. STEVENS.

PREFACE.

IN the following pages the author has endeavored to give an unbiased picture of the Russians and their country, as seen by him from the saddle, on a horseback ride of more than one thousand miles through the heart of the country, from Moscow to Sevastopol; thence up the Don and the Volga to Nijni Novgorod.

When in Moscow, preparing for the horseback journey, I was fortunate enough to enlist the enthusiasm of Sascha Kritsch, a young Russian who had just completed his studies, and was eager to distinguish himself by a noteworthy achievement in the saddle before joining the cavalry. He could speak English, and both as an interpreter and a companion I found him of much value. He accompanied me as far as Ekaterinoslav, about two thirds of the distance to the Black Sea, when the heat and fatigue of the southern steppes, together with the suspicions and vexatious interference of the police, caused him to dispose of his horse and return to Moscow by rail.

I may say that, in so far as I permitted myself the indulgence of preconceived ideas, my wish was to exploit the better, rather than the more objectionable, features of the government, and the economic and political conditions of the country. Before the ride was half finished, however, I found myself compelled to admit that matters were very bad, indeed.

The harshest feature of the many harsh sides of life in Russia, to an American, is the utter absence of constitutional rights.

Individuals have no rights in Russia. They exist in peace and breathe the air outside a prison cell solely on the sufferance of the police, whose authority over them is practically that of deputy despots in their capacity as representatives of the Czar.

When I first reached St. Petersburg, I wrote home of the agreeable impression that was made on me by seeing the Czar driving freely about the streets, with scarcely any escort. Before leaving Russia, however, I discovered that, in order to make this sort of thing possible, the Czar's Chief of Police summarily expels from the capital no less than fifteen thousand persons every year, or an average of over forty a day. Tourists and casual visitors from America and Europe see the Czar driving about in this manner, but they know nothing of the other side of the picture—of the steady streams of " suspects " and others driven from the city, three fourths of whom are probably innocent of evil intent, and so they come away with rosy and erroneous impressions, thinking they have seen Russia.

Those who have seen merely St. Petersburg and Moscow, have seen little or nothing of real Russia, nor even if they have made the grand tour across the country by rail, and up or down the Volga. These tourists have glided over the surface of Russia, their path made smooth and agreeable by the imported polish of the West; but they have not been in it.

Russia has within its vast area resources that should make its future as promising as the future of the United States. The development of the country from this time forward offers a field of profound speculation for prophetic statesmen and political seers. That a nation of 120,000,000 people, chiefly Caucasians, are to be kept in bondage forever is out of the question. Hopeless as the outlook seems at present for the masses of the Russian people, all history teaches that the day of their emancipation will, sooner or later, come. The best solution of the situation that could be hoped for, would, perhaps, be a progressive and liberal Czar, who would have sufficient courage and energy to give the country a constitutional government, a free press, and religious liberty. If this be too long delayed, and the autocracy should survive the fall of European militarism, which is inevitable, civilization will develop an "age of humanitarianism" when the American, the Englishman, the Frenchman, and the Teuton, will recognize the Russian as a brother, and see to it that he is relieved of his shackles.

THE AUTHOR.

CONTENTS.

LIST OF ILLUSTRATIONS.

THROUGH RUSSIA ON A MUSTANG.

CHAPTER I.

ST. PETERSBURG.

FOR the second time I was bound for the Land of
the Czar. But this time I was to enter it by a
different door, in a different manner, and for a different purpose. My previous entrance had been inci-
dental; this was to be special. In 1886, when on my
bicycle ride across Asia, Russian suspicion had barred
my road through Turkestan, and the Afghans had arrested me and turned me back into Persia, after I had
pierced into their forbidden country to within three
hundred miles of Quetta. So, in June of that year,
when, in order to overcome this hundred-league bar-
rier it became necessary to reach the free roads of
India by a roundabout journey of six thousand miles,
I saw something of Russia in the Caucasus and on the
shores of the Caspian Sea.

My impressions were not favorable to the Russian
rule. At the wharves of Baku, I, for the first time in
my life, had seen smart, uniformed policemen strike
people smashing blows in the face with clenched fist,
and kick them most brutally in the stomach, for what
in England or America would have called forth a mere
gruff order to " move on," or at most a threatening
push. From page 257, vol. 2, " Around the World on

a Bicycle," I quote, writing of my impressions of Baku :

" Everywhere, everywhere, hovers the shadow of the police. One seems to breathe dark suspicion and mistrust in the very air. The people in the civil walks of life all look like whipped curs. They wear the expression of people brooding over some deep sorrow. The crape of dead liberty seems to hang on every door-knob. Nobody seems capable of smiling ; one would think the shadow of some great calamity is hanging gloomily over the city. Nihilism and discontent run riot in the cities of the Caucasus ; government spies and secret police are everywhere, and the people on the streets betray their knowledge of the fact by talking little, and always in guarded tones."

Such was the impression made on the author by his first visit to Russian soil. Was this impression in any degree the result of disgust at having been humbugged by the Russian Minister, at Teheran, about permission to ride through Merve, Samarkand, and Tashkend ? That gentleman had promised me, with Oriental politeness of tongue, that " all obstacles should be removed from my road through Turkestan." With the innocence of one whose experience of Russian officialdom was yet of the future, I had believed that the tongue of a Russian diplomat, like the tongue of any other person, was given him to express his thoughts and intentions, and not to conceal them ; and so, on the strength of the promise, I rode three hundred miles across the Persian deserts, there to find that orders had been telegraphed to stop me at the frontier.

Commenting on this, a reviewer of my book in the

New York *Times*, himself a distinguished traveler, observed : "Possibly this reverse may have been still fuddling the clear spirit of our author when he reached Baku. . . . . Mr. Stevens was probably of the same way of thinking (just then) as that energetic traveler who wished that the last Russian would murder the last Turk, and be hanged for doing it."

Nearly four years, mainly devoted to travel and adventurous undertakings, had mellowed this gloomy reminiscence of the Russians, and had broadened my experience of mankind in general. Perhaps, after all, there might have been something in the book reviewer's suggestions, that I was not then in a sufficiently amiable frame of mind to do Muscovy justice.

However this may have been, such was not the case as the author stepped aboard an Atlantic liner, May 1, 1890, bound for Russia, on a special mission for the New York *World*.

For many years the people of America had taken a friendly interest in Russia. We had been, in trying times, the recipient of courtesies from its government, and our sympathies had gone out to it as a great nation of people groaning under the oppressive rule of an autocracy, which is the extreme antithesis of our own institutions. Our position in regard to its government had been peculiar. From our own point of view the Czar's government cannot appear otherwise than as a monstrous enemy to the very principles that are the life-blood of all that we hold dear and precious in the name of liberty, fraternity, and justice ; yet we have accepted courtesies at its hands as from the hands of a bosom friend. Now and then our sentiments in regard to it have been rudely shocked by revelations of a more or less revolting nature as to its methods of dealing with the people in its power. Our interest in it became painfully intensified as the Siberian revelations of Mr. Kennan were unfolded in the *Century Magazine.*

So revolting was this picture of barbarity and administrative corruption that many of our people, whose kindly remembrance of Russian courtesies influenced their prejudices and biased their better feelings in its favor, could not but receive them with a spirit of wondering skepticism.

The Russians were keenly sensitive to the criticisms of the people of America concerning them, more so than to the opinions of any other nation. A rebuke from us seemed to them like a rebuke from a friend. They are thicker-skinned in regard to England. Abuse and bias from the press and people of England, many Russians have come to regard as a foregone conclusion. They think the great dailies of England will publish eagerly anything and everything of a disreputable and abusive nature about Russia, and refuse, like the Jews in regard to Nazareth, to believe that anything good can come out of it. This is the inevitable consequence of the political tension between the two empires. But they expected from us, at least, an impartial judgment equally as to their good qualities and their imperfections. It was because they regarded America as a country with which they have ever been on the friendliest terms, that made the Russians feel apprehensive lest the Kennan articles should cause them to be wholly misunderstood, and blind us to the better side of their nature. One cannot, of course, say anything in this connection of the 119,-900,000, out of Russia's 120,000,000, who never heard of the *Century* nor Mr. Kennan, and who have as vague ideas of the world beyond the limited horizon of their village communes (mirs) as the Persian ryot in Khorassan, who once asked me if America was in London.

There was little to be learned of the true Russia in St. Petersburg. In Russia the investigator very soon discovers that he is sojourning in what may fairly be termed a dual country. There is the Russia of St. Petersburg, Moscow, the Czar, the army, politics, exiles, Siberia,—of which we read and hear from day to day,—and there is the Russia of the peasants, the villages, the country-side, "domestic Russia," of which we hear, and many of us know, next to nothing. By writing too confidently at the beginning, one may easily lay himself open to the sort of criticism bestowed on the English tourist, who rides in a parlor-car from New York to San Francisco and then goes home and writes a book about America.

Though St. Petersburg is deceptive as a glimpse of Russia, it is an Imperial city, magnificent as to churches and public edifices, statuary and monuments, and interesting in the life that ebbs and flows in its streets. St. Petersburg is the rouge and enamel that the sallow, ill-looking tragedienne of the mediæval part that Russia is playing in the drama of nations, wears, beautifying herself, and coquetting successfully with many who see her and fancy she is Russia. St. Petersburg itself is charming.

I sat for an hour one day in the window of a café

on the famous Nevski Prospekt. It was four o'clock in the afternoon, and a fine, sunny day. All the Russian world and his wife seemed to be driving, walking, hurrying, idling past the window on this Broadway of the Russian capital.

The most numerous passers-by, and to the new-comer the most Russian and interesting, were the drosky-drivers, the isvoshchics and their "fares." Like Washington, St. Petersburg is a city of magnificent distances. Everybody rides; fares are cheap; and there are twenty-five thousand public drosky-drivers in the city plying for hire.

The isvoshchic and his costume are peculiarly Russian. The latter has not changed for ages, and apart from youth and age, whiskers and no whiskers, there is not the splitting of a hair between any of the five-and-twenty thousand public "kebbies" in the Czar's capital. There are isvoshchics at fourteen, young in face but old in iniquity, and isvoshchics of seventy-five, bearded like pards and supremely artful, in bargaining with the foreigner about the price of a drive.

The summer costume of the isvoshchic is an ideal garb for winter from the point of view of anybody but a Russian. He is enveloped in an enormous overcoat of heavy dark-blue cloth that descends to his heels and is gathered about his waist by a gay-colored band. Top boots, heavy and prodigal of leather, incase his feet and legs; and even on this warm June day a dis-arrangement of the big blue over-garment revealed a sheepskin coat, of similar dimensions, underneath.

But the crowning glory of the drosky-driver is his

hat. Imagine a " stove-pipe " hat, six inches tall, with a very rakish brim and a very expansive crown, something like the hats of the ancient and honorable beef-eaters at the Tower of London, and you see any one of the 30,000 coachmen's hats of St. Petersburg. I say 30,000, because there are, beside the public isvoshchics, about five thousand private coachies, similarly dressed.

The only difference between the public and private isvoshchics is that the latter look about three times larger than the former. All the private isvoshchics are men of Falstaffian girth. Some are of a truly startling circumference ; their stomachs bulging out like barrels, and the breadth of their figure more than fills the seat of the drosky. The thinness of the face often contrasts ludicrously with the vast proportions of the body, for the amplitude of the latter is not flesh but padding. The impression that the private coachman desires to make upon the world at large is that he is the " well-fed servant of a generous man." To this end, huge pads, like pillows, are fastened about the body, and over them is wrapped the all-concealing overcoat. To complete the deception, the colored waistband pinches into the padding, as if the chief concern of the owner of this vast wealth of fat were to reduce his girth, if such an impossible thing were possible.

Whilst every private isvoshchic in Russia is thus a living lie in his figure, every public one is likewise a perambulating Ananias in a way that more directly concerns the pockets of the public. Every drive you take in St. Petersburg has to be bargained for in advance. The rates are cheaper than in any other European capital, being only fifty kopecks, or about thirty cents an hour. The St. Petersburg isvoshchic is known as the most reasonable of the fraternity in Russia ; he rarely demands more than three times his proper fare, and as a general thing not even twice as much as he is willing to accept.

He is good-natured and remarkably patient about finding an address. He is polite—of the Orient, Oriental. He rarely gives you a decided negative if he doesn't wish to drive where you desire to go, but takes refuge in his horse, telling you that it is weary, lazy, or ailing, and does not want to work.

The isvoshchic is superstitious and fearful. Every little way, as he drives you along, he passes an ikon or shrine, at each of which he removes his abbreviated cylinder and crosses himself at the forehead, mouth and breast. His fear is centered on the Chief of Police of St. Petersburg. The isvoshchic is rarely obstreperous, but if he is, "I'll tell Gresser" (or whoever happens to be chief), brings matters to a speedy conclusion by immediately reducing him to a humble and apprehensive frame of mind.

His horse is small and his vehicle little larger than the old-fashioned invalid chairs one sometimes meets, with gouty old gentlemen in them, in the parks at home.

A peculiarity of the "fares," if a lady and gentleman, is that the latter usually has his arm about his companion's waist. The Russian explanation is that without this precaution the lady might tumble out. The levity and penetration of the American mind,

however, refuses to accept this practical view of the
matter in all cases. And there certainly passed by the
café window many a couple who, oblivious of the public
eye, betrayed a decidedly sentimental interpretation of
the relations between waist and arm. So prevalent is
this custom that an exception excites attention.

About five per cent. of the ladies, old or young, who
passed by the café window were victims of the tooth-
ache and had a swollen and bandaged jaw. Tooth-
ache is the commonest malady of the St. Petersburg
fair sex. The St. Petersburg girl of the period stays
up late, lies abed till noon, takes no exercise, and lives
on sweets and pickles. Her punishment is the tooth-
ache, dentist's bills, a toothless old age, and a very bad
complexion. Good teeth are rare with city ladies, and
a fresh complexion is seldom seen on the streets.

Half the men who passed were in uniform and, warm
as it was, like the isvoshchics, wore big overcoats.
The wearing of overcoats in summer is a Russian
peculiarity. One of our popular impressions of the
Russian is that he can stand more cold than a polar
bear. Such, however, is not the case, at all events with
the city Russian. An American or European who
visits St. Petersburg or Moscow in the winter can stand
the cold better than a resident. He can stand it out-
doors with thinner clothes on, and is altogether less
sensitive to the nose-nipping Russian frost. The Russian ·becomes a polar bear in winter, not because he
can stand the cold, but because he cannot.

All the people in military uniforms who passed by,
however, were not soldiers. You see little shavers of
ten or twelve years old trudging along in military over-

coat and trappings.   These are young students, who are required to wear uniforms, conspicuous colors and trimmings for the different schools for purposes of identification.   The newsboys also wear uniforms.

A troop of Cossacks passed by, all big, fine fellows, belonging to one of the crack regiments, all riding splendid black stallions, sixteen hands high, spirited and glossy.

A private carriage, an English-built brougham, with a magnificent team, and gold-laced lackeys on the box, dashed by.   It belonged to one of the legations, and lolling in the seat, in a studiedly negligent attitude, was Madame, the Ambassador's wife, alone in her glory, *en route* to the Islands—Vasili Ostrof—for her regular evening drive.

A string of twelve droskies filed past, each one containing a big Russian greyhound and a keeper in a red shirt.   They belonged to some sporting nobleman, and were bound for the railway station to be taken somewhere out in the country to an estate for a day's coursing for hares.

A man in a suit of white coarse canvas, and with a brand on the back, tramped along between two policemen with drawn swords.   He was a prisoner.   His face was pale, showing that he had been in confinement some time.   Otherwise, he looked no different from his keepers, with whom he chatted freely as they walked past.

An aged couple tried to halt a tram, which, like the street car of London, carried passengers both inside and on the roof.   The conductor shook them a negative.   His car was carrying the number permitted by law, and no such confusion and overcrowding are allowed as in New York. Another one came along. The old couple tried it again and were again refused. Finally they hailed a passing isvoshchic, and, bargaining with him awhile, drove off.

An economical party of four from the country drove past, all piled in one small drosky, two women sitting in two men's laps. Workmen strolled along, nine out of ten in top boots and red shirts. The red shirts were outside the trousers. A waistcoat was worn, but no coat, and the trousers were slouchily tucked inside the boots. Mingled with the throng were moujiks from the country, visiting " Pater-boorg," perhaps, for the first time in their lives. They wore dirty sheepskin coats, shockingly bad caps, home-made foot-gear of the rudest pattern and material, and their shock heads seemed to have been trimmed for the visit to the city by placing a bowl on the top, upside down, and clipping around it. They looked like savages—as incongruous and out of place on the Nevski as Indians would on Fifth Avenue, New York.

Nurse-maids from Finland, or from Little Russia, rode by in the family carriage with their charges. They wore a wonderful dress of gorgeous colors and gold embroidery, and a sort of beaded brass, silver or gold crown on the head.

Young lady students passed in little troops or alone, carrying portfolios bearing the word " Musique." Music was the fad of the day in St. Petersburg. All the young ladies were raving over "musique." Next season the craze would be—who can say? I was told that one of the latest fads with them was the study of midwifery. Everything in the student life, especially the girl student life, is faddy and eccentric. It is the spasmodic attempt of the intellectual Russian youth to find some employment, some scope for their energy and ambition, in a field where there is next to no intellectual employment at all.

A small crowd was gathering on the street corner, as I left my window in the café. The Czar was coming in from Peterhoff and would drive this way. I did not wait, for I had seen him and the Empress before. The Emperor and Empress were almost as much in evidence as the President in Washington. When the Czar and the Italian heir-apparent, who was visiting St. Petersburg, drove down the Nevski, it was down a lane through the assembled and applauding populace, on which scarcely a soldier or a policeman was to be seen. The people were under less restraint than a New York crowd is at any popular gathering.

All this impressed me, a new arrival, with a sense of agreeable surprise.·

Yes; St. Petersburg, consummate actress and gay deceiver that she is, was bewitching, disporting herself, arrayed in the focused glories of an empire, to the admiration of an audience of pleasure-seeking tourists from everywhere. The pageantry of the Czar's capital was ever on the move across the stage. To-day the christening and launching of an ironclad; to-morrow a priestly procession along the Nevski, a glittering cavalcade of monks in golden vestments, in honor of the Emperor's name-day; the next day, a military review.

One day I resolved to leave this pomp and Imperial

greatness, and experience the contrast of a sudden change from the Elysian glories of Peterhoff to the huts of a typical village seventy miles away. Peterhoff is an Imperial summer residence on the gulf of Finland ; grounds peopled with gilded statuary, amid a magnificent system of fountains.

Mr. Steveni of the London *Daily Chronicle*, a resident correspondent, went with me to Tchudovo.

Tchudovo is about one hundred versts (seventy miles) from St. Petersburg, in the direction of Moscow, a village in the district government of Novgorod. A Russian village is in appearance the counterpart of many small towns in the Western States. The first impression of the writer, who knows the West very well, was that he had stumbled into one of those slowly decaying backwood villages in Missouri or Illinois that have fallen out of joint and behind the times because the railway didn't come through their section of the country. Tchudovo is situated in a country as level and dreary as the dreariest part of any of the prairie States. The land belonging to the village was a big clearing in a level forest country that presented to the eye no single point of interest beyond the people and their mode of life. The village was like all Russian villages, except that many of the houses were two-storied. It consisted of two rows of houses, between which ran Peter the Great's broad military road to Novgorod. A few of the houses were of brick, but most were of wood. Here as everywhere, though the uniformity of architecture was striking, evidences of wealth and poverty came within the orbit of a glance. Some of the houses were fairly toppling about their occupant's heads, and in no country of the world (and I had been in twenty-four), had I seen people so wretchedly lodged as part of the population of Tchudovo. Many, however, were good, comfortable board or log houses, comparable to the houses of eighty-acre farmers in the West. Half the houses might, perhaps, come under this description; one fourth of them would be considered by us as wholly unfit for human habitation, and the remainder were superior dwellings, from the American farmer's standpoint, including one which might fairly be termed a mansion.

There was a bakery, in front of which, on a rude bench, a row of huge rye loaves were exposed for sale. There were three or four general stores, the counterparts of the American corner grocery, and as many vodka and mead and kwass shops. There was the inevitable village smithy and a school; towering over all was a large white church, surmounted by four blue domes and a blue spire. Both church and mansion were of Græco-Corinthian architecture, a fact that led one to suspect that the founder of the church and the former occupant of the mansion, before the emancipation of the serfs in 1861, was the nobleman who owned the land and peasantry of the district.

We made our way to the blacksmith shop, here, as in the West, often the gossiping place of the village, and entered into conversation with the blacksmith, a man of fifty, his son and assistant, a young man of twenty-five, and a ragged moujik, all of whom took off their hats as we entered and sat down. As many of my readers already know, the Russian villages are communes of peasants who own their land in common.   Except for the disturbing influences of insolvent peasants who have recklessly got over their heads in debt, or from other causes, have become landless, the Russian village commune or mir is a collection of families and kinsfolk who own the right of tillage each to a certain portion of their common land.   This is the ideal mir. But with the mir as with everything else, in Russia as elsewhere, the real and the ideal seldom agree.

The mir of Tchudovo, the blacksmith said, contained 2000 people, of which something over 500 were " souls," that is to say, sharers in the land.   The rest were the children, small shopkeepers and vodka-sellers, the " pope " or priest, the grain merchant who lived in the mansion of the former nobleman, and landless " batraks," who worked for wages at anything they could find to do.   The blacksmith's son was the most intelligent of the three.   We asked him about the mir and the various things that make up the sum and substance of the Russian peasant's life.   The people of Tchudovo, he said, had been wiser than many of their neighbors.   The mirs had a right to borrow money from the banks or from private capitalists, giving the land as security.   Many had done this, and by pledging themselves to ruinous terms were in sorry straits, having hard work to keep their heads above water and pay their taxes.

" We have had better sense, though," said he, smiling with the peculiar grin of a simple rustic soul who is not to be easily taken in, " and have never borrowed money, and so our mir is very well off."

" If your mir is well off, why, then, are there so many

batraks (men without land who work for wages) here?"

" Men and mirs are very much alike," he returned; " some are wise and some foolish. Most men become batraks because they have foolishly borrowed money, and, being unable to repay, their horses and cows have been sold, and they have lost their power to cultivate any of the mir's land. Every member of the mir has the right to work a share of the land for the support of his family and the payment of his taxes, a large or small portion according to the number of persons capable of field-work and tax-payment in the family; but with the loss of his horses and the means of working land he is no longer a moujik, but a batrak, a man who would starve but for charity or work given him by others."

" What is the hardest thing about the way you are governed?"

" The taxes," sang out our hearers in one voice, and the countenances of all lit up, and tongues wagged volubly in eager rivalry to tell their tale of woe.

" So the government taxes you pretty heavily, does it?"

" No, no; the government gets but very little of it. If the government knew all that happens to the moujik, it would pity him. The government taxes the mir and the mir taxes the individual. The elders collect the taxes and go off to Novgorod and drink vodka and eat caviar with the Novgorod officials, then come back and demand more taxes. It would be much better for us all if the Czar could sweep away everybody that stands between the Imperial Government and the people, and have no elders, no officers of any kind. The more officials who have the handling of our taxes and the management of our affairs, the worse for us."

"But the mir has the election of its own officers. If the present starosta (mayor) and the elders are dishonest and grasping, why don't you elect honest men, like the blacksmith there, in their places?"

"The blacksmith doesn't know how to read and write," they laughed; "how could he be starosta? We have tried to remedy matters, but the educated people are too sharp for us; they always manage to keep in office whomever they choose, and the wisest moujik keeps his mouth shut closest. The elders assess each one of us the amount of taxes he has to pay, the amount of work to be done on the roads without pay, and have the regulation of everything in the mir. If I am their friend, they take care that my share of the taxes shall be light and my work on the roads easy, and when the Czar demands soldiers they will pass by my son and pick out the son of a moujik who has made himself objectionable to them by grumbling at them and voting against them at the elections. There are moujiks in the mir who pay next to no taxes at all, and moujiks who have to work away from home like batraks, besides tilling their land, to get money enough to pay their taxes. It is the same in nearly every mir. If every man had a good heart the mirs would be happy and prosperous, the moujiks well fed and clad, and our taxes would be light and easily paid. But every mir is a house of intrigue, in which the moujik is, in one way or another, cheated out of most of his earnings."

" Then you have nothing to complain of about the St. Petersburg government ? "

The group in the smithy had increased by this time to a half-dozen. The eagerness and intelligence which they all displayed in discussing their own affairs, in striking contrast to their ignorance of the outer world, was something remarkable. It was easy to imagine that if these peasants were only decently educated they would be a different people. They are born village politicians. Their faces were animated and bright, and from their eyes shone a light which was the lamp of an uncultured intelligence, which enabled them to understand, if not to remedy, their grievances. They were extremely good-natured about it all, however. A reform that they were looking forward to, and expecting great things of, was a distinct reactionary move in the direction of local autocracy. The periodical peasant courts were to be done away with, they said, and in their stead were to be individual officers, a species of cadi, appointed from St. Petersburg. The fact that they preferred to have their cases tried by a single judge, rather than in an organized court, was a significant straw showing the bent of the uncultured Rússian mind.

All the lesser cases among the Russian peasantry, both civil and criminal, are decided by the mir on the basis of custom and common sense, though it is very certain that the justice meted out by the elders and starostas of the mirs is, like the collection of the taxes, too often a warped and unjust thing, manipulated by the intriguers and wire-pullers of the commune. It was plainly evident that the group of poor ragamuffin moujiks in the blacksmith shop of Tchudovo would prefer to place all their affairs in the hands of one reasonably honest stranger than to submit them to even their own rural assembly. Yet theirs was a comparatively prosperous community. They stated with pride that their mir was free from debt, and with still greater pride they pointed to their church and told us that it was richer than even the churches in Novgorod.

"No," they replied, to our last question. "St. Petersburg doesn't bother us much. The Czar takes only five young men each year for soldiers. They have to be twenty-one years of age, and they are chosen by the starosta and elders of the mir."

They then went on, in reply to other questions, to talk about the Czar. The Czar Alexander III, they said, was a good man, who introduced many reforms (the peasants use a number of English words, such as reform, bank, per cent.), and if some of them didn't work very well for the moujik it was not his fault, but the fault of the local officials, or circumstances over which he had no control. They spoke affectionately of the late Emperor Alexander II, who, they said, freed "the Christians." The Russian peasants never called themselves serfs, but Christians, and so consider themselves. The term as applied to them originated with the Mongols, of Ghengis Khan. When the Mongols conquered and enslaved them, they called them Christians as a term of contempt. The moujiks accepted the appellation as a compliment and an honor, and have stuck to it ever since. To the moujik everything Russian is sacred. Russia is Holy Russia, the Czar is God's elected, the Russian army is the Orthodox army, the Church the Orthodox and only true church, and the Russians are Christians, as distinct from foreigners, who are heretics.

We asked them about America. They had heard of it, but knew nothing about where it was. They asked if it was a good country to live in.

"In America," I replied, "every man is his own Czar, and nobody has to be a soldier unless he wants to."

"That may be good for America," they said, shaking their shock heads, "but not for us. For us, our Czar is much better."

"Here you have to work for five rubles a month," I pursued; "in America a workman earns as much in one day. Why don't you go to America, like the Germans?"

"It is true that we work hard and get small pay, but it is better to remain in Russia and be poor than to live elsewhere and grow rich. It is all very well for the Germans, but we like Mother Russia best of all."

How devoted they seemed, these rag-bedecked. soft-spoken, polite peasants—how loyal to Mother Russia and the Czar! The only grievances you could wring from them by questioning on all points was against their own local and nominally self-elected officials.

We passed the night in the house of a moujik, who, from the peasant's standpoint, would be neither rich nor poor. His house was leaning sadly to one side and the back wall of it had disappeared, leaving the rear rooms exposed; but he owned a horse and rattletrap telega and cultivated land for two souls,—himself and wife,—and was assessed taxes proportionately. His taxes amounted to about fifteen rubles a year and whatever share of public work the assembly of the mir assessed him. When all the family were at home they numbered nine persons. The good wife prided herself immensely on having been a domestic in the family of "noble-born" people before her marriage. She and her husband; their eldest daughter and her husband; the mother, an ancient dame; two sons; a younger daughter, and a two-year-old embryo moujik, who took a tremendous fancy to the author, owing to the bestowal of a lump of sugar on our first acquaintance, all occupied two stuffy little rooms up-stairs.

The greater part of the space was taken up by a monster tiled stove, on the top of which, our hostess informed us, the entire family slept in the winter. It was difficult to see how so many people could manage it, unless some of them slept two deep; but the woman said there was plenty of room. The chief room was about ten feet square. In it was a bed, an old lounge, a table, three chairs, a chest of drawers, two large brass samovars, four ikons or holy pictures, before one of which was a cup with oil and taper. The ikons are heirlooms in the families of the Russian peasantry, as also are the samovars. These are the most precious of the moujiks' household gods. There is a saying among them, "If your house is on fire, save the ikon and samovar first, then the children." More children will come, they say, but if the ikon and the samovar are lost, the saints will be angry about the ikon, and a samovar costs many rubles.

The household cradle was a curiosity. The roof of

the room was low. A ring and staple were in the center. Through the ring was thrust a pole. At one end was suspended a cage-like cot for the baby, and the other end was above the mother's pillow. By reaching up and working the lever, the latest arrival in his cot could be danced up and down, or swung about, pendulum-fashion, by his mother.

CHAPTER II.

TCHUDOVO AND THE PRISTAV.

THE day was a holiday in Tchudovo.

We were seated on a rude bench, talking to the starosta, on the afternoon of May 28. Although it was neither saint's day nor Sunday, the peasants were arrayed in every bit of cheap finery they possessed.

The holiday was special. Sotniac Paishkoff, centurion, or captain, of 100 Cossacks, started May 7, 1889, on one of the most remarkable horseback rides that had ever been made. The greatest feat of this kind heretofore known to the Russians was that of a military officer a few years before, from Moscow to Paris, on which ride, however, two horses were used. Paishkoff's ride was from Albazinski, a station of the Cossacks of the Amoor, a day's ride from the Pacific coast at the mouth of the Amoor, to St. Petersburg. The distance is over seven thousand versts, or about five thousand miles, and the trip was made on one horse.

Orders had therefore been sent from St. Petersburg, during the latter part of Paishkoff's journey, to have every attention shown him, and police escort provided from day to day. A small convoy of Cossacks, from the "Czarevitch's Own" Cossack regiment, were dispatched to Novgorod to escort him in to St. Petersburg, a four days' ride, and a whole regiment was to meet him outside the capital. He was to be promoted and receive an order and a pension.

Paishkoff was expected to pass through Tchudovo that evening. The street was gay with colors, in which the red shirts of the moujiks predominated. A red calico shirt, black velvet trousers, and knee-boots, constitute the moujik's ideal costume. The whole population of the village was streaming leisurely in one direction. Fifty or more small boys were marshaled in a troop and, under the direction of the school-master, marched in very good step, singing lustily as they tramped, after the manner of Russian soldiers.

A deputation of old men came up where we were sitting and proposed to the starosta that, for the honor of the mir, he should proceed along the road at the head of the people to meet and welcome Paishkoff.

" Nay, nay, brothers," demurred the starosta, " when the Cossack comes I will have the samovar ready with tea ; but from Novgorod is a long ride, and perhaps he will not arrive before morning."

The starosta was right in his surmises. The Cossack rider didn't appear that evening. We passed the night in the moujik's house, and early next morning hired our host to drive us out on the Novgorod road to meet him.

We met the popular hero a few miles out, and, turning, kept pace with him back to Tchudovo. With him were the escort from the Czarevitch's regiment, an infantry officer from Vladimir, a rural mounted policeman, and a couple of Russian newspaper correspondents.

Paishkoff turned out to be a small, wiry man, twenty-

ROADSIDE VODKA-SHOP.

seven years old, with a pleasant face of almost mahog-
any darkness from the long exposure to the dry, wintry
winds of Siberia. He wore the Cossack lamb's-wool
hat, leather jacket and trousers, with a broad yellow
stripe down the latter, and heavy jack-boots. He was
armed with a British bull-dog revolver and a small
sword.

His horse was a big-barreled, stocky gray pony,
about fourteen hands high, the exact counterpart of
horses one sees by the score in the broncho herds
of Wyoming and Colorado. He was well chosen
for his task. He was all barrel, hams, and shoulders. His neck and head seemed scarcely to be
parts of the same horse. His pace was a fast, ambling
walk that carried him over the ground at five miles an
hour and left the big chargers of the Czarevitch's Cossacks far to the rear. The escort had to trot occa_
sionally to catch up. The gallant little gray was as
sleek and well-conditioned as if he had just come out
of a clover pasture.

Paishkoff raised his cap in reply to our salutation, and
when my companion said that I was from America,
lifted it again. "We belong almost to the same part
of the world," said he, smilingly, "only the sea is
between us. We have both traveled a long way, you
by ship and train, I on horseback." The Cossack
officer, though pleasant, was inclined to be rather taci-
turn, and we talked more with the newspaper men
than with him, calling upon him occasionally for con-
firmation. One of the reporters was Sergie Riskin,
from the Moscow *Listok ;* the other was the Novgorod
correspondent of the St. Petersburg *Novosti.* The

latter gentleman handed me a card, on which his name and profession were set forth modestly as follows:

"Neil Ivanovitch Bogdanoffsky, correspondent Northern Telegraph Agency, of the gazette *Novosti*, and of the Society of Russian Dramatic Authors and Operatic Composers, Novgorod. Own house and own horse."

The last item of Mr. Bogdanoffsky's identity meant that he lived in his own house and rode his own horse; that is to say, he was a free-lance as distinct from Mr. Sergie Riskin and kindred members of the profession, who are employees at a few rubles a month and a house to live in, and who, when called upon to undertake a horseback journey, have to ride a hired animal or one belonging to the newspaper.

Mr. Riskin did most of the talking. Alluding to the Cossack's taciturnity: "Paishkoff is a man of deeds," said he, "rather than words. He is small in stature, yet bigger than all the Cossacks of his escort put together."

Riskin had accompanied the Cossack from Nijni-Novgorod, sending daily reports of his progress to the *Listok*. Whether a man of deeds himself, he was most decidedly a man of words. He was jolly, yet in despair. His paper, he said, had given him 1500 rubles to cover expenses from Nijni-Novgorod to St. Petersburg, and, "posheevnoi!" he had but eighty left. All the money had gone drinking vodka and having good times with police officers and others along the route; and now what would he be able to do at St. Petersburg, where, for the honor and glory of his paper, he was expected to drive out in grand style to meet

Paishkoff as he neared the end of his ride, and make a lavish display of the *Listok's* wealth and enthusiasm?

Sergie rattled on, pausing very reluctantly and only for an instant now and then, to enable my companion and interpreter to ask a question. His nervous tension, and his effort to talk faster than the movements of his lips could frame his words and sentences, was almost painful. Paishkoff, he informed us, was a remarkable man in many ways. While he, his comrade of the *Novosti*, and almost everybody else he had ever met, drank vodka, the Cossack officer refused to drink anything stronger than kwass, a kind of weak beer made from rye bread.

"At Novgorod," said Mr. Riskin, "there was a grand service of prayer before a celebrated ikon in honor of Paishkoff's safe arrival, and after the prayers came a jollification, when the officers, the priests, and all of us got drunk and happy—all but Paishkoff. Paishkoff would drink nothing but kwass and tea; he's a wonderful man. He eats what he likes, just like other people. He wears undergarments of mineral wool; over that a linen shirt, which he gets washed every two weeks. During the winter he wore a cholera-belt to protect his stomach from the cold, and over all a leathern suit. He rises at five in the morning, pops a lump of sugar in his mouth, and drinks tea with lemon in it before starting.

"A few days after starting he was caught in a blizzard and got lost. He was nearly frozen to death, and would never have pulled through but for his horse's intelligence. He gave his horse the rein, and although it was pitch dark and the air full of blinding snow, the animal found his way back to the last station. He rode alone as far as Tomsk, from which point he has been assisted by the police. His only sickness has been a touch of influenza. He had experienced forty degrees of frost (about fifty degrees below zero, Fahr.) but thinks winter the best time to travel in Siberia; the roads are then hard and good, and the cold stimulates the horse to travel. He has met with no adventures beyond the blizzard. Wolves?—he hasn't seen a wolf, and he has never fired his revolver. He has promised to give me his notes and I'm going to write a book about his journey."

We turned from the versatile representative of the Moscow *Listok* to the hero of the ride. "Sotniac," said my companion, "Mr. Stevens wants to send word about you to America. Tell us the motive of your great journey. Is it to decide a bet?"

"No, no," replied Paishkoff, "only an Englishman or an American would do such a thing for a bet. My object is to prove the great powers of endurance possessed by the horses of the Amoor."

"How much will you take for your horse when you get to St. Petersburg?"

"Money again," returned the Cossack, reproachfully; "it would be a sin to exchange this horse for money, after what he has done. All the money in America wouldn't induce me to sell him. He will be taken great care of for the rest of his life—pensioned off."

"And you?—you, too, will be pensioned, I suppose."

"We shall know better about that at St. Petersburg."

As we neared Tchudovo, the whole population of the commune was assembled at the entrance to the broad, long street. A beggar rushed up to the Cossack's horse and flung himself on the ground before it, as if begging its rider to trample him under its hoofs. Paishkoff tossed him a coin without halting, and the pony swerved meekly to avoid stepping on the man.

The women crossed themselves and the men and boys removed their hats. The old moujiks·gave the cue and three hearty cheers went up for the bold "Kazak" as he rode past. He acknowledged the honor by holding his hand to his forehead. The eyes of the Cossack escort from the Czarevitch's regiment roamed wolfishly over the picturesque gathering of village damsels, turning in their saddles to prolong their scrutiny as the crowd followed behind. The school-master and his brigade of small urchins tramped solidly in ranks, four deep, singing noisily.

The starosta, true to his idea of remaining at his post and extending the hospitality of his samovar, invited Paishkoff and his escort to dismount at his house. They refused to halt, however, and the officer of the Cossacks paid him scant courtesy, as though rebuking him for not coming out to welcome them as the others had done.

The reporters sent word to their newspapers that an American had met Paishkoff and offered him 30,000 rubles for his pony, for the purpose of taking it to America to exhibit! That truthful item went all over Russia.

Before leaving Tchudovo, we made the acquaintance of the pristav, or chief of police, of the district. The pristav invited us to spend the evening at his house. Vodka, raw salt fish, salted cucumbers, cheese, tea, and cigarettes were provided by our host, who turned out to be a man of considerable education and of no mean order of intelligence. He had been a school-master, manager of an estate, principal of a reformatory for boys, and was now chief of police of a district about forty miles square, containing a population of 50,000 people. .I had, of course, designs on the pristav's knowledge of his country and its institutions, and led the conversation into that channel. He was a genial and communicative soul; a thorough Russian in that absence of reserve, when the hand of good fellowship had been given, that is one of the national traits. A Russian police officer is compelled, *nolens volens*, to suspect the stranger on principle; but approach him genially, drink tea or vodka with him, the social heart that beats universal in the Russian breast is touched, and he is yours, believing in you, confiding in you for the time, though he may grow suspicious again after you are gone.

In talking of international politics, the pristav of Tchudovo was as epigrammatic as interesting.

"The only enemy we have," said he, "is Germany. Austria is an ingrate. Several times have we stepped into the breach and saved her; and our reward is that she arrays herself against us. England doesn't understand us, and so she hates us. The Hebrew is our greatest economic question. The countries of the future are America and Russia. Our people have more good qualities than bad. Our faults are great, but our virtues are greater. Our prisons are good, and will, in time, be better than the prisons of any country in the world."

These were some of the poignant shots directed at the writer by the pristav, in reply to questions. Like all Russians whom I afterward met, he was enthusiastic and loyal to his country.

"People at a distance," said he, "remember our faults and forget our virtues. We have plenty of both. Our intentions are good, but our methods are faulty. As a people we have no talent for detail, and for that reason our administration is defective. We are the kindest-hearted people in the world, but a Russian is too easily contented with things as they are. We are not thrifty like the French, nor economical and plodding like the Germans, nor progressive and energetic like the Americans. You will see, if you travel through Russia, colonies of Germans scattered here and there, and you will be astonished at the contrast between them and our own people. The Russian peasant will be living in a tumble-down house, and his daily fare will be black bread and cabbage soup. The Germans will be better fed, better housed, better clothed, their fences will be neat, their gardens will be full of vegetables, and they will be rapidly growing rich. You would think that the Russian moujik would envy his prosperous neighbor and follow his example, but he seldom does. He even considers himself superior, and laughs in a good-natured way, saying, with pride, as he thinks of his hard fare, 'What is death to the foreigner is life to the Russian.' With plenty of rich land in his back yard, he doesn't even take the trouble to grow vegetables, as you have seen for yourself in

Tchudovo.   You may admire the German colonist and call him wise, but the moujik would win your heart for his good nature and generous impulses.   If you were to fall into the river the German would think twice before jumping in after you ; but the Russian wouldn't even stop to consider whether he knew how to swim before plunging in."

I felt very much like summing up all that the pristav had said about the moujik, except his generosity, in the one cynical comment "laziness," yet that same morning I had seen laborers at work at 2.30, and had been assured that in the summer season, the "white nights," when you can see to read a newspaper in the streets of St. Petersburg at midnight, the moujik is astir twenty hours out of the twenty-four.

On the subject of official Russia the pristav was on his own ground, and spoke at length.   He referred to himself as an unit of the system.   In him and his position, he said, we had before us a fair sample of the entire official system of Russia.   He was Chief of Police over a district as large as two American counties, and was held responsible for the acts of 50,000 people. Half the time he was on horseback or in a troika, and he had been without sleep for three nights at a stretch. He had more than a thousand documents pigeon-holed in his office that needed his attention, yet the authorities at St. Petersburg thought nothing of taking up his time in the most trivial things.   With hundreds of important grievances, criminal cases, and what not on hand, one half of which he would not be able to attend to if he never slept nor rested, he had just received orders from St. Petersburg to personally superintend the safe conduct of the Cossack rider, Paishkoff, through his district. For two days his precious time had been taken up riding ahead of Paishkoff, from village to village, arranging for his food, even cooking it himself, and seeing that everything was done for his comfort. Such things as these were more important in the eyes of some one in St. Petersburg than the affairs of his district, and it would be as much as the pristav's official head was worth to neglect them.

While he believed paternal government was the best for the Russians, he cited his own case as an instance of its faults. The people of his district came to him like children to a father, and for a father to listen to the grievances and adjust the differences of 50,000 children was a physical impossibility. They came to him about everything. The peasants are required by law to insure their houses. If a peasant neglected or refused to do this the starosta of the mir would send him a complaint. If there was trouble about the taxes it was the same. Forest fires were a stock nuisance that kept him riding like a Cossack from one part of the district to another.

Murders were one of the common crimes among the moujiks. These he had to investigate and report on. Domestic troubles were common. The young men, who married at eighteen or nineteen, would be taken away for soldiers at twenty-one. The young grass-widows left behind would behave scandalously, and the parents of the absent husbands would complain to him, expecting him to set matters right by putting them in prison. Ten men couldn't do the work he had to and attend to it properly, yet his salary was but seventy rubles a month.

The pristav scouted the idea that Russian officers were naturally any more dishonest than others. The trouble with most of them is, he said, that their salaries are simply not sufficient to keep them from starving. They are obliged to take bribes in order to live. Yet if they are found out, they are punished and disgraced. Of all the overworked and underpaid people in the world, the pristav thought, Russian officials walked off with the honors. It was the same in every district in the empire—thousands of cases pigeon-holed because there were not officers enough to dispose of them.

We spoke of prisons and Siberia. The pristav had never heard of Mr. Kennan or the *Century Magazine.* This was not surprising, as his information of the outer world was all obtained through the medium of the Russian press. Yet it seemed curious in a man of exceptional intelligence and good education, living but seventy miles from St. Petersburg. During the past year five people had been exiled to Siberia from his district. That was about the average number per annum. All of them were either criminals or rogues, sent away by the mirs for persistent worthlessness. Not one was a " political."

About the prisons in Siberia the pristav didn't know. He had never been there, he said, and so could not speak from personal knowledge. He had heard that some of them were not in good order. But the prisons of European Russia he knew, having been pristav in two districts and visited many others. He begged me to believe nothing that I might hear in condemnation of the Russian prisons proper, for he knew them to be as good as the prisons of any country in Europe. The authorities were continually devising ways and means of improving prisons and the treatment of prisoners, and he would be glad to show me the prisons in his district any time I wished to see them.

The next day I met him at the railway station, when the subject of prisons came up again. The pristav, afraid lest I might leave with erroneous ideas, invited me to inspect his Tchudovo prison before going. I was afraid of missing the train, however, and declined. I had no reason to doubt his word, nor was the condition of a provincial prison a hundred versts from St. Peterburg of much importance.

The pristav laughed at the idea of Russia wanting India.

"That was Skobeloff's idea," he said. "Skobeloff was a soldier, not a statesman. He found it a good thing to juggle with in our negotiations with England, but the idea has never been seriously entertained by sensible Russians. We hate England because she persists in hating us; but if we go to war it will be with Germany. She is our only natural enemy."

It is always interesting and instructive to hear the ideas of people about themselves and their country. It is a lesson one should always take, if possible, in a new field, before beginning the serious work of investigation on one's own behalf. My brief visit to Tchudovo, and the talks with the moujiks and the police officer were the preliminary steps to an extensive tour of investigation. I had determined to ride on horseback from Moscow to the Black Sea ; then return by way of the Don and the Volga.

It was deemed that the best plan of getting into genuine contact with the Russian people, and of studying them and the way in which they are governed, at close range, would be to take a long horseback journey through the country. This being an extraordinary proposition, and everything out of the ordinary being always regarded with suspicion in Russia, difficulties, of course, presented themselves at the outset. Kennan's exposures had prejudiced the Minister of the Interior against American correspondents in particular, and to approach him for permission to undertake an extraordinary ride on horseback, through the heart of Russia, would probably be equivalent to putting one's head in the lion's mouth. Permission would be refused ; or, if granted, care would be taken that everything should be prepared along the route, in advance, to prevent one doing anything in the nature of honest investigation.

It was resolved to ignore the authorities entirely, and—well, simply go ahead. This plan had proved successful in other parts of the world, why not in Russia also ?

CHAPTER III.

MOSCOW, then, was the first objective point, and along the length of Czar Nicholas's famous "ruler-railway," between St. Petersburg and Moscow, a few "impressions by the way" of Russian railway traveling may not be out of place. Every reader knows the story of how the St. Petersburg-Moscow Railway was surveyed in one minute by the Emperor, with a ruler, a pencil, and a map. A traveler once compared this road to the pyramids of Egypt as a monument of Imperial will. Times have improved, however, in the past five thousand years. It is still possible for a Czar of Russia to draw a straight line across a map and order a railway to be built along it, but these days not even the Russians would stand a pyramid.

To the American popular mind this railway is a gigantic freak of autocratic power, toying recklessly with the resources of a great nation. Those informed of Russian affairs are aware that the ruler-and-pencil survey was the result of the Czar's disgust at the efforts of the officials, intrusted to draw up the plans, to serve their own personal ends. A gentleman in St. Petersburg told the author that the preliminary survey, as laid before the Czar, twisted about the country like a serpent's trail, for no other reason than to enhance the value of the estates of the survey officers, and made the distance from St. Petersburg to Moscow nearer 1500 miles than 400. Like many other things, moreover, which from a distance assume fantastic proportions, the "ruler-railway" turns out to be less of a freak than one would imagine, upon a closer acquaintance.

It runs through a country almost as level as a floor, and with a population of but twenty-five to the square verst. Railways wind about to avoid engineering difficulties and to accommodate cities and towns. As there were none of the former, and next to none of the latter to consider, and as the termini were the two greatest cities of the empire, the Czar was at least as much of an economist as an autocrat in making his famous survey.

For an hour prior to the departure of the train the crowd at the station was enormous. There is as much leave-taking, kissing, and shedding of tears at the departure of a Russian train as there is at the sailing of an Atlantic liner. To nine tenths of the Russians a journey of a hundred miles by rail is a tremendous event, and each passenger has probably a dozen friends who have come to see them off.

The hum, bustle, and buzz as the time for the train to leave draws near is astonishing to an American. Rough men and stout old women hug one another with the fervor of bears, and half the people are either kissing each other or shedding tears. The average Russian face of the middle and lower classes is singularly vacant and devoid of sentiment. But at the departure of the train the overflow of emotion is a revelation to the foreigner. One is bewildered and yet amused at the many ways the people have of displaying their affection, one toward another, and the utter absence of restraint.

Not the least amusing thing to the beholder are the ludicrous mistakes of the uninitiated. Several warnings are given before the train leaves, and half the people think each warning the last. I remember one woman who was saying the parting words to her husband through the open window of her car. The bell rung. The lady passenger leaned out; the husband's arms twined lovingly around her neck; their lips met—one! two!! three!!!—ah! Between the first kiss and the third the woman's mouth had expanded from a tempting smile to a grin so broad that a fourth was impossible. So, drawing back into the car, both expected the train to move off.

The train didn't move, however, and an officer told the man they had fifteen minutes to wait yet and that there would be another signal. Instead of one, it turned out that there were two. And so this loving couple treated the subscriber, and an Englishman who was seeing me off, to the above delightful little tableaux no less than three times, two of which were the result of false alarms.

The Russian passenger coaches are a compromise between the English and American. You can pass from one end of the train to the other as with us, but by closing a door you can shut yourself up in a little apartment, as in England. Only forty pounds of baggage is carried free, but bundles are allowed to be taken in the passenger cars. The consequence is that every nook of the car is stuffed with bundles, band-boxes, baskets, and valises. Economical old peasants, who have been to the capital, perhaps, for the only visit of their lives, struggle into the car with a dozen bundles and boxes to avoid paying anything for baggage. The train is miles away ere the people get comfortably settled down.

Three fourths of the people travel third class. Second class is as comfortable as first, and your fellow-passengers here are military officers who live on their salaries, well-to-do merchants, and the better class of citizens generally. First-class passengers are foreign travelers or natives of wealth, ostentation, or distinction.

In a seat near me were a couple of students going to spend their summer vacation in the Valdai Hills. Both could speak English. They talked freely. One of them gave me a new version of a late trouble with the students—an outbreak in St. Petersburg and Moscow. One of the students, he said, had received a letter from a lady convict in Siberia, telling of the miseries she and others endured. The students thereupon drew up a memorial to the Emperor and presented it to one of the professors to be delivered. The professor advised them to trouble their heads with their own business, and tore it up. A row ensued, the police and Cossacks were ordered out, and "two thousand students were sent to Siberia."

Fortunately my experience of the East had familiarized me with the recklessness and unreliability of its people's tongues in regard to figures, distances, and time. The Russian seems as much an Oriental as the

Persian in this respect. The rest of the story was, not unlikely, true enough, but the "two thousand students sent to Siberia" was worthy of the Persian who, within a stone's throw of the mud walls of Teheran, told me that they were of marble.

Many of the exaggerated stories that reach us from Russia and the East are the result of the European correspondent taking the statements of the natives too literally.

If you are traveling in Turkey or Persia, the native, believing you to be anxious to get to your destination, will assure you that it is but an hour away, even though it be several days. In like manner, these Russian students, knowing that, as an American, I was probably interested in the question of students being sent to Siberia, evolved from their inner consciousness the story of the two thousand.

Neither Turks nor Russians expect you to accept their statements literally. A polite desire to please, to say something that they imagine will fall pleasantly an your ear, is the *motif*, in so far as there is one ; but with them both, the tongue is more often but the vehicle for the ventilation of the vaguest imaginings. Intellectual apathy is the explanation. Ask six different officials, about a railway station, as to the time of departure of a certain train, and, whether in Turkey or Russia, you will be very sure to get a half-dozen conflicting replies. Too careless to remember and too lazy of brain to reflect, the answer will be the time they happen to think of first. In our conception of the Russians we are, I think, too apt to neglect this trait of their character.

If the Russian is lazy, however, he is far from being dull. The number of people one meets who understand several languages is astonishing. Across the aisle from us sat an officer and a young lady companion. My attention was attracted to the latter, before our train had gone far, by reason of the number of cigarettes she smoked. She was almost a chain-smoker, lighting one cigarette after another from the stump of the one just consumed. The students, seeing that I was interested, made some remark about the custom of smoking as indulged in by the ladies of Russia. We talked on a while, and all agreed that the habit was more likely to grow on a woman than a man, and that for a young lady to permit herself to become a cigarette devotee was a mistake. At this juncture, the fair smoker could keep her countenance no longer. She had understood all that we had said! Before reaching Moscow I discovered that fully one half the passengers in my car knew English! Now, a Russian might knock about the United States for six months without falling in with anybody who could talk with him in his own tongue.

The idea these students had of Russia's international politics was that everybody hated her except France and the United States. It sounded queer that despotic Russia should find friends only in these two governmental antitheses to herself.

I asked them which they considered the better government of the two, that of the United States or Russia.

"Russia," they said.

"Why?"

" Because if one man kills another, you hang him. If a Russian commits murder, we only put him in prison and we don't care much if he escapes altogether ! "

" But you send political offenders to Siberia."

" It is true, for to plot against the Czar is treason, and treason in other countries is punishable with death." Strange to say, I had heard this same view of the case several times since my arrival in Russia. It is curious logic from our point of view that a government is good because it lays a light hand on the murderer and a heavy one on a political offender.

But I am wandering away from the railway.

The result of the Emperor Nicholas's arbitrary survey is that many of the stopping places are nothing but platforms for the taking on and putting off of passengers and freight for distant points. Such stations as there are, are of wood, comfortable and artistic structures, where painters with yellow paint seem to be always painting the sides, and painters with red paint always painting the roofs. Small parks and gardens, and even fountains, embellish the two or three more pretentious stations along the route.

At all the stations the buffets are excellent, and the service reasonable. The railway buffets are one of the best things in Russia. In the larger cities, a great many people go there to eat instead of to restaurants. The privileges of the buffets are let out to large caterers, like the Spiers & Pond railway buffets in England. The results in Russia are excellent.

The waiters are chiefly Tartars,—bright, attentive young men,—who, I believe, receive no salary, but depend on tips for their remuneration. The Tartars, who three or four centuries ago were dominating the country, and at one time enslaved and persecuted the Russians, have now become table waiters in the country. Nearly all the large hotels, as well as the railway restaurants, have Tartar waiters. They form a guild, or *artel*, and their numbers are regularly recruited by young boys, who are brought from the Tartar villages of the Volga provinces. Making themselves useful among the young men, at a big railway restaurant or hotel dining-room, you see two or three small boys, yellow-cheeked, oblique-eyed, and black-haired. They are young Tartars, learning to be waiters, under the watchful eyes of their elder brothers.

All the tips are pooled and the various sources of income go into a common purse, and the proceeds are periodically apportioned. An *artel* is a species of workmen's commune, by means of which the welfare, honesty, and earnings of each is the concern of all. Some of the *artels*, as the *artel* of bank porters and hotel employees, among other functions insures the honesty of its members. If one of its members steals money or property, the *artel* makes good the loss. Notices in the bedrooms of the hotels advise guests to deposit their valuables, not with the hotel clerk, as with us, but with the agent of the *artel*, who has an office and a safe in the hotel, and is responsible for any losses.

The grade of accommodation, to suit the length or shortness of the passengers' purses, is admirable. You can spend twenty rubles on a dinner, or you can carry your own provisions, tea and sugar, and buy a pot of boiling water, holding enough for six glasses of tea, for one kopeck. A gourmet's feast for a moujik is a glass of vodka, a big salted cucumber, a slice of smoked sturgeon, rye bread, a glass of tea, with a slice of lemon in it, and a cigarette.

At every station is a *gendarme*, with long sword and revolver, blue uniform with red trimmings, lamb's-wool hat with tall red plume—as gorgeous an individual as the rural carbineers one sees at the stations in Italy.

At every station, also, are peasant girls selling beer-bottles of milk, and members of the "Orthodox," in rags and tatters, humbly begging, "for Christ's sake," a kopeck. All true Russians are Orthodox, but the wan-faced wretch, with unkempt hair and bleary eyes, who wails for alms as the train glides slowly into the station, is peculiarly so. We toss him a coin, he crosses him-self a half-dozen times, calling down on you the bless-ings of many saints, then moves on to the next win-dow.

"For Christ's sake, a kopeck for the Orthodox," he repeats. The scene wafted me to similar scenes in other countries and alien religions. On the great pil-grim roads of Persia the half-starved devotee, footing his weary way a thousand miles without means to pay his expenses, begs for alms in the name of Mahomet.

"I am a good Moslem on a pilgrimage to Meshed," says he; "therefore give me alms."

"Give me alms," says the Russian peasant, "for I am a Christian."

In the north the Russian locomotives burn wood, in the south refuse petroleum. Pine forests cover about all the land between Moscow and St. Petersburg that has not been cleared for cultivation or burned off. Tremendous quantities of wood are piled up at the stations for the railway company and for shipment to cities. The piles are built up like cord-wood and at some stations cover fifty acres of ground. St. Petersburg and Moscow burn wood almost exclusively, and the provincial towns and villages know no other fuel. The quantity of pine wood consumed in the long, cold Russian winter by two cities, the size of Brooklyn, is enormous, and the cutting and transportation of the same give occupation to a large share of the surrounding peasantry.

At nearly every station was seen the inevitable drunken moujik, stupid and happy. One of them attempted to pass through our car. He stumbled over a bundle. " Nitchevo ! " he said in a maudlin voice, as he scrambled up. " Nitchevo ! " said two or three sympathetic souls ; " never mind."

Nitchevo is the most frequent exclamation one hears in Russia. It means anything of a negative degree. Nitchevo !—never mind. Nitchevo !—pray don't mention it. Nitchevo !—everything will come all right, Nitchevo !—the horse is dead, but God will provide another.

Our train plodded along, slowly but surely, like the tortoise in the race. It took twenty-three hours to carry us something over four hundred miles. We grew impatient as the day waned and mentally wished we had taken the " Courier train," which does it in twelve. But the noise of the engine, which in other countries seems to pant and puff with exertion, here bade us " Nitchevo !" and seemed to remind us reproachfully that time was made for man, not man for time.

Mackenzie Wallace, in his excellent work on Russia, tells us that the Russian merchant has reached the same level of commercial morality, on the road toward honest dealing, that is occupied in England by the horse dealer. It may be that the English horse dealer is grossly libeled by the comparison ; but, however that may be, there can be no two opinions about the character of the gentlemen who gain their livelihood by buying, selling, and swapping horses in Russia. A man may be a knave in any country without being a horse dealer, but the country has yet to be discovered where a man can make a success as a trader in horseflesh without an occasional breach of faith with his conscience. Certainly, an inquirer after an honest horse dealer for a museum of ethnographical curiosities would not turn to Russia. Least of all would he go to Moscow.

Moscow is the commercial Mecca of the empire, as well as the Mecca of its imperial and, next to Kiev, its religious traditions. The merchants of Moscow are understood to be the shrewdest and the wealthiest in Russia ; and the " Moskovsky " horse dealer has attained such a tremendous height in the scale of roguery, that he is regarded by provincial members of the fraternity with a degree of admiration amounting to awe.

When, therefore, the author turned his footsteps, one fine day in June, 1890, in the direction of a large open space in the ancient capital of the Czars, where these crafty gentlemen exhibit, for the benefit of possible customers, the accumulated results of life-long and hereditary trickery in selling spavined and broken-winded horses to credulous humans, with a view to buying a horse, a sensation as of venturing on exceedingly slippery ground may well be excused.

A slight knowledge of horse-flesh would be sufficient to prevent me being taken in much on the score of age, or other " points " visible to the eye; but, on the other hand, a stranger, knowing nothing of the language, nothing of the idiosyncrasies of Russian horse dealing, and very little about the prices of horses in Moscow, would be sure to be looked upon as a veritable windfall by every dealer who had on hand a "touched up" animal.

For the purpose of seeing Russia and the Russians to better advantage than from viewing them from the windows of a railway train, or on the streets of the cities, I had determined on taking a horseback ride of more than a thousand miles; a trying journey for a horse in the middle of summer. It was, therefore, very necessary that I should secure a sound, strong animal.

The probability of my doing so, within the few days that I intended to stay in Moscow, vanished like a , shadow as I reached the horse-market and approached a group of dealers. The apparition of a stranger, and apparently a foreigner to boot, coming their way, produced on these worthies a truly magical effect. I became the cynosure of a dozen pairs of the craftiest-looking eyes that ever attempted to look through and through, discover the inmost thoughts, size up the mental caliber, the horse knowledge, and the purse of a likely-looking victim.

The typical Russian horse dealer is a whiskered individual in wrinkled top-boots, loose black trousers, a black frock coat, and a black cap with a patent-leather peak. He is much given to wearing the shiny peak of his cap well down on the bridge of his nose, in order that he may furtively examine the horse-buying section of humanity from beneath it. If the subject of his scrutiny happens to be a person not given to close observation, the glint of the horse dealer's peering eyes will be confounded with the glint of his patent-leather peak, and he might easily be taken for a man engaged in the pious examination of his own conscience.

After looking at a dozen horses, I gave it up, and returned home to think up some other plan of getting what I wanted. Though I had not bought a horse, my ideas of the Russian horse dealer had undergone a decided change. As arrant a knave as ever preyed on the ignorance and credulity of others, his roguery is yet of an order so crude and palpable as to seem ridiculous in the eyes of one who has had dealings with the same fraternity in America.

I approached the Moscow horse-market in fear and trembling, and came away horseless, but very much amused.

There is one method of arriving at the price of anything, that seems to be applicable all over Russia. The seller asks twice as much as he is willing to take, and the buyer offers half as much as he is willing to give. Commencing on this basis, the vendor gradually comes down in his prices, and the customer warily advances, until a bargain is made. The Moscow horse dealers not only asked me five hundred rubles for horses worth two hundred, but they seemed to think the above method to be an equally fair way of arriving at a horse's age. They showed me a horse which they stated to be five years old, but which was in reality fifteen. I had already obtained a hint as to their methods, and by yielding at the fifteen year end, induced them to give way at the five-year end, a year at a time, until they reluctantly admitted that he might be nine years old.

The roguery of the Russian horse dealers consists largely in brazen mendacity, and in his reluctance to deal with you at all unless he can swindle you. You may know more about the horse you are trying to buy from him than he does, and prove it to him in a dozen ways, but he will haggle and dicker, argue and drink tea with you for a week, rather than let you take him at a reasonable price. As I had no inclination to waste a week on nothing, I looked elsewhere.

Dr. Carver, the celebrated champion shot, together with a troupe of cowboys and Indians, called "Wild America," happened to be exhibiting in Moscow at the time. I applied to them, and was thus fortunate enough to obtain a horse that carried me bravely through the trying heat of a Russian summer, in six weeks, to Sevastopol.

Texas was a Hungarian mustang, which the manager of "Wild America" had bought in Budapest, with a view to breaking him in to the wild work of the arena. Texas, however, turned out to be afraid of the shooting; afraid of the Indians; afraid of the cowboys; afraid of the band; afraid of the Deadwood stage; afraid of

the wild steers; afraid of the crowd; afraid of almost everything under the sun. That he was afraid of the shooting, I knew before buying him. All the other evidences of his constitutional timidity enumerated, gradually dawned upon me during the first few days on the road. I never ceased to be thankful that they didn't dawn upon me in advance, however, rather than as the result of experience, for had they done so he would have been passed over and probably a much worse animal secured.

It took me half an hour to get Texas over the first tiny rivulet, and, after crossing hundreds, he flinched at stepping into the well-nigh dry bed of the historic Alma, at the end of our long journey. With bridges it was the same. Between Moscow and the battle-fields of the Crimean war are hundreds of bridges, small and great, all of which Texas was forced to cross, always against his will, often under the lash; yet he attempted to turn tail at the last one, exactly as he had done at the first.

He shied at houses, people, cattle, dogs, sheep, hillocks, and sometimes at his own shadow. Left a moment to himself, his first idea was to get rid of his saddle, either by rolling, or by rubbing against tree, post, or railing. He objected to being led, unless another horse was ahead of him. When tired he was a stumbler. Five times on the journey he went down all of a heap from stumbling against some scarcely visible stone or other inequality, and sent me sprawling over his head. And nothing but unceasing vigilance on my part prevented the recurrence of this undignified, to say nothing of dangerous, performance fifty times instead of five.

Yet, with all this, Texas was a good sort of a horse. The only grudge born in memory against him is for blundering down on a piece of rough macadam road, and peeling his knees and nose, when but two days' march from Sevastopol, where I intended offering him to a horse dealer as an exceptionably fine animal. As such he would, undoubtedly, be passed on to the next customer by the dealer ; for he was as handsome a horse as ever wore a shoe. With all his faults he was parted from with a pang of regret. Before we reached the shores of the Black Sea he would follow me about like a dog, so long as one didn't lead the way across a bridge, or near anything that excited his suspicion.

From " Wild America " was also obtained a good cowboy saddle, made at Houston, Texas. It was the easiest saddle the writer ever rode in. At an early stage on the road, however, I decided that it was too heavy for the hot weather and the long journey, and exchanged it for a light Circassian seat. The Circassian saddle consists of a naked wooden frame, and a pillow-like cushion of soft Russian leather, stuffed with goat hair. The light frame rests on a thick pad on the horse's back, and the soft leather cushion is pinched tightly in the middle by a surcingle, that passes round it and under the horse, as a third girth. The natives ride with a stirrup so short that the leg is bent as in kneeling, and the foot plays no part in relieving the weight in the saddle. The position is at first extremely uncomfortable, and I preferred to lengthen the stirrups to getting accustomed to it.

The merit of the Circassian saddle is its lightness. It weighed less than half as much as the Texan. The cushion seat, too, is handy on a ride through a country where travelers are expected to provide their own bedding, for it makes a capital pillow. Whether it makes a better seat for a long ride than a hard saddle the writer is not prepared to say, never having given the latter a long trial. It is the saddle of Asia,—the home of the horse, and the nursery of equestrianism. Cossacks, Circassians, Kirghis, Persians, Tartars, Arabs— these are, and have always been, the finest horsemen in the world; they all ride, with slight modifications, this form of saddle.

The arrival of an American in Moscow, who intended riding on horseback from that city to the Crimea, was no sooner known than a candidate presented himself as a companion on the journey. The ambitious young man who made this proposition was a student in one of the Moscow universities, who had just completed his studies. As he could speak very good English I readily agreed to the arrangement. His brother would provide him with a horse and I was to bear all expenses of the trip.

Sascha turned out to be a typical Russian. As an interpreter on the road, and an explainer of the manners and customs of his countrymen, he was invaluable. But it was as an ever-present mirror and reflection of Russian character in his own person that he did me the greatest service. He was singularly warm and impulsive, and strangely unreliable, contradictory, quixotic, and inconsistent.

Never did a young man start on an undertaking

with greater enthusiasm, or brighter visions of advantages to be reaped from success. In the autumn he was to enter upon his military duties by joining a regiment of cavalry. The ride would win him fame and prestige among his comrades, and bring him to the notice of his superior officers. He would gain a knowledge of his country, and, by having some one to talk to in that language, improve his English. He would keep a diary, and upon his return write a book. In the eyes of his relatives and his *fiancée*, the daughter of a merchant of Tula, he would be a hero.

The keeping of a diary proved too irksome at the end of three days, so he gave it up and decided that it would be easier and better to wait until I had published a book in America, when he would translate it into Russian. A week's journey on our road we called on his *fiancée*. The young lady was delighted with him, for what he was doing was, in her eyes, an heroic performance. She presented him with a bouquet, and stuck rose-buds in his hat-band when we rode away. Scarcely had the roses faded, and the vision of his sweetheart's approving smiles grown dim, than he began to dwell on the contrast between the fatigue and discomforts of the road and the ease and pleasure of life in Moscow. And he eventually threw up the sponge and returned, when but twelve days' ride from the end of our journey.

In intellect, he was as bright as he was incapable of logical reasoning. He knew four languages and could quote Shakespeare by the page ; but could never be brought to understand why the Czar couldn't make Russia as rich as he chose, by simply ordering the mint to manufacture mountains of paper rubles. In money matters he was an understudy of the old race of Russian nobles, who used to ruin their serfs and estates at home in order that they might squander thousands of pounds ostentatiously on the green cloth tables at Monaco, and fling handfuls of Napoleons at waiters' heads in Paris. From all this, it will be seen that though fortunate in my horse, I was a great deal more fortunate in my companion.

CHAPTER IV.

THE START FROM MOSCOW.

IT was a warm, moist morning in the middle of June, when Sascha, the young student of Moscow, and the writer rode out of Moscow. The eminently respectable section of old Moscow's conservative citizens, the representatives of her wealth and beauty as well as of her mercantile pre-eminence, were still asleep. At the doors of the big mansions, and the fashionable apartment-houses, the dvorniks, curled up in their huge overcoats, were imitating the admirable example of the inmates.

A few of these watchmen, who had proved their fitness for their position by sleeping, through the night, the untroubled sleep of the righteous, craned their necks above the all-enveloping sheepskins, at the sound of our horses' feet, as a setting hen peers over the edge of her nest when apprehensive of intruders. And having satisfied their curiosity by a sleepy scrutiny of my American cow-boy saddle, drew their heads down again, once more in unreflective imitation of the hen.

We rode along a narrow street in the old Moscovite quarter, where the houses were painted in many bright colors and ornamented with woodwork, curiously carved. Balconies, where, a few hours earlier, the young bloods of Moscow, military officers, and visiting merchants from country towns, drank champagne, listened to the balalaika and the accordion, believing, in the intoxication of the hour, the place, and the occasion, that they were having a capital time, were now closely curtained.

In deference to the ignorance that still prevails in Russia, the shopkeepers of the cities are obliged to decorate their signs with pictures of what they have to sell, in addition to setting forth the nature of their business in words. The narrow street we were now traversing, being a part of the older section of the town, was curiously realistic in this matter. Painters and sculptors had lent their art, that there might be no mistakes by rich country merchants unable to read, and the curtained balconies were supported by statuary never intended to represent the saints. To this part of old Moscow, though it was six o'clock in the morning, night had only just begun.

We came to a quarter where there seemed to be nothing but boulevards, with avenues of young trees, big barracks, and equally big and gloomy-looking institutions of learning. Under the windows of the big commercial college, where my companion had lately graduated in the theoretical part of a profession that would enable him to hold his own against his mercantile countrymen, we halted a moment. Sascha was in high glee. Here also, he informed me, was learned the language that had been instrumental in bringing him my acquaintance, and had recommended him as a companion for the ride on which we were now starting.

His old tutors, as well as his comrades, came in for

a share of his attentions. Though absent in the flesh, Sascha declared he could still see them through the gray stone walls, and, stretching out his hand toward his old dormitory, he apostrophized the tutors in a most theatrical manner, declaring his keen satisfaction at the mighty change in his fortunes, that had transferred him from the world of stools and studies, to the saddle and the freedom of a horse's back.

Beyond the universities, we plunged into plebeian Moscow, the world of red-shirted workmen and cheap frocked women ; low vodka shops and bare, roomy traktirs, where the red-shirted workmen assemble each evening to gossip and swallow astonishing quantities of tea, inferior in quality and very, very weak.

Here was Moscow's social and material contrast to the big houses, with the sleeping dvorniks, and of the silent street of painted house fronts, curtained balconies and all the rest. Though day had not yet dawned for other sections of Moscow, it had long since dawned for the inhabitants of this. Employers of labor in Moscow know nothing of the vexed questions as to eight-hour laws, ten-hour laws, or even laws of twelve. Thousands of red shirts, issuing from the crowded hovels of this quarter, like rats from their hiding places, had scattered over the city long before our arrival on the scene; other thousands were still issuing forth, and streaming along the badly cobbled streets. Under their arms, or in tin pails, were loaves of black rye bread, their food for the day, which would be supplemented at meal times by a salted cucumber, or a slice of melon, from the nearest grocery.

For five versts, according to Sascha, who, Russian-like, had no idea, however, of the population and size of the city, though he had been born and educated in it, we rode over Moscow's execrable pavements, then emerged on to a macadam road. Workmen from the quarter we had just passed through had preceded us in this direction hours before, and were now met in the character of teamsters, bringing in petroleum from the big iron tanks that loomed up in the distance ahead.

Though Moscow can boast of its electric light .as well as of gas, it is yet a city of petroleum. Coal is dear, and, in the matter of electric lights and similar innovations from the wide-awake Western world, Moscow is, as ever, doggedly conservative. So repugnant, indeed, to this stronghold of ancient and honorable Muscovite sluggishness, is the necessity of keeping abreast with the spirit of modern improvement, that the houses are not yet even numbered. There are no numbers to the houses in Moscow ; only the streets are officially known by name. To find anybody's address, you must repair to the street, and inquire of the policeman or drosky driver, who are the most likely persons to know, for the house belonging to Mr. So-and-so, or in which that gentleman lives. It seems odd that in a country where the authorities deem it necessary to know where to put their hand on any person at a moment's notice, the second city of the empire should be, in 1890, without numbers to its houses.

The macadam road, though just without the city, and thronged with produce and petroleum wagons, was but a slight improvement on the cobbled streets. We were glad when we eventually found ourselves fairly in the country. Our way led through the estates of Prince Galitzin, a wealthy land owner in this part of Russia. Villages dotted the level landscape thickly, their positions being indicated by big churches painted white, with green spires and domes. Russia is a hedgeless country, and fences are confined to gardens and house grounds, or to special bits near the country mansions of wealthy landlords, such as Prince Galitzin.

This nobleman's country residence was a fine, large mansion, on the edge of a lake, several hundred acres in extent, which had been artificially created in the good old day of serfdom, princely squanderings in Paris, and a steady diet of champagne and sterlet at home. The serfs are " freed "; we hear nothing nowadays of Russian spendthrifts in Paris, and the land owners who can afford to entertain largely on the above named costly articles of consumption, have dwindled to a very small company indeed.

Who has profited by the mighty change? Popular supposition opens wide its eyes, in astonishment at the ignorance implied in such a question, and condescendingly replies, " The peasants, of course. Were they not formerly serfs, and are now free from the hardships of having to work without pay?"

The peasants—we rode through their villages ; and, bearing in mind this popular conception, one could but marvel at their condition, and wonder if, like so many other changes brought about under the directions of a too paternal government, their improvement was not theoretic rather than material.

But it is early on the journey to begin moralizing on the condition of the people whose acquaintance

we were only beginning to make, and whose appearance and manner of life were, as yet, matters of
curiosity.

The forests through which our road led were in
their happiest midsummer mood as to vegetation, and
the day being sultry, threatening thunder-storms, their
savagest as to flies. My companion's horse, who was
a tough old charger, obtained from a Cossack officer,
held his own stolidly among the myriads of hungry flies,
of many sizes and varieties, that assailed us in the
patches of primeval forest.

But I early learned that, among his other eccentrici-
ties of character, Texas considered the attack of even
a single fly so gross an insult, as to justify a combined
assault on the offender with mouth, feet, and tail. In
other words, Texas was remarkably tender-skinned, and
sensitive to a degree in the particular matter of flies and
mosquitoes. At this early stage of the journey, also,
he promptly asserted the authority of a horse to have
the first voice in the matter of his own comfort by
rolling with the saddle, when we halted for refreshments at a village. He was a persistent advocate of
horses' rights; and all the way to the Crimea never
neglected to remind his rider that horses as well as
women's rights women, had abstract rights that men
were bound to respect, regardless of their own judgment in the matter.

The villages about Moscow echo something of the
venerable atmosphere of legendary lore that hangs
about the ancient capital itself. Sascha pointed out
one village church where, at the approach of a procession of priests carrying a miracle-working ikon, the

big iron bell had suddenly disappeared from the belfry. Nobody saw where it vanished to, but it was
supposed to have flown into a near-by lake; for on certain nights a sound, as of a bell ringing, may be heard
issuing from the depths.

The flowers, the ferns, the grasses that carpeted the
forest, all served to conjure up in my companion's
mind scraps of peasant-lore, so keen and enthusiastic
was his enjoyment of these, our first few hours in the
saddle.

Rye and potatoes were the crops that lined the road,
in the big open fields, which were clearings in the vast
forest that covers the whole of northern Russia. Forest lands play a conspicuous and important part in the
economic affairs of the Russian country and people.
Russia is primarily a country of "land and timber."
The wealthiest Russians are those who own the broadest tracts of the one, and the most valuable and accessible patches of the other. The most desirable possession in Russia, setting aside choice mining or city
property, is a tract of heavy pine forest, accessible to
one of the large cities by rail or river. Facility of
transportation, however, is everything. A tree five
hundred miles inland from where a purchaser could be
found for it, becomes a mere encumbrance to the
ground, and an obstacle to cultivation; whereas, in
the part of Russia traversed by our first week's ride,
it is one of the chief sources of wealth.

In remote districts the peasants clear the ground by
burning up all but the choicest sticks of timber in a
patch of forest, and, by the aid of the ashes, produce
crops on soil that would otherwise be too poor for cul-

tivation. But on this first day's ride, and after, we passed many tracts of pine forest that had been set out, and carefully preserved from harm. Fir trees seem to grow best on barren soil, that would grow nothing else. It is customary for Russian land owners, with an eye to the future, to plant tracts of forest, for the benefit of their posterity. Many of these artificial tracts are beautiful to the eye, the young trees standing in straight, long rows, whichever way you look through the forest, like fields of maize in the West. These tracts of forest are often given by Russian land owners as dowry with a daughter. An heiress, in Russia, often means a young lady whose father will fit her out with a blooming trousseau and a " tract of forest." Sascha spoke to me of Russian heiresses with " dowries of 300,000 rubles in forest."

The important part played by these forests, in Russia, is continually thrust upon the notice of the traveler, whose business is to take cognizance of his surroundings. It is the fuel of St. Petersburg and Moscow and all the villages, towns, and cities of the northern half of the country. All summer long the canals of St. Petersburg are filled with monster barges, containing as much as four hundred tons apiece of neatly cut firewood. They are moored in the Neva ; they crawl along the canals and smaller streams, and are towed in long strings by stout tugs across the Gulf of Finland, Lakes Ladoga and Onega, and the smaller lakes of the adjacent provinces, all streaming toward the great northern capital. For eight months of the year, six of which are very cold, St. Petersburg has to be heated, and the fuel is wood. With Moscow it is the same, only the supply has to reach the old capital by rail and road.

The Russian peasants of these great northern forest regions are the most skillful axmen in the world, begging the pardon of the lumbermen of Maine and Minnesota ; and the forest is their good foster-mother, without whom they would have a sorry enough time of it, dodging the tax-collector's knout. The land is poor, and the amount allotted to them by the government when they were emancipated is often insufficient for their bare support, saying nothing of taxes. Since there is no escaping the latter, great numbers of these northern moujiks literally "take to the woods" for the greater part of the year.

All winter the ring of ax, and the buzzing music of the sawmills resound through the forests ; and men and teams transport fire-wood, railway ties, telegraph poles, lumber, and blocks for paving city streets, to the railways and river banks. With the thawing of rivers and canals in spring, a great movement begins in building huge rafts of timber, and starting off big barges of fire-wood. The barges are generally frail affairs, that are broken up at the journey's end.

Much of the forest is owned by the government, even about St. Petersburg and Moscow. "Government property" in Russia means something very different from the American idea of the same. No such liberty is permitted as with the unsettled domains of Uncle Sam. Everything available on government land is expected to yield a revenue, as on the property of an individual. It "belongs to the Czar." Why should the Czar permit liberties with his patch of forest on the right hand side of the road any more than Count Trotoff, on the left?

Whether you put up at a hotel traktir, or with a moujik on the Russian roads, all feed is supplied by weight or measurement. A primitive form of beam scales, with brass dots to accommodate the mathematical incapacity of the unlettered moujik, instead of figures, is produced to weigh your pood or half-pood of hay or cut grass, and measures are filled with oats and leveled off. Hay and oats are almost always to be procured.

The accommodation for man is not particularly inviting. The village traktir is a little better than a Chinese wayside inn, but not much. Doughy black bread, eggs, and tea are the refreshments, and in summer your rights to what you purchase are disputed by myriads of persistent flies. The Russian fly worries you all night as well as all day. The brief summer of his activity commences late and ends early, and he evidently believes his short life should always be a merry one.

The windows of the room to which you are shown are probably nailed up and were never intended to be opened. It is no joke to be thrust into an evil-smelling room, ten feet square, with a myriad of hungry flies, and the air of which has been boxed up since winter. The Russians thrive on this sort of thing, however, and one soon ceases to regard an over-crowded prison as a punishment to the lower-class Russian.

For travelers of sufficient importance, from a financial point of view, however, the landlord readily vacates his private room and arranges a comfortable shakedown with hay and quilts. The rooms of the traktirs all contain from three to thirty ikons, and at the hotels a small ikon sometimes hangs on the head of the bed, to insure sound and peaceful repose to the occupant.

The tipping nuisance is worse in Russian hotels than in any other country, not excepting even Egypt, the land of backsheesh. With few exceptions the hotel employees receive no compensation for their services beyond the offerings of the guests, and all tips are pooled and divided *pro rata.* Wealthy and open-handed Russians, dining at the big traktirs of St. Petersburg and Moscow, usually reckon to give the waiters one ruble for every five spent on a dinner. At the Hermitage Traktir, the finest restaurant in Moscow, wealthy and ostentatious merchants have been known to spend two hundred rubles on a dinner for two persons, and to tip the waiter with a couple of twenty-ruble notes. At the country hotels the employees swarm about you like hungry rats as the time arrives for your departure. People whom you have never set eyes on before, now present themselves with an awkward bow and with a look of eager expectancy that is positively embarrassing.

Few things on earth are more delusive than a Russian country hotel. In the two capitals the influence of Western European contact has brought about a better state of affairs; but the bill of a Russian provincial hostelry is a curiosity. We stayed over night at the Hotel London in the provincial capital of Tula. On calling for the bill in the morning, I learned for the first time that in engaging a room at the leading hotel in a Russian city you do not thereby always engage a bed to sleep in. The bedstead is reckoned as part of the room, and is always there for you to look at and wonder why it contains no bed beyond a naked mattress. After thinking it will be all right, till you are ready to retire, you ring for the chambermaid and mildly chide her for her forgetfulness.

Sheets and pillows are brought at your command, and next morning, on looking over the items of your bill, you perceive with astonishment that "two sheets, two pillow-cases, one counterpane," etc., have been added to candles, matches, and other "extras" charged up to you. It is the custom in Russia for the traveler to carry with him his own bed-linen, pillows, towels, etc. Only Russians who have taken to the ways of Western travelers ever think of traveling without all these things. All that the hotel is expected to provide, and all that the hotel-keeper feels called upon to include with the room, is bedstead and mattress. The better-class Russian is very much opposed to sleeping between sheets that have been used over and over again by the Lord knows who and how many passing travelers. The fact that they have been washed before being passed on to him makes no difference. His custom and the custom of his ancestors has been to carry his own bedclothes with him on his travels, and when some unforeseen circumstances brings him to a hotel without them, his idea is to borrow a set for the night from the proprietor and pay whatever is charged for their use.

In the court-yard of the hotel or traktir are always from one to three or four savage dogs. They are of a shaggy, wolfish breed, and seem but half domesticated. Usually they are chained up with a long, heavy chain.

Why the chain is always long the owners of the dogs are unable to explain, beyond the fact that chains and custom are alike hereditary; but the stranger who unwarily saunters into the yard and manages to hop beyond the danger circle by a few spasmodic jumps, as the dog springs at him, not unfrequently makes the mistake of jumping too far. A second wolf-fanged brute rushes at him from the other side, and, as he momentarily speculates on the chance of being torn down, a third tries to reach him from the body of the old sleigh toward which he has begun retreating. All three tug and struggle violently to break their tethers, and to menace them with stick or stone only serves to redouble their rage. The writer had a pair of trousers converted into material for the ragman by these savage sentinels, before we had been on the road a week, but no blood was spilled. After a couple of narrow escapes one becomes wary by instinct, and never enters a Russian court-yard without due precaution.

Away from the railways, the traffic one sees on the Russian highways is a far better index to the state of the country and the condition of its people and institutions than the mere tourist ever comes in contact with. Our route was along the main road between Moscow, Kharkoff, Kief, and other Southern cities. As far as Kharkoff and Kief it is a very fair macadam road. The vehicles are peculiarly Russian, and a picturesque feature are the troikas, with three, and the tchetvarkas with four horses abreast; the horses and the duga (the bow that connects the shafts) are hung with bells that jingle-jangle merrily as the teams sweep by at a smart gallop.

There is also the linega, an affair like the Irish jaunting car. The people sit back to back between, instead of over, the wheels, and the foot-board almost touches the ground. A large family or public linega carries as many as fourteen persons.

A primitive drosky is also commonly met, a four-wheeled low vehicle, with driver and passengers bestriding a long cushioned plank, which connects the fore and hind wheels. The telegas, or common country wagons, are met in long strings, taking produce from remote parts of the country. Goods of certain kinds are still hauled into Moscow several hundred miles by the lumbering telegas from districts that are far from a railway.

The Moscow-Kharkoff highway is a well-kept macadam with a reservation of greensward, forty feet wide on either side. On some of the communes through which the road passes the side reservations are rented from the government and preserved for hay; on others are herds of hobbled horses, tended by men and boys, with dogs, and whips that are one of the curiosities of the road. These enormous lashes are twice as large as the largest bull-whacking whips of the old overland days in the West.

It seemed to the writer rather picayunish, in a country so prodigal of land as Russia, for the authorities to "rent" the grass on these two narrow strips of side-road. Our horses, which we usually rode over the sward, might fairly be said to have walked through clover the whole distance from Moscow; yet we could not conscientiously permit them to dip down and take a mouthful, for where the grass was fit for anything, every blade had been paid for by villagers, who could ill afford to give away even a bite of grass. The Imperial Russian Government considers it beneath its dignity to sell its superfluous parks and palaces, but before the moujik may thrust his scythe into a bunch of grass growing on the big military road, which his taxes and his labor built and keep in repair, he has to purchase the privilege.

This seems rather overdoing the thing, in a government that considers itself, first of all, "paternal." That it fully deserves the name, however, in general, evidences were not wanting every hour of the day, as we rode along. On every house in the village is painted a rude picture of one or another household implement. On one is a bucket, a second a spade, a third an ax. These primitive hieroglyphics are the outward and visible signs of paternal forethought in the matter of fires. Every peasant is obliged by law to insure his house to the amount of seventy-five rubles. This costs two rubles a year. Beyond this he can insure to any amount.

As a further safeguard, every village community is organized into a primitive fire-brigade, and the pictures on the houses indicate to the occupant what he is required to do in case of a fire breaking out in the village. The man on whose house is pictured an ax, is required to bring one of those tools; a householder whose property is decorated with the sign of a bucket is to hurry to the scene of the conflagration prepared to carry water, etc. This is a primitive form of fire-brigade, suitable to the little clusters of log houses that pass for villages in Russia.

RESTING AT WAYSIDE INN.

CHAPTER V

ON THE CZAR'S HIGHWAY.

ON Sunday, June 29, we crossed the River Moskwa, where it runs through the broad, fat lands of the Nicolai Oograshinsky Monastery, over a rickety pontoon bridge, half-submerged. Bridges have, in Russia, an evil reputation among native travelers. The foreigner sees in them merely the possibility of broken bones, but to the native they are also the lurking-places of highway robbers. In troublous times and lawless districts, it is under the archways of the bridges that marauders hide, to pounce out upon passing travelers. Many Russian travelers make a practice of crossing themselves at bridges, by way of commending themselves to the special protection of Providence. This, I was told, is a relic of the old Tartar days, when the peasantry approached a bridge with fear and trembling, making signs of the Cross, lest it be the hiding-place of a band of marauding nomads.

No danger of robbers at the bridge across the Moskwa, however, unless they might also be amphibians, capable of keeping their heads under water an indefinite length of time.

Texas, as before mentioned, had a truly Russian horror of bridges. Among his notions of a horse's rights, was the privilege of turning tail at all sorts and

conditions of bridges, whether safe or unsafe, large or
small, wood, stone, or iron.   The Nicolai Oograshinsky
bridge consisted of planks that had once been spiked
to a set of rafts, but which were now mostly loose.
By dint of many cuts of the whip, and the assumption
of a truly portentous attitude by his rider, Texas suf-
fered himself to be urged a fourth of the way across,
though starting with spasmodic fear at every step.
Here, a viler spot than any brought him to a halt; and
when, prancing about under the goad of additional
threats and coaxings, water squashed up between the
loose planks and smote him under the belly, he gave
way to an impulse of terror, and, whirling round, bolted
for *terra firma.*

Then ensued a comical battle between his fear of
the bridge and his love of society.   The other horses
crossed and drew away in the distance.   Texas
neighed at them to come back, emphasizing the summons by vigorously pawing the ground; and at length,
finding that no attention was paid to him, ventured
across the bridge, and, demanding the rein, overtook
them at a gallop.

The Moskwa is a sluggish, meandering stream, and
like all Russian rivers, save the Neva, several times
larger in the spring and early summer than from June
to winter.   Wood, hay, and all manner of country produce is towed along it in big barges to Moscow.   The
government attempts, in a desultory way, to improve
its navigation by digging canals across its innumer-
able horse-shoe bends, levying tolls on the barges
to pay for the outlay.   It is one of the minor streams
of Russia, a tributary of the Oka, and is the cradle of

the Muscovite Empire, and of the traditions that center around Moscow, which it gave birth to and nourished into a capital city.

From the bluffs beyond the bridge could be obtained a splendid view of Moscow. Its many golden spires and domes glittered and twinkled in the sun like yellow stars, and the scene was as Oriental, on the whole, as anything the writer had seen anywhere in Asia. Even more than the tall minarets of the Stamboul mosques, or the beautiful temples of the Hindoo gods at Benares, the twinkling beacons of the golden domes of Moscow the Holy, impressed one as the metropolis of a people's religion. Surely, those beacons indicated a harbor where all who wished might find comfort and repose of soul in the calm waters of the "Orthodox Church." If anything were wanting to complete the Eastern character of the scene, it was provided by a band of pilgrims, who were gathered on the bluff, touching their foreheads to the ground toward Moscow, and making the sign of the Cross. These were people, who had come on foot, in rags and begging their way, from the distant confines of the Empire, making a pilgrimage to the shrines of the Saints at Moscow. Four years before I had seen Persian devotees, on the hills near Meshed, bowing to the earth at their first glimpse of the golden dome of Imam Riza's Mosque; vividly alike these two occasions seemed,—the yellow, twinkling domes and the bowing rapturous figures on the hills,—though one was a Christian, the other a Moslem scene.

We rode through many small villages, devoted to the cultivation of cherries, currants, and other small fruits;

and traversed for a few versts the road that Napoleon's army passed along after the evacuation of Moscow-Sascha and his brother, who rode with us that day, joked about Napoleon's discomfiture, and the devotion of the moujiks, who burned their produce rather than sell it to the French, much as though the whole affair were an occurrence of yesterday.

The talk was of wolves and bears, as our road led us through tracts of wild forest. Some of the tracts are several thousand dessiatines in extent, and in the depths of these both wolves and bears remain all summer. The wolves prey on the smaller animals; the bears live on roots and berries. During the summer they are invisible, but in the winter hunger drives the wolves to come out and commit depredations on the sheep and cattle of the surrounding villages. Three or four pairs of wolves, that have managed to rear their young without molestation in the depths of the forest during the summer, muster a fair-sized hunting-pack by the following winter.

Bear-hunting is the most ambitious sport in Russia. Winter is the season of bruin's undoing, for, though he hibernates, the art of discovering his lurking-place has been reduced to a reasonable certainty by a number of sturdy peasants, who devote their winters to finding bears and selling them to the sportsmen.

When the ground is covered with several feet of snow, the village bear-finders scatter through the forests. The sleeping place of a bear is revealed by a hole in the snow made by his breath. The finder of a bear, taking sundry precautions to " prove his claim " should others come to the same spot after his departure, hastens to notify a sportsman of his discovery. He offers to sell the bear, much as if he had it in a sack, safely secured ; with the understanding, however, that if bruin should have sniffed danger, and made off before he takes the sportsman to the spot, the bargain becomes null and void.

The usual price demanded for a bear is a hundred rubles. He is actually sold in his lair, and the peasant's services consist in guiding the sportsman to the spot and pointing out the breath-hole in the snow. Whether the sportsman succeeds in bagging the bear or not,—that, of course, being no fault of the peasant's,—he pays the price agreed upon. Many sportsmen have a standing agreement with the bear-finders of the surrounding district, that he is to have the option on any finds they make. And when a sportsman has earned a reputation among the peasants as a dead shot, they often prefer to sell the bears to him by weight, bargaining for so much per pound instead of a lump sum.

This is, in fact, the method preferred by old bear-finders, who have by long experience learned to judge of the bear's size by the dimensions of the hole in the snow. They shrewdly take advantage of their superior bear-craft to drive a sharp bargain at the expense of the city sportsman, selling the bear for a specific sum of money if they think the find a small animal, and by the pound if the hole indicates a big one.

When the writer was at Count Tolstoï's, the famous author showed me the scars of an old scalp-wound that had been inflicted by a bear. In his ante-literary days the Count was very fond of bear-hunting, and, on the occasion to which the scars bear reference, a wounded bear came perilously near cheating the world out of "War and Peace," "My Religion," and other of the Count's productions that we could ill afford to be without. He owed his life to the presence of mind of his brother, who was hunting with him. Tolstoï had shot at bruin twice, wounding him both times without disabling him ; and in return the bear had knocked him down in the snow and was standing over him, when the brother rushed up and put a bullet in its brain.

From bruin to Briton may, or may not be much of a digression, depending, of course, on the nature of the Briton in the case. For the sake of continuity, moreover, even more startling associations than these two may be permitted to the chronicler of a journey. It is well, however, when abrupt transitions of this nature occur, if one is able to disarm English susceptibility by introducing, after treating of bears, a gentleman as unlike one of those animals as it is possible for a human being to be.

We spent the heat of the day at the hospitable datscha of Mr. Hamson, a cotton mill-owner of Tzaritza. Mr. Hamson is a fair specimen of a type of Englishmen one occasionally comes upon in Russia. He was born in the country, of parents who had gone to Russia and started cotton mills fifty years before. Others went as managers in Russian mills, and in the course of time became partners and proprietors.

You see unmistakable English and Scotch faces among officers of the army and navy, and in centers of mining, manufacturing, and shipping industries. These are the descendants of Englishmen who flocked to Russia during the reign of Peter the Great to take service under him, and for various enterprises since. They take pride in being of Engli..h origin, though it may be but a family tradition among them. You can offer no more acceptable piece of flattery to the lady members of one of these Anglo-Russian families than to compliment them with having the English type of face. On one occasion I overlooked this delicate point, until reminded of the negligence by one of the ladies, who affected surprise that I hadn't mistaken her for an Englishwoman, on account of her face. Her father's grandfather or great-grandfather had come from England some time in the eighteenth century.

In St. Petersburg, army officers with English blood in their veins affect dinners at the Hotel d'Angleterre, where you may see typical English faces under the Russian military visors, or even in the incongruous setting of a Circassian officer's costume. Nearly every day, when the writer was at this hotel, a guardsman and a Circassian, both officers, used to come to lunch together at noon ; as typical a pair of English faces as could be found in all Britain.

Many will be astonished, as I was, to learn that in St. Petersburg, alone, are more than ten thousand English, nearly all of whom are British subjects. The majority of them are connected with the shipping and manufacturing interests in and about Petersburg.

Englishmen who become, as it were, isolated in the provinces, soon lose interest in the doings of the outer world, and surprise a passing countryman, who drops in on them, by their ignorance of current events beyond the Russian border. In this respect, the disreputable press censorship tends to drag them rapidly down to the level of the people among whom they have cast their lot. From the Russian newspapers they learn nothing but what a suspicious and tyrannical government permits the people to know, and in order to keep on good terms with the authorities it is advisable to receive no foreign publications whatever. It seemed curious to meet intelligent and well-educated Englishmen, like Mr. Hamson, who had never heard of what the foreign press was full of at the time of my visit, the *Century's* exposition of the evils of the exile system of Siberia. And it sounded even comical to hear him ask if it were true that " at the Penjdeh affair the English officers had run away ! " Such, it seems, is the story as it had been permitted to circulate in Russia ; where the truth in regard to such matters is never allowed to be published.

On the subject of cotton-spinning our host was more at home. Tariffs were high, he said, yet they couldn't compete with English manufacturers, owing to the incompetence of Russian workmen and the higher rate of interest on capital in Russia. In Russia, capital was worth eight per cent., in England, three ; and a Lancashire weaver was as far ahead of a Russian factory hand " as a race horse was ahead of a donkey." The Manchester man, he reckoned, would do the work of six to eight moujiks.

A great future was looked forward to, however, in cotton production and spinning. Everything possible is being done to promote the cotton growing industry of Russia's Central Asian possessions. American cottongins were being shipped to Samarkand by the dozen, and Americans had been employed by the government to proceed thither and instruct the people in improved methods of cultivation. The dream of Russian statesmen is to see the Trans-Caspian and Lower Volga regions develop into manufacturing districts that shall eventually supply all Russia with cotton goods. The idea is, that when Russia is able to manufacture sufficient for her own people, to keep foreign goods out of the market altogether by means of a prohibitory tariff. Cheap clothing, for the welfare of the masses, is of course, not for a moment to be considered in a country where the interests of the people are always made subservient to that of the state.

We spent Sunday night at a dirty traktir in Podolsk. Wayfarers, other than tramps and pilgrims, were mostly moujik teamsters, whose idea of cleanliness and comfort are on a par with those of the American Indian. The Podolsk traktir contained no bed for transient guests but the bare floor, which, however, the proprietor did something to improve by means of an armful of spiky hay. Sascha had his Cossack bourka, an ample cloak of goat-hair, and the writer had an English rug. With these spread over the hay, and the cushions of our Circassian saddles for pillows, our beds were at least as good as our supper of milk, black bread, and tiny raw salt fishes.

A dozen drunken moujiks, in an adjoining room, added to the sum of our appreciation by howling bacchanalian songs and arguing with each other violently till past midnight. Drunken peasants were an every-day feature of the road, as we pursued our way along the great military *chaussée*. Whether we halted for refreshments at a traktir, morning, noon, or night, maudlin moujiks drinking vodka, or having drunk all they could get, quarreling with the landlord because he wouldn't trust them for yet more, were sure to figure in the by no means attractive picture of Russian village life. In other countries, where drunkenness prevails among the lower orders, it is in the evening when most of the drinking is done, and a drunken man is rarely seen in the morning. Morning drunkenness impressed me, early on the ride, as being one of the national peculiarities of the Russians, though it would, doubtless, be more correct to say that it is one of the characteristics of the uncivilized boozer, that distinguishes him from his brother inebriates of more civilized, and consequently more regular habits. The lot of the Russian peasant is hard in many respects, but much of his burden of woe comes from his inability to resist the doubtful allurements of King Vodka. Without any brains to spare from his scanty equipment for the battle of life, his daily concern is to obtain the wherewithal to pour down his throat and steal away what little he has. Whether he is to be pitied more than blamed is a question that is applicable to individuals rather than to the moujiks as a class. The hopelessness of the outlook ahead of them, and what must seem, to the vast majority of them, the uselessness of attempting to better their condition in life, is, no doubt, largely responsible for the moral degradation of the Russian peasantry.

Indeed, it is hardly necessary to go to Russia for examples of men "driven to drink" for the want of opportunities to better their condition, though there is a limpness and a streak of recklessness in the Russian character that makes for moral surrender in the face of difficulties that the Teuton or the Anglo-Saxon would stand up to and attempt to overcome.

Undoubtedly the lower strata of the Russian population are the drunkenest people under the sun. Looking back over our road, as the thought occurs to me, I remember no village in which drunken people were not very much in evidence. At every wayside traktir where we stayed over night, the forepart of the night would be more or less of a pandemonium from the shouting and singing of roystering moujiks filled with vodka. I have seen gangs of gray-haired old men, see-sawing, flinging their arms about, and making fools of themselves generally, in the sight of the whole village, yet not attracting to themselves so much as the curious or reproachful gaze of a single woman.

On Sunday all the men seemed to be drinking and carousing, and all the women were sitting in little circles in front of the houses gossiping. The one sex seemed to be absolutely oblivious of the proceedings or even the presence of the other. The drunkenness was sad enough, but the indifference of the women to it was the saddest of all.

Sometimes, but not often, were drunken women. Near one village we met a crowd of drunken men and women, as merry and picturesque a set of subjects as Bacchus himself could wish. Hand in hand they reeled along and sang ; now and then they stopped to dance and to express their joy in wild laughter. They halted and sung for us a melodious bacchanalian song, well worth listening to, as we rode past. The men were in red shirts, black velvet trousers, and top boots. The women were in all the colors of the rainbow, with red well in the ascendency. Arriving at a little old, dilapidated ikon by the wayside, the merry-makers, one and all, removed their caps and crossed themselves devoutly, then, proceeding on their way, struck up another bacchanalian refrain.

Soon we reached the groggery. It was a cheap log house, roofed with tin, and with a little porch at the door. On the porch stood an old moujik with a gallon demijohn of vodka, from which he was filling glasses holding about a third of a pint. He seemed to be treating the crowd. One of these portions costs fifteen kopecks, or about eight cents. The best vodka is made from rye, the worst from potatoes. A moujik can get howling drunk for fifteen cents.

On Sundays and holy days the vodka shop is the rallying point of the male population. His rags may be insufficient to cover his nakedness, his house may be tumbling about his head, his family may be upon the verge of starvation, but the improvident moujik hands out his last kopeck for vodka, then runs in debt. He pledges his growing crops, his horse, his only cow, engages his labor in advance at a ruinous discount. He becomes insolvent, and is unable to pay his share of the mir's taxes.

But the moujik is not the only member of Russian society who contributes to the enormous revenue derived from the sale and consumption of vodka. Curious as it may seem to American readers, the Russian priests are notorious boozers. A village priest may get drunk as often as he pleases, and by so doing does not forfeit the respect of his parishioners. It is no uncommon thing, so I was told, for a priest to drink himself into a state of beastly intoxication. And the "black clergy," the monks who spin out an indolent existence in the five hundred monasteries of the Empire, drink brandy out of beer glasses.

But do not imagine that all Russia is shocked at this consumption of spirits by its priesthood—these "carryings-on," as we should call it. Nothing of the kind. The relations of priest and people in Russia are curious to the Protestant mind. The Russian is devoted to the Church, and demands of his priest that he be able to perform the rituals. Whether the priest is of a good moral character or the reverse has little weight with the worshipers. To them he is merely the automatic human machine, a necessary adjunct to the Church, to swing the censer and marry them, and say masses for them and bury them. He seldom attempts to influence their moral character, and they hold him in no sort of respect. As to vodka, if they trouble themselves about it at all it is to envy him his ability to purchase enough to get drunk on oftener than they themselves can afford to.

That vodka drinking is at the root of half the misery one sees in Russia, I was quickly persuaded. The evil is enormous, but the remedy is not so easily found. The revenues are correspondingly enormous, and the universal adoption of temperance by the peasantry would probably bankrupt the government. The revenues from vodka are said to pay the expenses of both army and navy.

A drunken moujik is a maudlin, funny creature.

He is recognized by all classes as primarily a lover of vodka and the music of the accordion. The toy moujik in the shops of Moscow and St. Petersburg always represents a drunken man with a bottle or an accordion. In groups, his wife is trying to pick him up from the ground.

On Tuesday night we put up at the house of a thrifty moujik in the mir of Volosovo. His was an ideal peasant family household, and Volosovo came near being an ideal mir. The ideal mir is one of the happiest arrangements imaginable for the people of the mental attainments and social disposition of the Russian moujik. Unfortunately, the real state of affairs comes far short, in ninety-nine cases out of a hundred, of the ideal, even as we found it in Volosovo.

The household I speak of consisted of an ancient moujik, more than eighty years old,—who remembered Napoleon's retreat from Moscow,—and three robust sons with their families. The house sheltered about eighteen persons. All three of the sons could read and write. I had noticed, when riding through Volosovo, that the houses were neater and better, and that the whole appearance of the place seemed more prosperous than other villages we had passed through. We inquired the reason. " It is because there is no vodka shop in the mir," was the answer.

We entered into conversation on the subject of the moujiks and their condition. Our hosts vied with each other in giving information. Were the moujiks better off since the emancipation than before ?

" Some of them are, and others are not," was the reply. " Everything depends on the man himself.

HARVEST TRAMPS.

There is no reason why all should not be much better off. Vodka was the only trouble. A moujik who kept away from the vodka shop and tended to his land and his work was infinitely better off than when he was a serf. For the man who cared for nothing but drink and neglected his family, serfage and the master's stick were better than freedom.

" The secret of the prosperity of Volosovo is that we voted to have no vodka shop in the mir—that, and nothing else. Every mir has the privilege of local option. (Since this was written, local option has been taken away.) It remains with the people themselves whether they shall admit a vodka seller to their midst or not. Vodka sellers get into the mirs by bribery, and by paying a good share of the taxes. A vodka seller will, perhaps, engage to pay five hundred rubles of the mir's taxes, which, let us say, amounts to one tenth of the whole. This being agreed to, the liquor shop is opened, the moujiks spend everything in drink, and the entire mir is demoralized. The vodka seller takes twenty rubles out of every moujik's pocket ; in return for which he pays twenty kopecks back in the guise of taxes. Now, in Volosovo we decided to keep our twenty rubles and pay our twenty kopecks taxes ourselves, and so, at the end of the year, we find ourselves nineteen rubles and eighty kopecks in pocket."

Thus far, my informant said, the government had been inclined to deal leniently with the moujik. If unable to pay his direct taxes, it was because he had drank vodka, and had thereby paid them, several times over, indirectly. So reasoned a paternal government that had delivered him from serfdom—a weakling to be nursed and borne with patiently. So had it borne with him for twenty-nine years, wavering between the duty of teaching him the lesson of a little self-reliance, by hard experience, and a reluctance to resort to extremes. Beginning with that year (1890), however, the moujik who failed to pay his taxes was to be flogged. From twenty to thirty stripes might be administered, and a fine of five kopecks added with every stroke.

Every mile of the way from Moscow the baleful effects of vodka drinking had thrust itself into our notice, and we asked our hosts why the Russian priests, like the priests of other countries, didn't exert themselves in the cause of temperance. The mass of the Russian population are swayed by the sentiments of devotion to the Church and its precepts. Two days out of every week, the whole of the seven weeks of Lent, three weeks in June, from the beginning of November till Christmas, or about seven months out of the twelve, the ignorant and reverential moujik starves his long-suffering stomach at the bidding of the Church. During all that time he denies himself even eggs and milk, nor deems the condition of his spiritual well-being hard. But though the Church would rebuke him for swallowing a glass of milk in fast time, it says not a word against, but rather encourages, the swallowing of an inordinate quantity of the fiery and biting vodka.

"Why this state of affairs?" we asked.

The devotion of the answer was almost pathetic. "It is bad for the people to drink vodka; but what would the Czar do without the taxes on its consumption?" they replied.

It was bad for the moujiks to ruin themselves, but for the sake of the Czar all things must be endured!

On Thursday we arrived at Tula. Tula is a city of about 90,000 inhabitants, two hundred versts south of Moscow. It is the capital of the province of the same name, and has been famous since the time of Peter the Great for the manufacture of small arms. Its chief reputation, however, rests on the manufacture of samovars and accordions. In every house and palace, and in every peasant's hut throughout the vast extent of the Russian Empire, is found a brass samovar, or tea-urn. These are largely made at Tula.

Like caviare and vodka, the samovar is peculiarly Russian. So excellent a household god, however, will not always be confined to one country and people, however large the one or numerous the other. Its use is spreading to all tea-drinking countries. To every post-station, and to the house of every well-to-do Khan in Persia, the Russian samovar has already made its way, and not a few of the readers of these pages have become familiar with its appearance.

But Tula and its output of samovars, accordions, swords, rifles, and revolvers was interesting to the writer chiefly as the first stage of the equestrian journey from Moscow to the Crimea. After a five day ride we arrived here, men and horses in good trim. I had no intention of riding against time, but to jog along twenty-five to thirty miles a day, keeping well within the capacity of our horses.

As before stated, while the ride would be interesting as a performance on horseback, the principal motive of the journey was to study the country and people. It was in order to do this to the best advantage that I took Sascha Kritsch, the young Moscow student, to interpret and explain as we rode along from day to day. In the writer's opinion there is no better way to study a country than to make a tour on horseback or bicycle, with an educated and communicative youth, from among its inhabitants, for a companion.

Thus far our ride had been chiefly, like the famous maneuvers of the Duke of York, up hill and down. Had that old martinet been in this part of Russia with his 10,000 men, he might have " marched them up the hill, then down again," all day long, by simply following the military road between Moscow and Tula. The country resembles the rolling prairies of southwestern Iowa, but the land is poor. Fields of rye, oats, and potatoes alternate with primeval or artificial forests. We saw not a field of wheat between Moscow and Tula; the soil is not rich enough to produce it to advantage. The system of agriculture followed is known as the " three-field system," by which every field gets three years' rest after six of cultivation.

We talked of the celebrated black earth country, where there would be wheat, wheat, wheat—nothing but wheat. The change would not be agreeable. I imagined, except for the interesting characteristics of the Little Russians, its inhabitants. An ocean of waving wheat fields is an interesting sight to gaze upon, but soon grows monotonous. Here the monotonous character of the country was relieved by the alternate lights and shadows of field and forest. Imagine a rolling country, half forest and half fields of tall, ripening rye, from the ridges of which are always visible from three to a dozen little clusters of peasants' houses, and through which the broad government road cuts a wide swath, and you have the landscape of central Russia, in June, before you.

You have seen it at its best. What it is like in winter, when the forests are bare, the fields a waste of snow, and the red-shirted moujiks asleep on their stoves, can be readily imagined. Even in the holiday garb of June there is a tameness and a sameness in the beauty of the landscape that rob it of half its charms. One longs for a valley or a mountain, and I was constantly reminded by the observations of my companion, that for thousands of square versts, in any direction from Moscow, there is the same dearth of variety. A gully a hundred feet deep, or a ridge a couple of hundred feet high, stirred the adventurous soul of Sascha into an expression of wondering delight. Nor could he quite understand why it was that I viewed these trifling variations of the earth's surface without emotion.

The country passed through sustains a population of forty-five to the square verst. Villages were small, but numerous. We rode through no less than fifty-seven villages, a village for every three and a half versts. They seemed about as thick off the main road as on it. A village usually consists of two rows of log houses, straggling disjointedly along either side of the road. Nine tenths of the houses are unpainted log cabins, thatched with straw; the tenth would be roofed with tin, and with the house painted red and the roof green.

Some of my readers, though not all, will be surprised to learn that each of these villages is a tiny republic, and that the real Russia, the Russia that I am endeavoring to investigate and explain, consists of hundreds of thousands of these miniature peasant republics, to the members of which St. Petersburg is as remote as the heavens, and the Czar a demi-god, as infallible as Jove. These village communities are known as mirs (meers), and their number in all Russia is somewhere near a half million.

A mir consists of a cluster of peasant families, and the land allotted by the government for their support. In Russia are no separate farmsteads, as the term is understood in America. Sometimes, on the outskirts of a village, in the most picturesque situation round about, we saw pretty villas, as superior to the dwellings of the moujiks as heaven is superior to the earth. They were not the dwellings of peasants, however, but the "datschas," or country residences, of rich city merchants, or the owners of large estates. The moujik never isolates his house after the manner of the United States farmer. The inhabitants of the mirs are all clustered together in villages. Usually a dwelling consists of a four-square building, inclosing a court-yard. One side of the square is the house and the other three sheds.

In 1861, when the serfs were emancipated by Alexander II., three and a half dessiatines, in certain districts more in others less (two and a half acres to a dessiatine), of land were allotted to each liberated "soul," or head of a family. At the entrance to a village may be seen a sign-post, stating the number of souls and the number of houses in the community.

To the St. Petersburg government the mir is an administrative and financial unit. Instead of collecting taxes directly from the individual, the government collects them from the mir. The mir, not the individual, is assessed ; and if the community contains one or fifty "souls," incapable of meeting their obligation, the burden of their delinquency has to be borne by their neighbors. The taxes are collected by the starosta, or mayor, of the mir, and paid over by him to an agent of the provincial government.

CHAPTER VI.

WITH COUNT TOLSTOÏ.

ON Friday, July 4, our road from Tula led through Yasnia Polyana, the ancestral estate of Count Leo N. Tolstoï, the novelist. We had ridden out to Tula that morning, and striking the great Moscow-Kharkoff highway, turned our horses' heads toward the south. For some distance our road cut a swath through a magnificent forest. A stone pillar, surmounted by the imperial arms of Russia, told us that it was government property. We turned to the left, and a short distance from the road we came to a pair of circular pillars at the end of an avenue. It was the entrance to the Tolstoï estate. Both pillars and avenue seemed sadly neglected, to one accustomed to the neatness of England and America. The former were in decay, and the latter was overgrown with weeds and vagabond tree shoots. We seemed to be entering the domain of fallen grandeur rather than the abode of Russia's greatest and best known novelist.

On the plastered wall of a tumble-down little lodge, near the pillars, was chalked, in Russian, "Come to the house." We rode up the avenue to the house. It is a white two-story structure of stone and wood—a roomy, though unpretentious abode. The only striking feature about it was a very broad veranda, with rude carvings of horses and birds on the railings. It was six o'clock in the evening, and on the portico sat the Countess and several young ladies. The Countess was doing the honors behind the samovar, and the party were regaling themselves with tea and strawberries. The author sent in his card. Our horses were taken to the stables, and in five minutes we were of the interesting party about the samovar. Beside the Countess were the eldest daughter, the Countess's sister, two nieces from St. Petersburg, and two or three others.

"The Count has been mowing hay this afternoon," said the Countess, "and has not yet come in. I have sent him your card. He will be here in a minute."

Every person at the table could speak English, some of the young ladies so fluently that it was difficult to believe they had not been born and brought up in an English-speaking community.

Presently there appeared on the steps of the portico a thin, sun-browned man of medium height, clad in a coarse linen suit. His bushy eyebrows thatched a pair of kindly yet shrewd blue eyes, and his gray beard and long gray hair looked like a peasant's. A cheap home-made cap, of the same material as his suit, adorned the head to which the world is indebted for "War and Peace," "Anna Karenina," and other masterpieces of the Russian realistic school. Rude boots, as ungainly as the wooden shoes of Germany, attested mutely to the eminent novelist's skill—or lack of it—as a cobbler. Both cap and boots were the Count's own handiwork. The linen trousers were loose and the shirt looser. The latter was worn, moujik fashion, outside the trousers, and was gathered about the waist with a belt of russet leather.

"I am very happy to see you," said Count Tolstoï, cheerily. "I hope you will stay some days. We have had American visitors occasionally ; you are, I see, from New York."

"We are riding from Moscow to the Crimea," I said, " and, of course, couldn't think of passing without calling to pay our respects."

The Count looked thin and worn from a recent illness, but said he was now in good health. He was taking a season of "koumiss cure." At Samara, on the Volga, is an establishment for the manufacture of koumiss, to which the invalids of Russia resort. Count Tolstoï did not care to spend the summer at Samara, so he had set up a little koumiss establishment of his own.

"Come and see it," he said, " and take my koumiss. I have been mowing hay. I must now drink koumiss. I drink it six times a day, and take nothing else but a little soup or tea."

At the end of another short avenue, we came to a round wattle hut with a conical roof. It was a nomad aoul, or tent, of the steppes, improvised out of the best material at hand instead of the felt matting of the tribes in their own homes. Three yourg colts were tethered to a rope outside, and three big, fine brood-mares, their dams, were grazing in the orchard.

A family of Bashkirs occupied the aoul—husband, wife, and two small children. They had been obtained from the koumiss establishments of Samara and brought to Yasnia Polyana. The three mares each gave about a gallon of milk a day, the Count explained, and the foals were allowed to run with them at night. They were milked several times a day, and gave a pint at each milking.

Inside the aoul the Bashkir woman was plying a dasher in a horse-hide churn of milk. A big jar of koumiss stood on a table. The Count poured some into a wooden bowl.

" See how you like it," he said.

It tasted very much like buttermilk, and betrayed to the palate no suggestion of alcohol.

" I thought it had to be fermented," I said.

" It is fermented," returned the Count, " and if a man were to drink enough of it he would feel it go to the head."

" And so you have been mowing hay. You do not, then, like Mr. Gladstone, confine yourself to one form of manual exertion ?"

Tolstoï is an admirer of Mr. Gladstone, but freely criticised the motive of that statesman in chopping down trees as compared with his own ideas of why everybody should work. He had nothing to say against Mr. Gladstone felling trees, but thought it would be better were he to ply his ax for less selfish reasons than to exercise his body and maintain his health. Mr. Gladstone should wield his ax, if he prefers to chop down trees rather than to dig potatoes or mow hay, not merely for the same reason that an athlete goes to the gymnasium, but to earn his living.

" Every man," said the novelist, " ought to do enough work each day to pay for the food he eats and the clothes he wears. Unless he does that he is sponging his living off the labor of other people, and is doing an injustice to his fellow-men. Some days I mow, others I sow grain, plow, dig in the garden, pick berries or apples, or, like Mr. Gladstone, fell a tree. I live very simply. I make my own boots, and if my women would let me, would also make all my own clothes. I do not have to work very long hours to pay for what I consume, and so I find plenty of time to write and study. I am only sixty-two years old, and intend to write a great deal. My only concern is that life may prove too short to enable me to finish all I wish to do."

"What particular literary work have you in contemplatation?"

"Oh, I have many things! My future works will be on educational rather than on purely social matters."

"Will you advocate a new system of education, or only suggest improvements in the present methods?"

"The present system is all wrong," replied the Count. "The foundation of the system which I shall advocate will be the purity and perfection of the parents. In the shadow of paternal perfection the boys will attain perfection, and the purity and goodness of the mothers will be transmitted to the girls. This will be the foundation of a better system of rearing and educating children than the world has yet seen. The present system is full of evils. People have become so used to evils that they are no longer capable of distinguishing the evil from the good. Or, if they recognize an evil, they have been used to it so long that they have lost the sense of proportion, and it seems to them less real and grievous than it is. I hope to expose the evils of the present system and to point out the way to a better order of things all round."

I asked the Count when he expected to bring out his first work on education. He could not say, he replied. Possibly it would not appear during his lifetime. All would depend on circumstances. Tolstoï thinks it would be a good thing if every author would pigeon-hole his manuscripts and publish nothing during his life.

"Then," said he, "there would be less printed paper in the world, and people would find time for reading what was really good."

No author, he argued, ought to receive any compensation for his work, either in money or fame. His reward should be the satisfaction of having done, or having tried to do, something for the improvement of his fellows. He has never willingly seen any of his work go to the publishers, but has always yielded to the importunities and wishes of his friends. His "Kreutzer Sonata," he said, was an unfinished work, and was not intended by him to be published in its present form. But his friends took it, and against his better judgment it was given to the world. He was then preparing the epilogue to it that shortly afterward appeared. He was also writing a treatise on intemperance, setting forth his ideas regarding tobacco, alcohol, opium, hasheesh, rich food, romantic love, and various other indulgences that come under the ban of his creed.

We talked of Siberia, and of the methods of the Russian government. Tolstoï said, "The government is altogether bad. It is a monument of superstition and injustice. As for himself, he went on in the even tenor of his way, doing whatever his conscience approved of, regardless of laws and governments. They usually let him alone, but collisions sometimes occur. The previous winter his eldest daughter had opened a school for the children on the estate. The village pope (priest) sent a memorial to the government asserting that the instruction given in the school was not orthodox. The Governor of Tula, Tolstoï's personal friend, was obliged to come down to Yasnia Polyana and order the school closed. The winter was then about over, and the children had to go to work in the fields anyhow, so not much harm was done. His daughter intended to open the school again, however, the following winter, and to reopen it as often as the authorities might close it up. So, unless they tore it down, stationed a policeman at the door, or exiled the daughter, the school would be carried on.

"The government sins most against the people in the matter of education. None of the concessions it makes are of any value. They are only makeshifts. Schools are in every village, but nothing is taught but 'nonsensical catechism' and the 'three R's.' Yet, with the government restrictions dragging on the heels of the people, a great improvement had taken place since the emancipation of the serfs. It is now possible for every peasant to learn to read and write. All the people need, to make themselves heard, is a free rein to learn what they choose," continued Tolstoï.

The Count called to him a bright little peasant girl, in a blaze of red clothes. "Look here," he said, "how intelligent these children are. The moujik children are

always brighter than ours, brighter than the children
of the rich and noble, up to a certain age.   My daughter
proved that last winter, and it is a fact well known to all
of us.   But after ten or twelve years they begin to get
dull and fall behind.   It's the hard life and the drudgery
of toiling in the fields."

We talked of Africa and its people, the Count having heard of my adventures there the year before.   He
listened with intense interest as I told him that among
the uncivilized Africans, as well as the moujiks of Russia, the children were brighter than the grown people.

I intended to send the Count a copy of " Looking
Backward" that I had in Moscow.   He had already
read it.   He didn't know whether the government permitted it to circulate in Russia, but he had received a
copy through a friend.   The story was very well told,
he said, but that was all he could say for it.

" To be of value, the book should have shown how
the results which are portrayed were to be arrived at.
Without that 'Looking Backward' was nothing but a
fairy tale.   Then, men should live a life as happy and
perfect as that which Mr. Bellamy describes, of their
own free will and spontaneous goodness, and not require government regulation for all their actions."

Of the governments of the present day Tolstoï thinks
the United States government a long way ahead.   It
is almost a mistake, he said, to call it a " government "
at all in the general acceptation of the term.   Certainly,
it was not to be thought of as a " republic " in the
sense that France is a republic.   The French government is a " republican form of government " : the people of the United States have a " natural govern-

ment "—they govern themselves. A people who are simply living under a " republican form of government," because they think it better than any other, may possibly change their minds in time of some great public excitement and think that a king or an emperor would be better after all, but no such change is possible where the government is really and truly a government of the people—" natural government."

We stayed all night, and the next morning the Count and the writer took a long stroll about the estate. On our return three pilgrims were standing outside the house waiting for alms. On the roads of Russia one meets every hour of the summer day little bands of ragged, sunburned men or women, toiling wearily along or sitting down resting by the way. These are people making pilgrimages to Moscow or Kief, as good Mussulmans make pilgrimages to Mecca or Medina.

The three specimens who appeared at Tolstoï's were uncouth members of the species ; their faces were a dirty yellow, their hair and beards were all over their faces and shoulders, and their garments were a mass of rags and dirt. We came up to them, and the Count stood looking at them for a minute with a smile of admiration. Then, with a sweep of the hand, such as an artist might make toward some long-worshiped masterpiece of art, " I like very much these people," he said.

He ordered a servant to give each of them a coin, and then questioned them. One of the men, he explained, was very well off and owned a large farm near Kief. The life the pilgrims lead was his ideal of a perfectly happy, peaceful existence. The only lamentable thing about them was their superstition. They were not influenced by correct motives. They believed that there was virtue in visiting the ikons at Moscow or Kief; whereas the real virtue of their condition was that, in imitation of the Saviour, they were not afraid to start out on their long pilgrimages without so much as a single kopeck in their purses. This man, who owned a farm, had actually started out without a piece of money. The Count said he could, with the greatest pleasure, sever all the ties that bound him to his present mode of life and become a pilgrim.

"It is less of a tumble than most people think," he continued, "to descend from wealth to the bottom of the scale. In Switzerland, a boy who was running in the dark, fell into a hole. He clutched frantically at the edge with his hands and managed to hang on. For a long time he shouted for help, and bruised and lacerated his hands struggling to keep from falling to the bottom, which he supposed was a terrible distance below. At length a man came and told him to let go. He did as he was bid, and to his astonishment found that the firm, safe bottom of the hole was but a few inches below his feet. It is the same with a rich man. He struggles frantically to keep himself up, thinking the bottom means death or worse. Finally, he is compelled to let go, and, like the Swiss boy, is agreeably surprised to find the change a very small one."

The Count told a story of a young man of good family, whom he had known in the Cadet Corps in St. Petersburg, who once turned up at his house as a pilgrim, as road-worn a specimen as any of the three before us. He had been a pilgrim for a year. After staying with Tolstoï awhile, and tasting the sweets of a comfortable life, he one morning suddenly disappeared, without a kopeck in his pocket, and again became a pilgrim.

In a sense, the Count thinks all travelers are pilgrims; and while the person who travels for pleasure or on business is not to be compared for righteousness to the pilgrim who sets out without purse or scrip, yet all travelers are worthier than stay-at-home people. Their virtues consist in their contempt for a life of ease. With delicate flattery he complimented the writer on being " almost a real pilgrim."

It was hot, sultry weather at Yasnia Polyana, and rain and thunder and mud among the untrimmed vegetation about the house made a somewhat gloomy framework for the setting of Tolstoï at home. There were snatches of sunshine, however, in the morning prior to our departure, when the avenues and neglected grounds seemed a trifle more cheerful. From the Russian point of view, the Count's estate, probably, was in very good trim.

We sat on the portico talking until eleven o'clock on the day of our arrival, and we wandered about the estate and chatted next morning. Many subjects were touched upon. The Count likes to talk and to draw out the ideas of his visitors and compare them with his own.

I found him predisposed in favor of America, and the fact that I had just come from New York, and represented an American newspaper, was an open sesame to his sympathies and good will.

It requires but a few minutes' social intercourse

with him to discover that, like the rest of us, he has his weak points. The Count does not altogether disdain notoriety, though he may not be conscious of it. He seemed to me to possess a fair share of " author's vanity." In spite of the humiliation of the spirit and suppression of human exaltation, which is the chief foundation of his creed, Tolstoï likes Americans, because of the English-speaking world, we were the first to translate, read, and appreciate his productions. The taste for Russian literature was acquired in the United States before it spread to England.

There have been visitors to Yasnia Polyana who have carried away the uncharitable conviction that the peculiarities of the Count's daily life are theatrical; that he acts an eccentric part. Sometimes, during our conversations, I, too, thought him knowingly affected, but eventually decided that all his peculiarities come from sincere convictions and honest eccentricity of character.

At times, when talking, Tolstoï leaves the visitor momentarily in doubt whether he is not imposing on your credulity and trying to fathom your understanding; but the final impression is that he is sincere. There is a curious mixture in him of a deep knowledge of the world and the innocence and confidence of a child. Nobody would try to practice a deception on him as a man of the world, because he would feel in advance that Tolstoï would be sure to see through it. But by appealing to the benevolent side of his character, it required little penetration to see that the applicant would have him at a great disadvantage.

The young man who acted as a butler at the house,

and whom I questioned about his master's habits, told me that the moujiks often imposed on his benevolence and shamefully abused his charity. From all the country round the peasants came to Tolstoï with their woes and grievances, much as the freed negroes of the South used to appeal to the St. Clairs among the former slave owners, after the war. A short time before our visit a moujik come to Tolstoï with a very long face and asserted that his horse had died and that he was unable to cultivate his land. The Count gave him a horse out of his own stables to plow his ground and get in his crops. The moujik, who was a worthless fellow, took the horse away, sold it, and spent the money on vodka. Only recently, too, the overseer of the estate had caught a moujik in the act of cutting down and carting off trees from the Count's forest. He brought the thief to Tolstoï and proposed to take him before the court. " Let him go, poor fellow," said the author of 'Christ's Christianity.' "The trees are as much his as mine. I neither planted them nor cut them down."

Neither the timber thief nor the man who swindled him out of the horse was punished. The wonder is that Yasnia Polyana does not become a nest of worthless vagabonds and that the Tolstoï estate is not stripped as bare as a desert. The latter possibility would disturb the Count's equanimity little. He would, in fact, utter no word of protest at the spoliation of his property, and only the stand taken by the Countess and the children prevents the family possessions from melting entirely away.

The estate consists of 1000 dessiatines, or 2500

FEMALE PILGRIMS.

acres of arable land and forest. Part of it is the old family estate, given to the Count's grandfather, General Tolstoï, by Catherine II., as a reward for military services. The remainder has been acquired chiefly from the literary earnings of the Count. All economic affairs he leaves entirely in the hands of his wife. He seems scarcely a member of his own family. By residing in a good house and retaining land and property more than sufficient for his bare support, Tolstoï lives in perpetual violation of his own conscience. This state of affairs he submits to for the sake of his family, who are only partially in sympathy with his creed.

He believes not only that he has no right to the estate, but that it would be an act of pride and presumption to take upon himself even the right to divide it up and give it away. " How can one have the presumption to give away what doesn't belong to him?"

In the matter of land-ownership, Tolstoï declared himself a great admirer of the theories of Henry George. He declared George the greatest American citizen of the present time. He believed, however, in a system of communal, rather than a national, ownership of the land. The ideal state of society would be, to him, the simple, rural communes, in which every family would have the right to till soil enough for its own support. There would be no taxes and no government. The Count believed that all forms of government are humbugs, and that the whole machinery of law and lawyers, courts and judges, is a barbarity, and an excuse for setting one man above another, and enabling the privileged few to rob the many.

Governments he regards as the root of nearly all evils.

Tax collectors he considers highwaymen, who are able to rob people without bloodshed, simply because the tax-payers know that it would be useless to resist the powerful organization of which they are members. He was looking forward to a day when men would see through the fiction of government and would no longer consent to be robbed of money, nor to be instructed in the art of murdering one another in war.

He admires America because we have only a handful of soldiers, and the bitterness of his soul went out to the armed camps of which Berlin and Paris are the centers. In his younger days the Count was an officer and saw service in the Crimean war; but since his conversion the earth contains for him no more monstrous thing than a body of men drilling and practicing every day to perfect themselves in the art of killing the largest number of their brothers in the shortest possible time.

The accumulation of vast possessions by individuals the Count regards as one of the great evils that people have become so accustomed to seeing that they deem the wrong far less than it really is. He believed, however, that the mission of the large American millionaires would be to hasten the climax, when the eyes of the people will be opened by the display of tremendous contrasts. The moral consciousness of the people needs a rude awakening, he thought, and only the development of abnormal contrasts in wealth and poverty is likely to bring the people to consider seriously the equal rights of all. Just as the undue development of the military will one day result in general disarmament, so, he believes, will the vast accumulations of the few and the poverty of the many open the people's eyes to the fact that banks and government treasuries are robber's caves, in which is hoarded the money that has been taken from the people.

The Count, however, didn't think the equalization of property will be brought about by violence, but by a general moral awakening. Millionaires will become convinced that they have no right to the property that they now regard as their own, and will give it up ; just as he would be willing to move off the family estate at Yasnia Polyana. America, he thought, will one day set the example. England will follow; then Russia. The thinkers of Russia, he said, are already seriously studying the problem of doing away with the private ownership of land.

One could not talk with Tolstoï for any length of time without the subject of religion coming to the fore. Only foolish people, he said, trouble their heads about whether there is or is not a personal God ; or whether Christ was or was not more than human. We have our conscience for our guidance, and the only thing is to do right. People are mistaken in doing good here in the hope of future reward. This is the essence of selfishness. It prostitutes the best in humanity to the level of commerce. There is no merit in making a bargain by which you are to receive a ruble some time in the future in return for giving a poorer brother a kopeck or a crust of bread to-day. This is not charity, but usury pure and simple. In Russia the best Christians are those who never go to church. Priests, ministers, and churches the Count holds in scant esteem. The priests he considered as part and parcel of the governmental machinery for grinding the faces of the poor and living without work. To swing a censer and chant senseless masses is, in his opinion, stage-acting. The time wasted on this buffoonery, if devoted to planting and digging potatoes, would suffice them to earn their bread, and then there would be no need of preying on the ignorant and the superstitious.

Preachers should talk less about the future state and devote themselves, firstly, to earning their own livelihood by growing grain and vegetables, and, secondly, to bringing about the kingdom of heaven on earth. The Count had no patience with sectarianism, nor with preachers who are sticklers for certain forms of administering baptism or the sacrament. The spirit of hostility that brings ministers of the gospel on to the debating platform, he said, is not the spirit of Christ, but of Satan. Preachers and religious teachers should devote their energies to the work of compromising and the bridging of differences rather than disputing.

The world has more need of living examples than of weekly sermons. If all the preachers in the world would quit their fine houses, refuse their salaries, and take to sowing and reaping, and preaching every-day sermons of Christ-like lives, they would do more good in a week than they do now in a lifetime. According to the Count, a minister of the gospel who accepts a salary and lives off it, is a robber. The only difference between him and a footpad is that, whereas the latter knocks you down and rifles your pockets, the minister gets at the pockets of honest people by a more ingenious, if less violent, process. In both cases the results are the same: both minister and footpad eat food that they never produced and which, consequently, cannot possibly be theirs by right. Such is the Count's creed.

I found Tolstoï a vegetarian, and convinced that the ideal physical life is that of the Brahmins of India. He believed in reducing one's wants to a minimum, and in producing, so far as possible, with one's own hands the wherewithal both to feed and clothe the body. A state of society in which the condition of one would never be such as to excite envy in another is the secret of true social happiness. In Russia, the pilgrims who roam the country over, depending for their support from day to day on the alms of the people, approach this ideal, and Tolstoï would, so I inferred from his remarks, become a pilgrim himself were it not for the restraints of family ties and considerations.

When he took me into his little koumiss establishment to give me a drink of the beverage, he said with enthusiasm, that with an acre of grass land and a couple of milch mares, a man would possess ample property for his support. The mares would live off the grass and the man could milk them and live off koumiss.

Temperance finds in the great novelist an enthusiastic supporter. He neither drinks intoxicating beverages nor smokes, and he includes in the term many other indulgences that the ordinary advocates of temperance consider apart from their creed.

In his creed romantic love is also intemperance.

The tender passion that has from all time been the theme of the poet and the novelist, Tolstoï deems a species of moral depravity, on a par with gluttony, the smoking of opium, or indulgence in strong drink. A person finding himself, or herself, in love, particularly before marriage, should fight against it as against the opium habit or any other pernicious thing.

Theater-going, dancing, romantic literature of all kinds, anything, in short, that excites the imagination to thoughts of love, is intemperance. Cupid is the devil in his most artful guise.

In speaking of the relations of the sexes, Tolstoï talked with the same freedom from restraint as if he talked of digging potatoes or mowing hay.

The Countess and her sister from St. Petersburg sat at the other end of the table on one occasion, when the Count was particularly inquisitive about the natives of East Africa. To an ordinary mortal the situation would have been embarrassing in the extreme. The ladies, however, were busy chatting together, and their ears, of course, were closed to anything the Count or I might have said.

Tolstoï was deeply interested in the social life of the Masai and requested that a copy of "Scouting for Stanley in East Africa" might be sent him.

His interest in the relations of the sexes seemed to me to be abnormal, almost morbid. Men and women, he insists, should love one another only as friends or as brothers and sisters. Matrimony brought about by romantic love is an unholy and unnatural alliance, that in nine cases out of ten resulted in unhappiness for both parties to the contract.

The keynote of the Count's peculiar creed is "no violence." If cuffed on one cheek, he would turn the other. No matter what another person may be doing, the utmost force that is permitted to be used against him is passive resistance or persuasion. "If a man robs you, who are you that sets yourself up to judge him whether he is in the right or the wrong? One man has no right to judge another, nor to assume the office of executioner by using violence against him. If a man knocks you down, who knows but you have deserved it?

"One person has no right to use violence against another under any circumstances whatever, not even to oppose violence. There must be no self-defense beyond passive resistance. To subdue the passions and gain the upper hand of our human pride is man's first duty to himself and to his fellows. After that, all the rest will come easy enough."

After listening to such talk the Count's advice to keep away from the churches sounded oddly.

An American minister from New York once visited Tolstoï at Yasnia Polyana. Did I know him? I did not; and although Tolstoï spoke with every mark of respect for his visitor as a man, he let it be very plainly understood that the less the rising generation had to do with the modern expounders of the gospels the better for their comprehension of the true religion as he conceives it.

Previous to his conversion the Count had been an atheist. About ten years before there was a census of Russia. It is the custom of the government to impress the students of the universities to assist in taking a census. Tolstoï's eldest son was then a student in Moscow, and the father accompanied the son in going his rounds to number the people.

The task took them into some of the Moscow slums. The scenes of squalid poverty and wretchedness that the Count was then brought in contact with was the turning point in his career. For fifty years he had lived a life of selfish ease and pleasure. He had been through the whole mill of gay, fashionable existence. As a youth, he had been dissipated ; as a man, well-to-do and successful. The world had been to him a pleasure-ground, and the future a subject of philosophical speculation.

He went home a changed man. It seemed as if all his life had been utterly wasted. The selfishness of a life that had been largely devoted to pleasure and self-seeking now seemed to him an enormity of error and wrong. How should he expiate the great crime of fifty years of wrong-doing?

He sought consolation in the existing forms of religion. He said he found them worse than honest atheism. He turned to the Scriptures and independent research and harkened to the teachings of Sutaieff, a free-thinking peasant of Novgorod, who had been persecuted by the priests for independent action in the matter of baptizing his children. He drew inspiration from the child-like simplicity of the peasantry on his estate. He brought to bear on his observations and researches the mind of a cultured man and the intellect of a genius. The result has been the teachings that the world now recognizes as the Tolstoïan creed.

After he had become convinced that salvation lay in

living a Christly life in a truly unselfish sense, the Count was for getting rid of his property forthwith by distributing it among the peasantry. His plan was to descend at once to the level of the poorest of those about him, and earn his living with the plow and the hoe. That this was not done was due entirely to the Countess and friends of the family.

Such, then, was the apostle of this new religion, or, as he would say, of the Christian religion rightly interpreted, at home. Practical people in America would find in many of his ideas the vagaries of an ill-balanced but brilliant intellect.

Genius-like, he was not always logical and consistent. In discussing the merits of Bellamy's "Looking Backward," he condemned the author's judgment in presuming that such a state of society as he describes would be possible with human beings, possessed with the weaknesses and frailties of our kind. Only angels, he said, could exist under such conditions. Yet in the case of these same human beings, with the same weaknesses and frailties that would be the stumbling block in Bellamy's new social world, he advocated " no government, no police, no prisons, no army, no church, no judiciary, no punishment for wrong doing."

The Count's ideas of what is best were still in a state of development. A couple of years before my visit Mr. Stead, of the " Review of Reviews," paid him a visit. At that time he told Stead that he regretted every moment that he did not feel he was dying. He longed to have done with this world and to fathom the mystery of the next. Now he had changed his mind and told me his only fear was that he would not live long enough to finish all the work he wanted to do.

The wife of Tolstoï is a buxom lady, who looked about forty. She has a broad, matronly figure; a kind, motherly face, and was the daughter of a St. Petersburg physician. She is the mother of thirteen children, of whom nine were living. The eldest daughter and the two youngest children were at home. The others were traveling or away visiting, and the eldest son was officiating as Secretary on a Commission at the Prison Congress, which was then sitting in St. Petersburg. He had just written a letter to his mother, expressing disgust at the round of speeches and dinners that appeared to him to be the only probable outcome of the Congress.

The Countess acted as her husband's amanuensis and copyist. She copied and corrected all of his manuscripts. She seemed to be a most excellent woman.

The family life appeared to be altogether charming. Both wife and children fairly idolize the Count. The nieces also think their uncle the embodiment of wisdom and goodness, and the only point on which they openly take issue with him is, naturally enough, on the subject of romantic love as denounced in the "Kreutzer Sonata."

These young people do not always fathom the Count, but they never doubt the wisdom of his actions or the goodness of his motives. Everything he does is right. If you venture to criticise anything the Count has said or done, in their hearing, they defend him stoutly.

We stayed to lunch at twelve, then rode away. In

the house of strict temperance, where the master lives on curds and koumiss, cutlets and a bottle of wine were set out for the visitors. We ate the cutlets but left the wine untouched.

"I thank you very much for coming," said the Count, as he shook hands and advised us to be careful of our horses.

"I wish you a pleasant journey to the Crimea," said the Countess, "and a safe return to America."

Russia is a country where fantastic religious ideas seem to find a congenial soil. The dwarfing of the people's intellects in matters political, is productive of curious expansions in other directions. Between Moscow and Tula I stumbled upon a truly queer religious idea. None but a logical mind could, however, have conceived it. It is intended chiefly to comfort and console people of a doubting and skeptical turn of mind. People who are so unfortunately constituted that they don't know whether or not to believe in the existence of a personal God, and are forever casting about for light on the subject, are instructed by the new religion to "pray to the power that is responsible for their existence." By adopting this broad ground, all fears of missing the mark, so to speak, are done away with, and none need be afraid of going astray through ignorance or misconception.

CHAPTER VII.

AMONG THE MOUJIKS.

FROM Moscow to Count Tolstoï's our road was through the northern forest zone, where the moujiks are poor and superstitious. In many of the windows of the peasants' cottages were dead branches and faded wreaths of ferns and twigs. These were reminiscent of the Whitsuntide celebrations, which the Russian peasantry keep up with many curious cere-. monies, remnants of their old heathen rites.

Games that were formerly celebrated in honor of the Goddess of Spring, have now been transferred with changed names and certain modifications to the Whitsuntide festivities. On the Thursday before Whit-Sunday the peasants flock to the forests and devote themselves to singing and making merry. They cut down a young birch tree and dress it in gown and garland in rude imitation of a female, whom they furthermore garnish with bright ribbons and scraps of rag. This is the Goddess of Spring, in whose honor they now feast and make merry under the trees. In the evening they carry the goddess home with them, singing and dancing before her on the way, and install her as an honored guest in one of their houses till Whit-Sunday. Visits of ceremony are paid to her by the inhabitants of the village on Friday and Saturday, and on Sunday they take her to the nearest pond or stream and throw her in.

On Whit-Sunday the Russian churches are decorated with green as ours are on Christmas; and the flowers and branches are preserved and taken to their homes by the peasants, who believe them to be efficacious in keeping out witches, strange domovois, and epidemic diseases.

Many strange customs still obtain in different parts of Russia in connection with spring, which have come down from the ancient heathen worship of the vernal Deity. All over Russia is held on Thursday, in the seventh week after Easter, the feast, called Semik. In most places, the Spring Goddess takes the form mentioned above. In others, however, the handsomest maiden of the village is chosen to represent Spring; she is enveloped in boughs and blossoms and carried about by the other girls. In the evening the girls and young moujiks join in a circling dance, known as the khorovod. The maidens wear floral wreaths and the youths sport flowers in their hat-bands. After the dancing is over, the girls repair to the nearest water and toss in their wreaths, watching them anxiously to see whether they sink or swim, float ashore, or turn round in a circle. If a wreath doesn't run ashore, the lucky damsel who has been wearing it will have long life and a happy marriage. If it circles round, the wearer will become the victim of unrequited love; and if it sinks she will either become an old maid or meet with an early death.

When going to the forest to manufacture the goddess from a young birch, or to envelop the chosen one in foliage, the maidens sing an ode addressed to the trees, which is evidently a relic of ancient tree-worship. The oak is the Summer tree, and the birch the tree of Spring. They first address the oaks, singing :

> Rejoice not, Oaks ;
> Rejoice not, green Oaks.
> Not to you go the maidens,
> Not to you do they bring pies, cakes, omelettes.

Then turning to the birches, which are the Semik or seventh week (after Easter) trees, they sing, raising their voices to a shout :

> Io, Io, Semik and Troitsa (Trinity) !
> Rejoice, Birches, rejoice green trees!
> To *you* go the maidens,
> To *you* they bring pies, cakes, omelettes.

At the present day, in India, the natives of remote villages, in which there is no large idol, place offerings of food at the foot of trees that have been made sacred to certain of their gods. And a common enough sight is to see the people bowing to the ground, apparently worshiping these trees. In reality they are paying their devotions to the god, whom the tree, in the absence of the idol itself, is believed to represent. The above song of the Russian village maidens seems to point to a time in the past when offerings of food were also made to trees in that country.

From one end of Russia to the other there is one form of amusement that is common to the whole people. It is the circling dance known as the khorovod. It is common also to the Slavs of other countries, being in fact a Slav dance, which gives it a broader geographical and ethnographical meaning. The writer has seen more of it, indeed, in the villages of Crotia and Slavonia, Austria-Hungary, than in Russia. The ride through Russia was made during hay-time and harvest, the busy season, when the young peasants have little time for khorovods on a grand scale. But the children are given to dancing khorovods of an evening, and the writer also saw one danced by a troupe of Little Russians in one of the summer gardens of St. Petersburg.

Near every village is an open spot, where on holidays the young people, arrayed in their brightest costumes, assemble to perform khorovod dances. They form themselves in a circle, as in the old-fashioned game of kiss-in-the-ring, and commence moving round and round, this way and that, singing songs appropriate to the season and the occasion. There are spring khorovods, performed at Easter and Whitsuntide; summer khorovods for midsummer, and autumn khorovods after harvest. Sometimes, in a large village, two khorovods are formed, one at each end of the broad, long street, of which there is only one in a Russian village, as has been observed. At a signal, the two khorovods, which may be a verst apart, begin moving toward each other, preserving the circular formation in the broad road, singing and circling, until they come together in the middle of the village.

The songs are legion, and on every phase of Russian rural life: love, marriage, death, harvest, mother-in-law, and what not. There is the " Millet-sowing khorovod," the " Beer-brewing khorovod," and one called the

"Titmouse." The titmouse khorovod, as well as many others, has a sort of minor dramatic character. The *dramatis personæ* consists of the Bullfinch, a young man, or a girl with a man's hat on; the Titmouse, his sister, and any number of marriageable maidens, who join hands and form a ring around them. The Bullfinch wishes to get married, and the Titmouse has assumed the responsibility of finding him a suitable spouse.

The khorovod begins to circle and to sing in the sad, low cadence peculiar to Russian village maidens:

> Beyond the sea the Titmouse lived ;
> Not grand, nor sumptuous, was her state, etc.;

chorusing observations on the character and peculiarities of many different birds. A feast is held, at which, according to regular Russian tradition, the man looking for a bride may pick and choose among the many who are to be present.

> The widow Owl, though uninvited, came. . . .
> The Owl caressed the feathers of her head. . . .
> Why ever don't you marry Bullfinch, dear ? . . . etc.

The Bullfinch passes various shrewd opinions on the merits or demerits of the several candidates : " I'd take the Magpie—but she chatters so,"—and finally winds up by choosing the Quail, a plump and useful, rather than ornamental, bird.

Generally the songs of the khorovods, when not devoted to any particular theme, deal with the old, yet ever new, story of love. A peculiarity of these village love songs is that they seldom treat of the sentiment in

GIRL HOSTLER.

a joyous, triumphant mood; but deal almost exclusively with its sad and melancholy phases. It is a maiden repining for her lover, who has died or gone away; a youth lamenting the perfidy of his sweetheart, who has jilted him for the sake of a richer suitor; a young couple whose parents forbid them to marry; a young wife whose husband has died or been drafted into the army; a maiden carried off by marauding Tartars; a hard mother-in-law, who ill-uses the young bride—these are the melancholy themes of the love songs of the Russian peasants. The melody of the songs, too, is in harmony with the sentiments, being sung in a' sad, low, wailing tone,—a lamentation rather than a song.

The songs of the khorovods, indeed, are in keeping with the whole character of the Russian land, life, and institutions. They are in harmony and color with the monotonous gray of the level steppes, and the boundless wilderness of the northern forests; level, sad, and melancholy to the senses. From Archangel to Astrakhan there is neither mountain nor beauteous valley; in the equally broad realm of Russian popular song the general tone is correspondingly monotonous. In spirit, the songs breathe the tragedy of the people's life and history. The story of the Russian peasantry is a melancholy history of toil, sorrow, suffering, and despair. Their songs are a reflection of their history; and where they sometimes aspire to comedy, a hollow, counterfeit, almost pitiful ring may readily be detected. Their humorous efforts treat almost exclusively of the universal vice of drunkenness among the moujiks, and of wife-beating.

A fair specimen is the khorovod " A Wife's Love."
A youth, and maiden, who represent the husband and
wife, are surrounded by the circle of singers. The husband offers his wife a present, which she seizes and
flings contemptuously to the ground. The khorovod
singers, amazed at this exhibition of wifely insubordi-
nation, sing:

> Good people, only see!
> She does not love her husband at all!
> Never agrees with him, never bows down to him;
> From him turns away!

The husband goes to the bazaar and buys a whip,
which he offers his wife as a more acceptable present
than the one she threw on the ground. When he
brings a whip in his hand, she receives him with every
mark of affection ; and after a blow with it she bows
very low and submissively, and rewards him with
kisses. The khorovod singers laugh approvingly and
change their song :

> Good people only see!
> How well she loves her lord!
> Always agrees with him ; always bows down to him ;
> Gives him kisses, even.

But the subject of wife-beating is not always treated
of humorously in the khorovods. One popular song
runs thus :

> Beat not thy wife without a cause ;
> But only for good cause beat thy wife ;
> And for a great offense,—etc.

These circling choral dances are believed to be of
very remote antiquity among the people of Russia.

They seem to be allied to somewhat similar dances performed by the Greeks, and doubtless had their origin in pagan ceremonies, when the devotees formed in circles round their idols. Near Tula, the first large town we rode through after leaving Moscow, is a ring of stones, which, according to a legend of the district, represents a khorovod of singing maidens, who, while circling round, were suddenly transformed into stones.

In the winter, when the khorovods or other outdoor games are out of season, the young people indulge in social gatherings at each other's homes, called in some districts Besyedi, in others Posidyelki. Special evenings are appointed by the social leaders of the community, and one of the moujiks offers them the use of his house for the occasion. The maidens usually take some light work with them, such as knitting, or spinning wool or flax. The young men who may be possessed of musical talents bring their instruments, which are usually a rude sort of flageolet or flute made of lengths of reed, or the balalaika of Little Russia, a simple stringed instrument. Refreshments, consisting of kwass and rye cakes, or if the entertainers for the occasion are able to afford the luxury, piroghi, a sort of meat pie, that Russians of the better classes eat at the beginning of their dinner with the soup, are provided. The evening is spent in singing songs with a rousing chorus, dancing, and listening to stories from the lips of long-tongued old women, or garrulous old moujiks with a reputation as story-tellers, and depositories of folk-lore and tradition.

The dances consist of standing in rows or in a circle,

forming a sort of indoor khorovod, while several of
the number take the middle of the floor, turning alter-
nately to one another their backs and faces, meanwhile
singing and stamping time with the feet.   The songs
of the Posidyelki gatherings treat chiefly of the sentiments of love and marriage :

> Remember, dear, remember,
> My former love,
> How we two together, my own, would wander,
> Or sit through the dark autumn nights,
> And whisper sweet secret words.
>> Thou, my own, must never marry.
>> I, the maiden, will never wed !
>> Soon, very soon, my love has changed her mind:
>> Marry, dear, marry !   I am going to wed.

In Little Russia, more particularly, these social
gatherings last all night, the party breaking up at
dawn.   People who have seen something of the flirta-
tions of the young burlaks and servant girls in St.
Petersburg, where after ten o'clock of an evening,
while walking the streets, you are constantly stumbling up against young workmen hugging and kissing
their sweethearts in the untrusty shadows of porches
and doorways, need only to be told that flirtation is
one of the recognized privileges at the Posidyelki, and
that the village moujik's ideas of flirtation are even
more crude than the burlak's.

In some districts it is customary, instead of holding
the Posidyelki at each house of the village in turn, to
select the largest and most suitable, and rent it for the
evenings of the entire winter.   The young men pay a
couple of kopecks an evening, or a quarter of a ruble

for the season. The moujik who owns and lives in the selected cottage derives a revenue of ten or fifteen rubles from the enterprise each winter, and considers himself very well recompensed for the trifling annoyance of having his home converted into a pandemonium of dance and song about every night for several months.

CHAPTER VIII.

SCENES ON THE ROAD.

FOR the first week of our ride the weather was sultry, and occasional thunder-showers, and sometimes dismal rainy days, contributed to the discomforts of both horses and riders. Green-head horse-flies attacked Texas and his companion by the hundreds; and their ravenousness was intensified by the stormy character of the weather to such a degree that nothing but a blow would cause them to relinquish their hold. Texas, being a peculiarly thin-skinned and particular sort of animal, danced and capered along, kicking, striking, and biting at them every step of the way, the very picture of equine misery. Occasionally he considered himself worried to a point that would justify him in lying down in the road and rolling, regardless of the fact that a human being was in the saddle ; and he would pause and impudently essay a certain significant and time-honored movement of the legs, peculiar to his tribe, preliminary to carrying out this heroic method of ridding himself of his tormentors.

Perhaps it was owing to the flies, but along these early stages of the journey he developed a remarkable fondness for sidling up against Sascha's horse and endeavoring to persuade that more sedate animal to halt and permit him to rub himself against him as against a tree or fence. Finding these cajolings of no avail, owing to the objections of every other member of the party, he eventually took to scrubbing up against him as we rode along. Our fortunes at night were various, though always of a degree calculated to humble us to the level of the rude, uncivilized life and unrefinements of the moujik. Sometimes we stayed at traktirs, but in the smaller villages, where the prospective consumption of vodka and weak tea would not justify the establishment of a house of public accommodation, we had to seek refuge with a moujik.

Traktirs, as everything else in Russia that is patronized by the commoner subjects of the Czar, are regarded by the authorities chiefly as teats from which the largest possible yield of taxes are to be milked. A roadside traktir, according to a proprietor of one whom we questioned, pays a tax of 500 rubles a year and upward ; and a courtyard for the accommodation of teams, 250 rubles.

No wonder these people are picayunish and over-reaching in their small way, and disposed to make the utmost of any casual stranger who comes along. The moujiks presented a somewhat less monotonous level of commercial depravity than the proprietors of the traktirs ; but the general level of all was disagreeably low. The tendency of all from whom we were compelled to seek accommodation for man and beast, seemed to be to get the utmost possible number of kopecks out of us, and part from next to nothing in return. Most of them would simply speculate on our necessities, and take advantage of the fact that we had to accept what they chose to supply us with or go without.

The writer's preconceived idea of rural Russia was, that it would be found a country very poor as to ready money, but, nevertheless, a rude plenty in the matter of horse-feed and coarse food. The first proposition turned out to be singularly correct, and rye bread was tolerably plenty, but it was occasionally impossible to get a feed of oats for our horses, and I doubt whether Texas had a half-dozen feeds of decent hay on the whole journey. The "hay" was almost invariably nothing but weeds; and, in striking contrast to the American custom of supplying it to a traveler's horse in generous armfuls, a pair of scales would be brought forth, and "skoolka pfund?" (how many pounds?) would be the question. And, regardless of its glaring worthless-ness, the amount called for would be weighed as critically as though it were the most precious and valuable commodity, the veriest pinches being deducted to avoid over-weight. A particularly annoying advantage that was as often as not taken of us, in the bargain, was to select the moldiest and most utterly worthless armfuls that could be found, with the choice of that or nothing at all. The idea seemed to be to take advantage of strangers, to dispose of what they couldn't very well get rid of to regular customers.

In the matter of food, they were, almost without exception, abominably lazy, and reluctant to put themselves to extra trouble, even for the sake of earning money. Milk was easy to obtain, for the reason that no trouble was required beyond fetching it out of the cellar; and it was often of excellent quality and acceptably cold. A suggestion to cook a chicken, or even to fry us eggs, invariably brought a positive negative as to the chicken, and a counter-suggestion of "samovar" on the question of the eggs.

"Samovar" meant that it would. be less trouble to cook the eggs in the same water that was being boiled to make tea, a handy, slip-shod method exceedingly congenial to a shiftless, reluctant mind. There were exceptions, however, and they are as memorable as fresh little oases on a journey across a desert, no less from their scarcity than from their striking contrast.

After leaving Count Tolstoï's, the nature of the country and the character of the villages underwent a change. We were leaving the region where all had formerly been covered with forest, and were getting into the borderland between forest and steppe. The houses of the moujiks were no longer built exclusively of wood; but, commencing with Yasnia Polyana itself, at least half the number in the villages were of brick. The moujiks make their own bricks, and for the most part build their own houses. In work of this sort, which in most countries would be performed by professional bricklayers and carpenters, the moujiks are probably cleverer than the peasants in almost any other country in the world. To a man, almost, they are expert with an ax, and can hew logs and build a house far neater than the American backwoodsman.

In building a log-house, the walls are calked with hemp, twisted up like a hay rope and punched tightly into every crack and crevice. The house is put together close to where it is to stand, and then moved into its proper position by means of rollers and levers. Whilst in process of building, a rude wooden cross is erected close by, presumably as a measure of protection against the interference of evil spirits and witches.

Curious ceremonies are performed in connection with occupying a new house, varying somewhat in different parts of Russia, but all clearly allied to the rites and ceremonies of old heathen times.

It is believed that if the builders call out the name of any one whilst delivering the initiative blows of the axes, the person denominated will immediately go into a decline and quickly die. By-standers are particularly deferential toward the builders during the preliminaries of putting up a house, lest offense might be given ; and the former are expected to call out the name of some bird or animal, in proof that they have not maliciously brought evil upon any of their neighbors.

In many parts of Russia the foundations of the new house are sprinkled with the blood of some victim slaughtered for the purpose—nowadays, a fowl or young kid ; but in ancient pagan times, probably a human being. The head of the slaughtered fowl or animal is cut off and buried under the corner of the new edifice that is to be occupied by the ikons, the most vener-ated part of the house.

Another part of the new house, to which great ceremonial importance is attached, is the threshold. Precautions are taken to prevent any one crossing it until it has been crossed by the oldest member of the family who is to occupy it, and a cross is made on it to bar the ingress of witches and objectionable spirits. In various provinces some venerable household god, such as a small ikon, or relic of a saint, that has been for a long time an heirloom of the family, is buried under the threshold ; and the more superstitious of the peasants are extremely reluctant to sit down on the threshold of a house. In some places, if a child is still-born in the house it is the custom to bury it under the threshold ; and when a child has been baptized, it is held over the threshold for a minute or two on the way home from the church. To wash a sick child over the threshold is also believed to be almost as efficacious a remedy as sprinkling it with holy water.

When a family are moving out of an old house into a new one, everything portable is removed from the former residence, and a fire is kindled in the stove by the oldest female member of the family. At midday, the embers of this farewell fire are put in a jar and carefully carried to the new domicile and placed in the new stove. The jar is smashed and the fragments carefully collected and buried in the same corner that has been honored with the head of the sacrificial cock or lamb at the laying of the foundations.

When peasants migrate long distances, and the jar of embers cannot possibly be managed, they are careful to take with them a relic of some kind from the old stove, to be incorporated with the one they expect to build in their new home. In connection with the house-changing ceremonies, moreover, great importance is attached to certain formulas addressed to the domovoi, or house spirit, who is cordially invited to accompany the family to their new home, and is welcomed at the threshold of the new house by the heads of the family with bread and salt.

The removal of the domestic ikons is a matter of considerable ceremony in many places, where the moujiks seem to have gone little further in their con-

version to Christianity than to transfer their heathen
conceptions and ceremonies from the household idols
of their ancestors to the holy ikons of the Orthodox
religion. A cock and hen are carried into the new
house and turned loose, whilst the head of the family
respectfully holds the ikons until the cock crows,
before placing them in their new corner. As great
misfortune would come upon the family should chan-
ticleer refuse to lend his support to this all-important
ceremony, care is taken to ascertain beforehand the
crowing proclivities of the various members of the farm-
yard flock, so as to select one that may be depended on
to make himself heard in no uncertain manner.

On the ninth day of the ride we crossed the second
provincial boundary line, which took us out of the
province of Tula into Orel, and we passed through the
town of Msuesue. Strange to say, we here discovered,
among the moujiks, a local peculiarity that one is almost
sure to find among the peasants of certain localities in
any Eastern country. In reply to our inquiries about
distances, they always replied that it was a " verst and a
half," regardless of the actual distance. You find the
same thing in Persia and in Asiatic Turkey. It is simply a curious phase of Oriental politeness, which leads
the people to give the traveler an answer such as they
imagine will fall pleasantly on his ear. In certain parts
of Persia, the writer found it next to impossible to
learn the actual distance to any given point ahead,
owing to this extremely annoying peculiarity. They
take it for granted that the desire of the questioner is
to arrive as quickly as possible at the end of the
fatigues and discomforts of the road, and so they sim-

ply give rein to the nonsensical politeness of misinform-
ing him as to the distance, in order to minimize it
and win his momentary approval.

In Orel we, as a matter of course, excited the suspicions of the police, who, however, contented themselves
with merely keeping a close watch upon our movements until we left the city. The streets of Orel were
disreputably rough even for a Russian provincial city,
and the whole place seemed such a wretched dust-hole
that we halted in it only long enough to get dinner
and to give our horses a few hours' rest. As in any
other Russian town the conspicuous objects were the
churches and the prison. At the doors of the churches
stood old men, mechanically jingling little hand-bells,
and extending to passers-by, for donations, alms-re-
ceivers decorated with crosses.

A peculiar feature of religious fanaticism and men-
dicancy in Russia are certain old men who sometimes
take their stand at favorable points in the cities, and
sometimes wander about all over the empire, from village to village, like the wandering dervishes of Persia.
These men have taken vows to collect money enough
to build a church for the salvation of their own souls,
or they hold commissions from one or other of the big
churches of Moscow or Kiev to collect money for re-
pairs or other purposes. They simply devote their
lives to wandering about and begging for money, and
because it is not for their own use, but for religious purposes, they are able to accumulate large sums.

Here, it seemed to the writer, newly impressed at
this time with the financial slipperiness of the people
along the road, was a particularly fine field for the ex-

ercise of small knavery, by collecting donations from the Orthodox and easily-gulled moujiks, under the pretense of wishing to build a church. It seemed to me that this would be an exceedingly congenial game to any number of Russians; but my companion assured me that this class of fraud was positively unknown among them, owing to their dread of incurring the wrath of the saints. There was probably no mistake whatever about this explanation. One who might be the biggest rogue in all Russia in dealing with his fellows, would tremble in his boots with fear at the suggestion of bamboozling the saints by collecting money falsely in their name. And on the road, in any dangerous part of the country infested by Orthodox robbers, the toe-nail or shin-bone of a saint, bearing the " hall-mark " of Holy Kiev to prove its genuineness, would be a better protection to the traveler than a whole arsenal of revolvers.

All through the provinces of Orel and Kursk, our ears were gladdened,—evening, night, and morning,—by the singing of an astonishing number of nightingales. The forests seemed alive with them, and of an evening fairly rang with their sweet melody. Whether influenced by the cheeriness and the example of these forest songsters, or whether this particular part of Russia is blessed with some mysterious property of earth or air that inspires the vocal muse in humans as well as birds, seemed a reasonable enough fantasy in which to indulge one's mind ; for here, too, we heard more singing from the village maidens than at any other part of the ride. Nightingales are, indeed, said by some authorities to be more plentiful in this part of Russia than in any other country. It would be interesting to know what attracts such numbers of them to this particular locality.

In the villages we now began to see small and temporary rope-walks, and the cultivated landscape, which farther north presented chiefly fields of rye and potatoes, here displayed broad areas of hemp, one of the great staples of Russian export. The village rope-walks were the property of itinerant rope-walkers, who wander over the country from village to village to ply their trade. They usually have a horse and telega to convey their rope-making paraphernalia, and in all respects live the life of gypsies and tinkers. They make the hemp crops of the moujiks into rope of various sizes for a small amount per pood, and, when they have exhausted the stock of customers in one village, pull up stakes and move on to the next.

It was in the village of Subazhna where a youthful assistant to one of these rope-makers gave me a new idea of the extent to which the curse of vodka-drinking has undermined the moral perceptions of the rural Russians. It was a wet, miserable day, and we were compelled to remain over at the village traktir. It was some sort of a holiday, and the traktir was full of roystering moujiks, spending the day, as moujiks spend all their holidays,—drinking themselves into a beastly state of intoxication.

I had taken a little table out under the shed and was writing a letter, when there came reeling out of the back door the youth in question, well-nigh helplessly drunk. He was not more than twelve years old, and was endeavoring, in a pitifully maudlin way, to make a display of jollification. Over and over again he fell sprawling in the mud, and it was pouring with rain. At length, after staggering about the yard and falling a number of times, insensibility or helplessness overcame him, and, already drenched to the skin and plastered with mud, the poor little wretch fell like a log into a puddle of mud and slush, the most pitiable case of "drunk and incapable" that it had ever been my misfortune to see.

This was not later than ten o'clock in the morning. And a particularly revolting sight was to see full-grown men, still in the possession of their senses, taking no other notice of this child, lying there drunk in the pelting rain, than to make some trifling and quite in-different attempt at jocularity at his expense. Sascha and I carried him under the shed and laid him on some hay, a proceeding that attracted ten times as much notice as did the condition of the precocious bibber, from the men whom he had beaten in the reck-less race to get into the gutter and thereby glorify the saint in whose honor they were spending the holiday.

When we had been a couple of hours on the road, next day, Sascha suddenly discovered that he had lost his passport; and when, at noon, we reached a village, it seemed indeed a curious verification of the old maxim that "misfortunes never come singly," that we should for the first time on the ride make the un-welcome acquaintance of an uriadnik.

Of all the vast multitude of bureaucratic satellites that revolve about the throne and the sacred autoc-racy of the Great White Czar, to prevent it being blown over by the breath of public opinion, my readers are commended to the uriadnik, as a valuable study in the science of paternal government as it is understood at St. Petersburg.

The uriadnik first appeared on the stage in 1878; and in the great Russian drama of "The Czar and his Loyal Moujiks," plays the part of rural autocrat among the latter. Commencing in this picturesque rôle, he has succeeded in working his way up to the distinguished position of first villain in the Russian tchin. His most critical and competent judges are the moujiks, whom his existence and the exercise of his talents mostly concern; and from one end of Russia to the other, the writer could get from them but one verdict, which was that the uriadnik is the prettiest combination of police-tyrant, bribe-taker, blackmail-levier, and all-round scourger of his children, that their amiable and well-meaning father, the Czar, has allowed to be laid on their backs. The very word "uriadnik," is indeed likely to always remain in use among the Russian peasantry, even should they and the entire *dramatis personæ* of the paternal government one day disappear, and it will be as the synonym of as many attributes of rascality as could possibly be crowded into the character of one person. The wearers of the title have become a by-word among the moujiks, who have, since their introduction among them, been brought into closer touch with the governing body than they were before.

As the Czar is autocrat of Russia, and a Governor-General of his province, so is the uriadnik autocrat of the village community. Prior to 1878, the moujiks were left very much to the management of their own village affairs, and if they paid their taxes promptly, and allowed their minds to remain dormant on the perilous questions of State politics and religion, were not likely to be annoyed and harassed in their daily life. When the Nihilists commenced to stir things up, however, prior to the assassination of Alexander II, and a particularly active crusade was inaugurated against them, a full share of the repressive measures fell on the people for whose liberation the desperate knights of bomb and pistol professed to be working. A force of near 6000 uriadniks was organized and scattered throughout rural Russia, and given police powers in the village communes ; and in Russia "police powers" means well-nigh anything under the sun in the shape of tyrannical and irresponsible interference with the private citizen.

Like all Russian officials, the uriadnik is underpaid, and would find it very difficult indeed to keep up appearances consistent with the importance of his official position, if he had no other source of income than his salary. The office of uriadnik is worth 200 rubles a year, or about $10 a month. Yet you see these gentlemen sporting gold watches, and they appear, on the otherwise monotonous and colorless field of Russian rural life, full-blown, well-nourished, even gorgeous flowers. They have far more tyrannical power over the peasantry than has the Turkish zaptieh among the villages of Asia Minor.

Though "paternal," the Russian government scarcely seems, in any of its relations, part of the same family as the people. In a constitutional country the policeman, despite his uniform and baton, always gives the impression of being in familiar touch with the people, even those whose heads he may be on the point of cracking ; and there is a subtle spirit of apology in his bearing and movements. It is as though he were saying to his fellow-citizens, whom he is ordering to " move on," "It's my duty, you know, and I have no option but to order you about ; otherwise I should be very happy to let you loiter and look in the windows or do anything else you please."

All this is reversed in the Russian police. They, forsooth, are anything but the servants of the people, and they always impressed me as invaders and conquerors of the country. They represent the Czar, the autocratic power ; and their bearing is insufferably insolent, or condescendingly tolerant, according to the disposition of the individual policeman or the status of the person before him. The uriadnik in the peasants' village has the same arbitrary powers of domiciliary visit as the highest police authorities have in the cities. He can invade the houses of the people without warning or preliminary preparation of any kind, at any hour of the day or night. On the grounds of his own suspicions, he is empowered to make nocturnal visitations, and to tumble people out of their beds, search their houses from roof to cellar, and play bull in the china-shop, generally, among the people. Even the most malignant Turkish zaptieh has no such powers as these.

He is required by the powers at St. Petersburg to exercise the same paternal authority over the everyday affairs of the people as villagers, as they do in a national sense. His duties embrace such supervisory tasks as compelling the moujiks to throw open their windows for purposes of ventilation, to keep their floors swept clean, and all manner of sanitary and inquisitorial inspection. In theory, this sort of inspection is no doubt rather to be commended than otherwise ; the trouble is, that not one Russian in ten thousand is fit to be intrusted with powers that practically leave the people at his mercy. The writer has slept in rooms in Russian villages where the windows had evidently not been opened from one year's end to another, for ventilation seems as unnecessary and uncongenial to a moujik, and even to many Russians of considerable education, as to a mole.

The " best room," in nearly every village traktir we stayed at over night, was notoriously in need of being thrown open for ventilation by the uriadnik. The writer found the air in them, that had been boxed up all summer, so insupportable that I used to go and sleep, by preference, under the shed with the horses. Sascha, however, didn't seem to care ; or, at all events, it seemed to his Russian mind " so much like a moujik to sleep with the horses," that he preferred the dangers of suffocation in foul air. I expected to get up some morning and find him a ghastly corpse ; but, somehow, he survived to the end.

It is not the proprietors of traktirs, however, not the gentleman whose cellar contains barrels of vodka, and who owns a half dozen samovars, always ready to be steamed up for the making of tea, that ever feels the inconvenience of the inquisitorial powers of the uriadnik. In one village, where the traktir sleeping-room had to all appearances been sealed up since winter, we heard a queer story of a moujik whose window had been thrown open nearly every day during

the long bitter winter by an over-zealous uriadnik, in this case over-zealous for reasons that would not be very difficult to guess.

One hardly knows what quarter to turn to for the responsibility of the uriadnik. Considered apart from the motive that prompted his creation and distribution among the peasantry, the Russian government certainly committed no heinous crime in organizing a rural constablery, a privilege well within the rights of the most liberal of governments. Considering also the criminal indifference of the moujiks in sanitary matters, one can hardly blame the authorities for ordering summary lessons to be given them in elementary sanitation and the like. Here, however, the tolerable ends ; and despotism begins with the right of domiciliary visit, without warrant or responsibility.

But the chief responsibility for the evil reputation that attaches itself to their office, rests on the uriadniks themselves. And the underlying explanation is to be found in the lamentable fact that it is quite out of the question to find in Russia a body of men equal to the moral obligations of an honest performance of the uriadnik's duties. Were the entire tribe in possession of the field to be suddenly seized and hanged, and a fresh batch of average subjects of the Czar told off to fill their places, in six months the new gang would be as ripe for the hangman's noose as their predecessors.

As a general thing, the uriadniks content themselves with accepting small bribes, which are given to them by people by way of propitiation, in order to be allowed to live in peace, and to blackmailing such persons as seem to be reluctant and unmanageable in the matter of bribes. There are uriadniks, however, who, like the domovois on the 30th March, are given to fits of wanton deviltry, seemingly out of spontaneous and irrepressible exultation over the opportunities of their position. Stories are current of uriadniks entering moujiks' houses, and, on the ground of defective sanitary practices, upsetting jars of milk and tubs of picked cucumbers on to the floor.

In many of the villages south of Tula, one of the standing precautions against fire that the moujiks are required to maintain is to keep ready to hand, beside the water-buckets, axes, etc., previously mentioned, a swab attached to a long pole, which is to be dipped in water for flogging a blazing roof. An uriadnik is said to have once discovered attached to one of these fire poles, instead of the regulation swab, a dead magpie, which the owner of the house had fastened there as a precaution against witches. The zealous officer was naturally indignant, and determined to make an example of the offender that would be remembered for some time, carried it into the house and added it, feathers, corruption, and all, to the kettle of cabbage soup which the house-wife was boiling for the family dinner. As the magpie is a bird which was cursed centuries ago by a Moscow metropolitan, and is therefore unholy, the kettle of soup had to be thrown away.

But to return to the narrative of our own experiences on the road, our first uriadnik, who had turned up in so curious a manner at the exact moment when we could least afford to have anything to do with gentlemen of his kidney, as though uriadniks had the faculty of scenting from afar the vulnerable points of the rest of mankind, as buzzards scent from astonishing distances a carcass, turned out to be a reasonable sort of a chap after all. After considerable bargaining and casual references to the smallness of an uriadnik's salary, he finally accepted the trifling sum of three rubles, in consideration of which he would close his eyes to the fact that Sascha had no passport at all and mine was "irregular." The least we could do to show our appreciation of this extremely moderate demand was to take him into the traktir and set up a friendly samovar of tea.

CHAPTER IX.

INTO MALO RUSSIA.

ON Sunday morning, July 13, we rode into the provincial capital of Kursk ; and applied at the police station for a renewal of Sascha's passport. Strange to say, we were not received with anything beyond a mild and reasonable degree of suspicion by the police authorities of Kursk. The population of Kursk, however, is pre-eminently Orthodox, and the principal business of the police officials being, in consequence, of a monotonously routine character, their bumps of suspicion are of less abnormal development than in localities intellectually wider awake. The chief features of the police station were the vast number of documents piled on the tables and desks, and an exceedingly pompous gentleman, whom we immediately decided must be no less a personage than the Governor-General, but who afterward turned out to be the assistant chief of police, with a salary of, perhaps, 2000 rubles a year, or $20 a week.

One of the stock grievances that the Russians have against the Germans, is, that a German officer, with the salary of a journeyman tailor, will assume airs and ape the hauteur of a prince with an enormous income. It must not, therefore, be supposed that in speaking of the tremendous personalities seen among the police officers of the Russian service, that these worthy gentlemen are guilty of imitating the people whom, of all others in the world, they most cordially hate. It is true that they also sometimes outshine princes with enormous incomes, while drawing the salaries of journeymen tailors, but they manage to do it in a different way from that of the Germans. The difference is, that whereas the German official manages to do it on his salary, it cannot be reiterated too often that the salary of a Russian police officer has very little bearing, indeed, on the size of his income.

But all this has nothing whatever to do with the portly and theatrical gentleman whose personality made the police station of Kursk a memorable spot on our ride ; he being, no doubt, an exceptionally honest and trustworthy official. Far be it from the writer to express the smallest suspicion to the contrary, seeing that the gentleman in question, instead of taking a cynically suspicious interest in us, appeared chiefly desirous of exhibiting, for our edification, the pompous and portentous aspects of human vanity, thereby hoping to make such an impression on our minds as would cause us to remember him to the end of our lives. That he succeeded in this, seems very probable, since, whenever my mind happens to revert to the subject of the Russian police, the figure that invariably looms up in the foreground is that of a remarkably pompous gentleman, six feet or more in height, weighing 400 pounds, and clad, July 13, in a heavy gray ulster overcoat, warm enough for January 13, that reached to the floor, who issued from the inner *sanctum sanctorum* of the Kursk police station, and startled the numerous underlings about the room nearly out of their skins, by stamping impatiently with his foot. Having startled the scribes, secretaries, and policemen in this manner, the assistant police master beamed inquiringly in our direction a moment through his spectacles and then passed out.

In Kursk, as in most provincial Russian cities, the motive that prompts anybody to seriously take up their residence in it is a positive enigma to a foreigner. In summer the people seem to exist chiefly for the purpose of assembling every evening in a little public garden, illumined with colored lamps, where they circle round and round a fountain and peer into each other's faces to the music of a military band, kindly provided by the courtesy of His Excellency the Governor-General of the province. On this particular Sunday evening there were to be extraordinary doings in the little garden, in virtue of which a small admission fee was charged. Rockets and bombs, which exploded and hissed in fiery flight about 6 o'clock P.M., announced to the city that the performances for the evening had begun.

We made our way thither and mingled with the gathering throng. We called for tea and cigarettes at the garden restaurant, and, seated at a table, watched the proceedings with considerable interest. There was a sack-race around the fountain for an accordion ; and any number of abortive efforts on the part of men and boys to climb to the summit of a greased pole, the prize being in this case a samovar. The proprietors of the entertainment seemed to have taken good care that the pole should be so thoroughly covered with grease that they would have been quite safe even had they put up a prize of a million rubles.

There were more rockets and bombs, and then everybody paused in their circular promenade around the fountain to witness the dispatch of a tissue-paper balloonlet. At the flight of the little messenger to the clouds there was an universal clapping of hands, and everybody looked supremely happy. All then resumed the serious business of walking round and round. There were a good many ladies, the *élite* of Kursk, and a good many more who seemed to be even more ele-gant ladies than the real ladies; some were pretty, and a good many more owed their pretensions to the same to the kindly influence of the colored lamps and the charitable twilight of the ending day.

The military and the police were in the majority among the gentlemen, and private citizens seemed to be nowhere. Our friend, the assistant chief, was very much on hand, overcoat suspended cavalierly from his shoulders like a Spanish cloak, he, evidently, having better use for his arms than to thrust them in the sleeves. The arms were utilized as he walked,—not round and round, as everybody else was doing, but at eccentric angles, from one part of the garden to another, for the purpose of greeting his many friends with a glad and sudden surprise—utilized to bulge out the coat to such ample breadth that he seemed to require as much space as a full half dozen ordinary, private subjects of the Czar.

The greater part of the following morning was spent in endeavoring to overcome the prodigious difficulties of dispatching a valise off by rail to Ekaterinoslav. By means of a vast deal of patience, and efforts that came near being superhuman, we succeeded in eventually getting the railway employees to exchange a receipt for our money, and to take the responsibility of forwarding the valise. There were no suspicions here, however, to overcome—nothing but red tape ; skeins of that precious claptrap commodity having to be unraveled at eight different desks and departments ere a common traveler's valise could be sent away.

At the police station we obtained, for rubles, a genuine Russian responsibility-shirking document for my companion ; a sort of a "house-that-Jack-built" paper, stating that he had come there and said he had lost his passport, which he said he had obtained in Moscow, in which city he had said he resided, and in which city he had said he had received his education ; together with a whole string of other "saids," but which as a passport was of no account whatever.

South of Kursk we began to find a decided and exceedingly welcome improvement in the interiors of the people's houses. Here and there we were, at first, astonished to find houses that were clean and sweet within, and before reaching Kharkoff we were among a people who whitewash their interiors every six weeks, an improvement indeed upon the moujiks of the northern forests. We were getting into the famous "black earth region," and a change, too, came over the life to be seen in the fields. Men were harrowing newly plowed fields with as many as four harrows strung one behind another ; and on the road we met single teamsters in charge of as many as ten telegas.

Wheat, rye, and oat harvest was in progress, and the fields were alive with moujiks and their wives and children, all taking a hand. As a general thing, the grain was cut with cradles, swung by the men, and the women did the binding. There were, however, many females who wielded reaping hooks. Regular camps were formed in the fields, since the fields were often many versts away from the villages; and a novel feature of the camps would be the babies in swinging cribs suspended to rude tripods, and the toddlers next in size taking care of them. Occasionally might be seen the mothers, leaving their reaping or binding to kneel beside the cribs and indulge themselves and infants, the one as truly gratified to give as the other to receive.

Near the town of Oboiyan, both men and horses came near scoring a catastrophe in a stream with a bottom of quicksand. Texas, being the livelier horse of the two, managed to scramble out almost before he was in; but Sascha's animal got fairly into it, and whilst plunging about pitched his rider heels over head into the sand and water. Luckily both horse and rider escaped with no greater damage than a wetting and a fright.

Beyond Oboiyan the northern moujik and his red shirt began to gradually fall into the background, and the white-shirted peasants of Little Russia to take his place. The moujik of Malo (Little) Russia cuts a less picturesque figure in the fields than his Muscovite *confrères* of the north. In the fields of the forest zone the red specks conjured up the comparison of poppies, and in our gayer moods it was by this floral title that we would call one another's attention to them. But by no stretch of the imagination, nor by any enchantment born of distance, would it be possible to call the moujik of Malo Russia a flower.   His raiment consists of a coarse white shirt and loose black trousers, top boots, and almost any kind of a hat that comes his way.

" Poppies " were yet reasonably numerous, however; and at noon on July 11, we halted for refreshments at a wayside traktir, kept by a very energetic old lady, who immediately took us into her confidence in regard to the laziness and all-round worthlessness, of a young gentleman in a red shirt to whom she bore the relationship of mother-in-law.   The old lady was one of the singularly few persons I came across in Russia who seemed to have positive, rather than negative, qualities of mind and body ; and almost without asking us what we wished to eat, she set about making us a big omelette, and boiling potatoes.   Her son-in-law, she avowed, was the disappointment of her life.   She was a farmer as well as proprietor of the traktir, and her ambition had been to secure a husband for her daughter who would make a success of the farm whilst she attended to the traktir.   As it turned out, she and her daughter had to perform most of the work, whilst the son-in-law did little beyond eating what they earned, drinking vodka, and sleeping on top of the stove.

When we rode up, both daughter and son-in-law were out in the harvest field ; but the old lady assured us that it was the daughter alone who was doing any work.   The son-in-law, she said, would be found snoozing beneath a shock of grain, pretending to be ill.

A couple of hours after our arrival, the object of the old lady's wrathful denunciations turned up to sharpen his scythe and eat his dinner.   He turned out to be a poor little sallow-faced chap, who looked the very picture of misery. Suspecting that he was, probably, more sinned against than sinning, and she likely to turn out the finest specimen of " mother-in-law " we should stumble upon, we asked him what was the trouble between him and his wife's mother. He replied that the old lady never gave him a moment's peace ; that she wanted him to work night and day, and was for-ever accusing him of being unkind to her daughter.

" My wife," said he, " is a good deal bigger and stronger than I am, as you can see for yourselves ; how, then, can I be unkind to her? Is it possible that a small, weak dog, should treat unkindly one that is half as big again, and twice as strong, as it?"

The mother sometimes kicked up such a row, he added, that there was nothing left for him but to try and take his own part ; in which case, sometimes, mother and daughter got him down on the floor and beat him. The daughter, who had also returned to the house, was of a truth the bigger and stronger of the two, and in the matter of energy she seemed a worthy chip off the maternal block. We asked the son-in-law why he didn't seek happiness in flight, and the answer we received appeared to indicate that the mothers-in-law of Russia, like the police, have a powerful ally in the passport regulations of the country. He couldn't leave without a passport, he said, and this it would be quite impossible for him to obtain without the consent of his wife and mother-in-law.

" But your mother-in-law wishes you were dead," we protested ; " surely she would place no obstacle in the way, if you wished to clear out."

"Pooh! she only talks that way," returned he; "the reason she wouldn't let me go is because I do more work than both of them together."

This young man was well-nigh the last of the "poppies" seen in the roadside fields, though red-shirts are numerous in the cities of the South as well as in the northern part of the Empire.

All through this part of the country an article in great request among the moujiks was paper for the making of rude cigarettes. Shepherds, particularly, would come running to the road from considerable distances to beg pieces of paper. One day we asked one of these shepherds whether it was likely to be wet weather, the shepherds being regarded as the best weather-prophets in the country. His test, in reply to our query, was to moisten his forefinger with his mouth, then hold it up for a few seconds,—a primitive sort of barometer, indeed.

CHAPTER X.

SUSPICIOUS PEASANTS.

ON the evening of July 19 we arrived in Kharkoff, a city of 200,000 inhabitants, and one of the university towns of Russia. About 3500 students find accommodation in its various institutions of learning. It is the metropolis of Little Russia ; and on its streets are seen more handsome women than in any other city of the Empire, save Warsaw. It has numerous splendid churches, with interiors all ablaze with riches, and of its one hundred versts of streets, fifty versts are execrably paved and the other fifty not paved at all.

This glaring difference between the wealthiness of the churches, and the poverty or indifference of the municipalities in Russian cities, was always a matter of controversy between myself and companion. His explanation was that the St. Petersburg government was actively at the back of the churches, whilst the cities had to look after their own streets. Special medals are given for donations of 5000 rubles and upward to churches, and as these medals are much coveted by wealthy merchants, who have no other means of obtaining decorations, the churches simply roll in wealth. It seemed, indeed, that this ingenious method of coaxing donations from wealthy parvenues, might with equally happy results be applied to the far more needful improvement of the streets, which in all cities, save St. Petersburg, are simply abominable.

We bought a Kharkoff morning paper of the date of our arrival in that city. It contained this delightfully accurate piece of news:

Mr. Thomas Sveepos, an American gentleman who is riding on horseback from Moscow to the Black Sea, will leave Kursk this morning, *en route* to Kharkoff. He is accompanied by a Moscow student, A. Krega (Sascha's name was Kritsch). After completing this novel undertaking, Mr. Sveepos intends riding around the world on a bicycle (!).

On the way out of Kharkoff we were honored for the space of a·couple of hundred yards with the company of a gentleman with an exceedingly rusty coat, an exceedingly husky voice, and an exceedingly purple nose. His nationality was as uncertain as his gait, though we judged him to be a Russian of French or Italian descent. Seeing us pass by, he issued from a vodka-shop, and hailing us as "Franzositch correspondenta" offered, for the price of a drink of vodka, to sing us a song from Lermantoff. This tempting offer was not to be resisted, and so we immediately took him up, stipulating that he should sing it while keeping pace with us. Receiving his reward, he doffed his hat and, bidding us *bon voyage*, returned to wet his whistle in our honor, never doubting that we were " Franzositch correspondenta."

That night we stumbled upon the only genuine expression of hospitality, beside our hospitable reception at the country mansion of Count Tolstoï, that revealed itself to us on the journey, until I, after Sascha's return, got among the Crimean Tartars.

At the village of Babayi there was no postayali dvor, and the family of a Rostoff shipping agent, who were spending the summer there, offered us the hospitality of their datscha for the night, and in the morning insisted on us remaining a day to rest. It was in company of this family that we paid our visit to the convent-monastery of Karashavitch, an account of which is found in later pages. In the summer nearly every Russian city family, who can afford the luxury, spend three or four months in the country. Here the ladies pass the warm period of summer in a life of well-nigh ideal lotus-eating. They take their meals under the trees about the grounds, and indulge their love of cigarettes and tea to the last " papyros," and the last cup, demanded by the limits of utter satisfaction. They gossip and read Zola, play cards, and take long drives in the family linega.

If there is water near, they indulge frequently in swimming and wading in it, and get the waterman to row them about in his leaking wherry. In inland Russia, boats always seem leaky, vehicles ramshackly, harnesses old and patchy, fences broken, hedges gappy, and indeed well-nigh everything out of joint.

An interesting member of this hospitable family was a young man who wore the uniform of the Imperial navy. He had, to some extent, worked out his own career, and had entered upon it under very extraordinary circumstances. When he applied for admission to the naval academy, it was to discover that he was debarred on account of being, according to the rules, one year over age. Nothing daunted, he, in the teeth of all persuasions as to the folly of so doing, wrote a letter direct to the Czar, stating his case, and begging that an exception might be made in his favor. To the astonishment of everybody, he received, fifteen days later, an Imperial document which secured to him the coveted permission to enter the academy.

He had passed his examination and had been on several cruises in and about the Black, Mediterranean, and Red Seas.

This young officer gave the writer an amusing insight into some of the mental conceptions of the Russian sailors and younger inferior officers. They liked the French sailors better than the English, he said, because the French sailors kissed them, whereas the English sailors were always punching their heads. There is, it seems, a species of personal assault familiarly known in the Russian navy as being " boxed by a John." English sailors are the " Johns," and boxing, as it is " understanded of the Russian sailors," appears to be less of a scientific operation and more of the pummeling order of assault and defense than is permissible by the actual rules of the ring.

Once—this young officer and *protegé* of the Czar went on to say—his vessel was stationed at Alexandria, at the same time that an English vessel was stationed there, and every day, sailors, after leave ashore, used to come aboard with blackened eyes and broken noses, all evidences of having been " boxed by the Johns."

My informant was a very intelligent young Russian, but in common with a good many Russians, even of fair education, deep down among the bottom layers of his convictions and beliefs were scraps of fanaticism that belong to the days of Peter the Hermit, and seem

startlingly curious in these days of well-nigh universal
enlightenment among the Western nations. In speaking of the different navies, he seemed thoroughly conscious of the superiority of the British navy over the
Russian; "but," said he, "if a British ship were to
attempt to run down a Russian ship, God would interfere on behalf of the Russians, and before the English
ship could reach them it would go to the bottom."

One can understand how the Russian authorities
manage to foster such beliefs in the soldiers, who are
never allowed to come under any outside influence,
but it was something of a revelation to the writer, that
a young officer who had knocked about in foreign
ports should still seriously entertain such fanatical
ideas as this.

We were now fairly in Little Russia, and at Kharkoff we had reached the end of the broad *chaussé*,
which we had followed all the way from Moscow.
The difficulty of finding our way across a country
threaded with small roads that seemed to lead to
nowhere in particular, during our first day out from
Babayi, afforded Sascha exceptional opportunities for
the display of one of his peculiarities of disposition.
This peculiarity consisted of assuming the looks and
the language of utter despair, on the smallest possible
provocation. Any difficulty about finding the road,
getting food to eat, or a place to pass the night, or the
likelihood of being overhauled by the police about our
passports, would bring from Sascha the exclamation,
" Now *what* to do ? " with such a tremendous emphasis
on the " what," that at first I used to look at him with
astonishment, supposing him to be in a frame of mind

akin to that of a man who has just been sentenced to
death.   After no end of these "now *what* to do's,"
and an hour or so of floundering about in a sort of
morass, we eventually struck a broad and well-defined
road, though the roads were now nothing more than
a broad swath of land across the country, preserved by
the government as " the Czar's highway."

We stayed that night at a postayali-dvor, where we
experienced the welcome novelty of a clean white
table-cloth, and clean pillows to repose our heads on,
though we slept out of the house, Sascha in the stable,
I by the side of a hay-rick in the orchard.   The secret
of the clean linen was, that the proprietor of the
place had married a French governess, who seemed to
have taken charge of the management by preference, as
Frenchwomen in France delight in keeping shop.
The contrast between her and the Russian women
belonging to similar establishments along our road,
was remarkably striking.   The women were lazier and
even more indifferent about getting us anything to eat,
or putting themselves out of the way in any shape or
manner for our accommodation, than were the men.
And this churlish heedlessness of character grew to be
worse, and productive of more and more discomfort to
us, as we progressed into the heart of Malo Russia.
Here, we were among a people who could scarcely
be got to give us a civil answer in reply to our
questions about the road.   The moujiks seemed
particularly morose and disinclined to show us any
courtesy.

At Constantinograd, a small town, two days' ride
south of Kharkoff, we were getting well into Malo

Russia. The most striking feature of the landscape were big fields of sunflowers.

All Russia nibbles sunflower seeds in its moments of leisure. Imagine half the citizens of the United States carrying, habitually, a supply of peanuts around in their pockets and nibbling them continually, and you have a hardly exaggerated idea of the ubiquitous part played by the sunflower seed in Russian life. In the circus, in the theater, in the offices, the shops, the tea-houses, the city streets, the village door-stoop, men, women, girls and boys, peasants, nobles, merchants, soldiers—everybody, everywhere, nibble sunflower seeds.

It is to supply this universal taste that thousands of acres of those gorgeous flowers are cultivated on the northern border of Malo Russia.

People who have only seen the big sunflower as a garden ornament can have but a dim conception of the magnificent sight afforded by a forty-acre field of these gorgeous yellow blossoms. I first saw a field of them in the morning, when every big round golden face, without an exception in all the myriads, was looking toward the east. The scene was striking, and suggested a vast multitude of floral Aztecs worshiping the morning sun. Not being acquainted with the habits of the sunflower I wondered all the morning whether all those worshipful faces would, in the evening, be turned toward the west. So I watched other fields as we rode along, and learned, what every other reader of these pages very likely knows already, that the sunflower always turns its face to the east.

Here the mind naturally reverted to a period of the

past, when a slim gentleman in knee breeches, long hair, and with a big sunflower in his button-hole, emerged from the fogs of London to create a passing furore in America in favor of the floral monarch of the Little Russian steppes.

The sunflower crop is one of the best paying in Russia. A good crop is worth, as it stands in the field, 100 rubles a dessiatine, or about $25 an acre. The seeds are sold by the farmer for one and a half to two rubles a pood. Then the merchants retail them for four rubles a pood, and at about every street crossing in Russian provincial cities are stands and peddlers with baskets, selling to the passers-by the product of the big sunflower. In the field the sunflowers are sowed in rows like the " drilled corn " of the Kansas farmer, and, like corn, are cultivated and hilled up with shovel plows.

The peasants of Little Russia seemed to be even more superstitious than the moujiks of the northern forests. Once we halted for noon at a little village when the men were all away at work. The fields belonging to a village are often several versts away. So uneventful is the life of these people that the appearance of a couple of strangers, on horseback, dressed differently from themselves, is an event of portentous possibilities.

The woman from whom we demanded shelter and feed for our horses crossed herself several times and turned pale. She opened the gate, however, and brought us hay. Afraid to approach us, she placed the hay inside the gate and retreated. We went into the house to see about getting a samovar to make tea.

COSSACK CEMETERY.

The poor woman was quaking with fear, but was too frightened to oppose us in anything we might wish to do. The children avoided us and watched us furtively from a distance.

On entering the house we failed to cross ourselves before the ikons, or holy pictures, in the corner. This sacrilegious omission struck new terror to the heart of our unwilling hostess, who decided then and there that we were a pair of antichrists, come to " steal away the souls of the family." She crossed herself several times whenever we spoke to her, and dispatched one of the children to summon a neighbor.

The neighbor arrived, in the form of an ancient crone, who was probably the village znakharka, a mysterious individual to the villagers, half witch, half quack, but, to the better educated, wholly knave. After surveying us awhile and talking the matter over, the znakharka prescribed a piece of bread wet with holy water as the most likely thing to counteract any evil designs we might have on the household.

On January 5 every year a quantity of water is conveyed to the churches of Russia, where it is converted into holy water by the blessings of the priests. Every Orthodox Russian carries home a bottle of this water and keeps it in the house. It is supposed to be efficacious for many ailments, both bodily and spiritual.

The poor woman now produced her precious bottle of holy water, and, pouring some on pieces of bread, gave a piece to each of the children and to a young calf that was in the room. She then ate a piece herself.

Her terror of us was so genuine that I bade Sascha

try to calm her fears. He produced from his bosom the miniature ikon that had been given him by his mother at the beginning of the journey, and assured the woman that he also was a Christian. For a moment her suspicions were allayed, and for very thankfulness she knelt and crossed herself many times. Then it seemed to occur to her that Sascha's ikon was probably worn for purposes of deception; why else had he not crossed himself when he first entered the house ?

All her suspicions were intensified. Tears rolled down her cheeks. In vain Sascha tried to reassure her. Her house would burn down and the souls of the family would wither away as a consequence of our visit. When we departed she was afraid to take money directly from my hand, but motioned us to lay it down.

Though less superstitious than the women, the men regarded us with a different order of suspicion. To some we were mysterious strangers, spying out the country; to others we were secret police. In either case we had sinister designs on the people.

The most common form of suspicion was that we were secretly engaged in numbering the people and assessing the property for the purpose of increasing the taxes. An attempt to photograph a house produced considerable excitement. To the peasants this was proof positive that aggressive measures, in the nature of heavier taxes, would be the outcome of our visit. The peasants themselves were as chary of the Kamaret as the most timid and suspicious of the East African tribes which the writer met the summer before.

Their timidity and suspicions, it is fair to say, were not always the result of superstition. In some cases superstition and ignorance formed the groundwork of their objections, but their chief fears were that we were agents of the government. In one small village the people were so convinced that we were government spies secretly assessing their property that a delegation of elders waited on us and naïvely offered to pay us for undervaluing their belongings. The peasants are always in dread of some new scheme of squeezing more money out of their pockets. The traveler finds among these people the same dread of government officials as in Turkey, Persia, China, and other countries where the officials are notoriously corrupt, though not in the same degree. The evidence of bad government, which finds expression in the servile prostitution of the peasantry before the minions of the governing power, is seen to the best advantage in the Armenian villages of Asiatic Turkey. The arrival of a Turkish officer in a village creates as much consternation among the people as if they were rats in a pit, and the man in uniform the terrier, who is heavily backed to kill them all in a certain length of time. Nine tenths of them are invisible from the time of his arrival to his departure; the other tenth hover about, watchful and alert, to anticipate his every wish. The state of affairs in Russia is a decided improvement on this; but when the worst fears of the peasants take the form of suspicion that the stranger who comes among them is an officer of the government, something evidently is wrong.

One sees less of the military element in provincial

Russia than might have been expected. There are camps at every good-sized town—a tented field—for in Russia the army goes into camp all summer. But garrison towns are few and far apart, and it is only by bearing in mind the vast extent of Russian territory that one can come to accept as probable the numerical claims of its army.

It is curious to see soldiers in uniform working in the harvest fields or mending the roads. The pay of the Russian soldier is only seventy kopecks a month—less than Uncle Sam pays his boys in blue per day. As an offset, however, the Russians are permitted to hire out as laborers or artisans—anything they can find to do. In the cities, the soldiers of the garrison usually have the preference over others as supers in the theaters, and among them are often found amateur actors, singers, and musicians of considerable talent. In the provinces they work at harvesting, plowing, ditch-digging, or anything the large landed proprietors can find for them to do.

In every village are young men who have returned home from their three years' military duty. The Russian peasant dreads going into the army, but when he returns is immensely proud of his service. He then considers himself far superior to those whom three years before he would have given an ear to change places with in order to remain at home. The secret of his exaltation is that while in the barracks he has received a rudimentary education, and knows a thing or two more than the rustics about him.

The military burden, apart from the expenses of keeping up the army, seems to sit lightly enough on the population. Neither the eldest son, nor a son on whom depends the support of his parents, is required to serve. The young man who can pass a certain examination is required to serve only one year in the regular army as a volunteer recruit.

Between Kharkoff and Ekaterinoslav, the crops were a failure. From April 1 to June 1 there had been no rain, and all along our way were fields of grain too poor to repay the expense of cutting. The country seemed to be farmed mostly by large proprietors; villages were becoming scarce and the mansions of big land-owners became a prominent feature of the landscape. Jews and sectarians began to be more prominent in the towns.

At Constantinograd, the proprietor of the traktir was a Jew, and on the wall of our room hung a steel portrait of Sir Moses Montefiore. This portrait of Sir Moses is to be seen on the wall of every Jewish family in Russia, who can afford the luxury of a picture.

It was not always easy to distinguish, readily, Hebrew proprietors by their features, in Malo Russia, for many of the Little Russians themselves are dark and Israelitish in appearance; but the absence of ikons and the presence of the portrait of Sir Moses Montefiore in the room would immediately put us right.

However it may be with the Jews of Russia as a body, the writer is bound to do them the justice of recording the fact that such few specimens as I came in contact with, chiefly keepers of village traktirs, were a decided improvement, as regards cleanliness and willingness to put themselves to trouble, on the Orthodox traktir-keepers. And only in one instance did it seem to me that they were in the slightest degree "smaller" and more grasping as to kopecks. As between the two, though both were decidedly picayunish in their dealings from a Western point of view, if the writer ever got satisfactory accommodation in return for the charges made, it would be from the Jew proprietors rather than the Russian. The Jews were, certainly, shrewder, but not a whit more grasping and inclined to petty exactions; and the superior spirit of enterprise was at least productive of a decent place to sleep and something beyond weak tea and ancient hard boiled eggs to eat.

They were suspicious, however; even more so than the moujiks. At this time the Russian government was giving one of.its periodical twists to the Jewish screw, and these people were comically suspicious that we might be secret agents of the government. Sometimes this continual suspicion of both Russians and Jews would grow irksome, and the annoyance of it would be aggravated by the boorish reluctance of a Russian traktir-keeper to move in the matter of satisfying the cravings of a traveler's hunger; and the hunger and the annoyance would give rise to vengeful imaginings, in which the Jews were permitted to ruin all the moujiks, and the moujiks then permitted to rise up and massacre all the Jews! The condition of a man's stomach has more to do with his frame of mind than many people who have never known semi-starvation are aware of.

Near Pereschepinsk men were ducking, in a marshy tract of country, with old Catherine II match-locks, and huge flint-locks tied to stakes driven in the mud. Others were ambushed among the reeds and flags with flails, with which they smote the unwary quackers with unerring blows, born of long practice. Wild ducks were offered us at seven kopecks apiece; but it was useless to attempt to get one cooked. By this time I was well-nigh beginning to believe that the real secret of why the lower orders of Russia live on rye bread, salted cucumbers, and stewed buckwheat, is because they are too abominably lazy and shiftless to cook anything else.

All through this region of drouth, rye bread seemed to be abundant and cheap, while oats or horse-feed of any kind was difficult to obtain. It was the famous "black earth zone," where wheat and rye seemed to have driven out oats. At first Texas turned up his snip nose disdainfully at rye bread, and looked around with an almost human look of inquiry for oats, but he eventually came down to it, merely stipulating that the first couple of feeds be lightly sprinkled with salt.

At one of the postayali dvors we found the proprietor a comparatively rich land-owner, a young man whose father had left him 500 dessiatines of land. He and his better half were about the worthiest couple we had happened across on the road, for traktir-keepers. Our bed this night was in the hay-loft, and an hour or so after I had returned, Sascha made his appearance in such a jovial frame of mind that I decided he and the host must have been drinking one another's health with something more of ardor than discretion. Inquiring the cause of his hilarity, however, I learned to my astonishment that it was all because our genial host had rewarded him for the yarns he had been spinning about our experiences on the ride, by using the endearing "thou," instead of the more formal "you," in talking to him.

At Novo-Moskovski we once again came under the meddlesome suspicions of the police. The "lion" of Novo-Moskovski was a wooden church with nine small domes, which had been put together without using a single nail. Everything was done by dovetailing and with wooden pins. We were looking at this church, after having put up our horses at the postayali dvor, when up stepped a police officer and demanded to see our passports. They were, of course, declared to be "irregular." Mine was not in language that they could understand, and Sascha's house-that-Jack-built document was no passport at all.

Though an ispravnik, and several "niks" higher in the scale of the Tchin than our useful friends the uriadniks, this official was afraid to peep into the little view-finder of my Kamaret, and he was thoroughly mystified by the pictures in a copy of an American magazine, which he discovered in my saddle-bags. His suspicions of this magazine were, indeed, so remarkably comical that it was with great difficulty I could keep my countenance. He demanded a minute explanation of several plans of Japanese theaters that it contained, evidently suspecting that they might be plans of Russian forts.

Another of his suspicions was directed at a Russian cap which the writer had found preferable in the hot sun, to the one I might otherwise have worn. The fact that a foreigner was wearing a Russian cap smote him as an additional reason why we should be regarded with suspicion, and subjected to annoyance.

After detaining us till eleven o'clock next morning, they announced that the chief objection to allowing us to proceed on our way was Sascha's house-that-Jack-built paper. This was a plain enough bid for a modest contribution to the official pocket, and as the quickest way of settling the difficulty we applied for a paper that would enable him to avoid any further interference. The result was that we obtained another responsibility-dodging document, stating that Sascha had appeared to this police-station with a paper which he said he had obtained at Kurskh, where he had said that he had lost his passport, which he said he had obtained in Moscow, in which city he had said he resided, and in which city he had said he received his education, etc., etc., etc. (!)

CHAPTER XI

NUNS AND CONVENTS.

BEFORE continuing our ride toward the Crimea, let me ask the reader to retrace a few versts of our road, and visit a Russian convent.

A few miles south of Kharkoff is the convent monastery of Karashavitch. It occupies a picturesque knoll overlooking the rich bottom lands of the River Donetz, and contains quarters for both monks and nuns. Sascha and I were enjoying the hospitality of the Rostoff merchant's family before spoken of, and it being Sunday we paid a visit to the monastery.

Monks I had visited in the Alexandra Nevski Monastery at St. Petersburg, and the Nicholai Oograshinski Monastery near Moscow, but this was the first opportunity that had presented itself of seeing something of the manners and custom of the " brides of Christ " in holy Russia. In most countries it is difficult for a male biped to gain admittance into a convent, but the holy Sisters of Russia are extremely liberal in their ideas; and the monastery of Karashavitch, the grounds being occupied in part by monks, was as easy of access to one sex as to the other. Its very name, Karasha, in fact, signifies literally, " all right."

We timed our visit so as to see the nuns at dinner, which we were told would be the most interesting event of the day. We arrived, however, in time for the morning service in the church as well. A visit to a Russian monastery carries the visitor back at once to the Middle Ages, and no sooner were we inside the irregular high wall that crowned the summit of the knoll than our eyes were riveted on a scene worthy of "The Hunchback of Notre Dame."

A nun in black robes and black velvet helmet-shaped head-dress was up in the open belfry of the church ringing a clamorous peal of three bells, by means of ropes manipulated in a curiously skillful manner, with both hands and one foot. One of the bells was a regular "Big Ben," with a funereal boom that must have been the terror of aerial demons for twenty miles around; and in the task of putting them to flight this bell was ably seconded by its lesser, but by no means small brother, the middle bell of the peal. The little bell joined in with a quickening "tinkle-tinkle-tinkle," voicing its imperative mandates half a dozen times to Big Ben's one, as though, in the work of routing the enemy, it was determined not to be outdone by the others. Lucifer himself would have stood no chance against all three, and even had he braved the bells, a glance at the weird-looking figure in the belfry would have convinced him of the folly of bravado in the presence of so skillful and vigorous a holy Sister.

The black figure against the blue summer sky, with black-draped arms outstretched and one foot working a treadle, the whole body bending and swaying in muscular unison with the curious medley of the bells— could that possibly be a woman? A woman it was, however—one of the older nuns; and her performance in this belfry was worth traveling half across Russia to see.

In response to her summons, the shaded walks of the monastery grounds suddenly became alive with black-robed figures. They were the nuns and novices flocking to church from all directions, singly and by twos. The belts of the black frocks were well up between the shoulders, and worldly gewgaws, save black ribbon, had been rigorously eschewed.

Only the head-dress could be called fantastic. The older Sisters wore close-fitting helmets of black velvet and the novices a tall, pointed head-dress of the same material, in shape not unlike that of the Pomeranian Guards of Prussia. A pardonable concession to the world, the flesh, and the devil was permitted in the display of remarkably fine lengths of hair. Russian women have their fair share of this chief glory of the sex, and the young novices were allowed to indulge in single braids which, like a Chinaman's queue, often fell below the waist, and were tied at the end with little bows of black ribbon.

There was nothing noteworthy in the service except the singing. Imagine the offices of the priests in a Roman Catholic church performed by the older nuns, and you have a sufficiently clear idea of this service.

But the singing was soft and sweet and sad,—the plaintive melody that characterizes the popular songs of the Russian people, chastened and refined.

As before stated, most Russian popular songs are tales of sorrow, bewailing the loss of a sweetheart, or the death of cherished hallucinations, and their music is a melancholy plaint. "John Brown's Body," in Russia, instead of a humorous production, would have been a veritable dirge. In sacred music it is the same.

While our churches ring with songs of triumph, praise, and glory, the churches of Russia are filled with sweet, sad plaints for mercy.

By purchasing a small ikon from a grateful little old Sister who kept a stall for the sale of holy pictures, we gained admittance to the dining-room to see the nuns at dinner.

They filed in from church or from their cells, greeting each other affectionately as they came into the room, and stood up in rows along the walls. While waiting the dinner hour they chatted and smiled, and laid their heads together, and formed little gossiping groups, the queer head-dresses bobbing and turning, bowing and nodding. The novices had donned white aprons.

The table being ready, the nuns clustered together, and, turning their faces toward Jerusalem, sang a paternoster, afterward taking their seats. Four nuns had to eat from one plate and drink from one glass. Each had a square piece of black bread, a tiny cellar of salt, and a wooden spoon. Decanters of kwass were on the tables, and seemed to be in more demand than anything else. Whether they were thirsty after their singing, or whether the kwass was irresistible in itself, those who got a first chance at the decanters gave small heed to the rights of their sisters, many of whom got next to none. Kwass, black bread and salt, cabbage soup, and a porridge of grain was the meal. Four of the plumpest of the young novices were waiters, while others handed in the bowls and dishes at a door. Throughout the meal one of the nuns stood and read aloud from the lives of the Saints, while another also stood in a corner as a punishment for some slight breach of discipline.

It was all very interesting, and when, on returning to St. Petersburg after the ride to the Crimea, a lady invited me to accompany her to one of the largest convents in Russia, I readily accepted. This was the Monastery of Novodaiveètsa, in the eastern suburbs of St. Petersburg. This visit turned out to be even more interesting than the other.

We took with us a little tea-set to present to a nun with whom my friend was acquainted, and who, it was believed, would show us over the place. A ninth-day service for a young lady who had been buried in the convent cemetery was going on in the church when we arrived. There was the same plaintive singing by a choir of novices as at Karashavitch, only, this being a mass for the dead, two patriarchal priests performed the rites. The head-dresses were of a hussar, rather than Pomeranian Guard pattern, and veils of black crape flowed to the ground. In one corner, facing the choristers, was an old lady weeping bitterly, the mother of the young woman for whom the service was held. One of the nuns presented her with a loaf of holy bread.

Sister Salavioff, recognizing my companion, came over and kissed her several times, first on one cheek, then on the other, and saluted the author with a bow. Hers was a pale face, and, save for a roguish twinkle in a pair of remarkably lively black eyes, might have served as a model for a typical holy Sister. After the service it was her duty to extinguish the candles, when she said she would show us everything worth seeing in the convent.

We followed the priests and the choristers to the grave of the dead girl to see the services there. The grave was hidden beneath piles of flowers and wreaths, and the priests swung censers over it as they led the services.

"God have mercy upon our sister's soul," wailed the nuns in the same melancholy yet melodious strain.

The poor mother and a small gathering of friends stood at one end of the mound of fading flowers, and wept and made signs of the Cross. The services being ended, a big dish of boiled rice was produced and set on the grave. Everybody ate a spoonful, and the rest was scattered over the grave.

This cemetery was the most beautifully kept and interesting I had ever seen. Sister Salavioff showed us over it, explaining everything. In their family life the Russians are an affectionate people, and they do their best to follow their departed friends into the spirit world. "They think more of the dead than of the living," said my companion.

And, indeed, this convent cemetery was to me a revelation of how far superstition and religion combined may carry people in their striving to penetrate the mysteries of the future life and link them with the present. The ambition of every Russian is to be buried in a monastery, and those who are rich enough invariably find a resting place within this sacred boundary.

Rich merchants, who are, in Russia, often as ignorant and superstitious as the peasants, leave large sums of money to the monasteries in return for choice burial plots and future masses for the welfare of their souls.

A grave costs from 500 to 1000 rubles for positions

near the cemetery church, down to 50 rubles for remote situations near the outer wall.

Over many of the graves are built beautiful little houses, chiefly of glass and ornamental marble or iron, like small summer-houses.   These houses are cosily furnished with rugs, tables, chairs, etc., and the windows are embellished with fancy curtains or made of stained glass.   Photographs of the dead hang on the rear wall, which is not of glass, and sometimes busts stand on a shelf.   Easter eggs, religious books, and other mementoes of the departed are on the table.   Pots of flowers stand around, and ikons and holy pictures hang up or stand on a shelf as in the houses of the living.

In one of these houses sat a woman reading a book, and with a samovar of tea on the table.   "A disconsolate widow," explained Sister Salavioff, "who comes twice a week to spend the day in reading or knitting, and drinking tea in the company of her departed husband."

In another house were a family party, also with a samovar, and luncheon brought in a basket.   Some of the family were smoking cigarettes.   They, too, were enjoying the company of such members of the family as had "gone before."

These houses over the graves are peculiarly interesting, as being a distinct survival of heathenism, which the Russians have clung to and shaped to their conceptions of the Christian religion.   The pagan Slavs used to build wooden huts on the graves of their ancestors for the accommodation of the spirit when it chose to return to earth and visit the body, and also for the use of the relatives when they came to mourn on the grave. In spite of ecclesiastical prohibition, the peasants of remote districts still erect log huts on the graves, and in the case of those who have rubles to bestow on the monks and nuns, full liberty to indulge this ancient custom seems to be given.

Eating from a dish of rice around the grave, and scattering the remainder over it, is likewise a relic of paganism. The heathen Slavs used to feast and revel on the graves of the newly buried and leave portions of the food for the use of the departed. In modern Russia the feasting is observed at home after the visit to the grave, but the formal eating and scattering of the rice is decidedly pagan. Whether the old heathen builders of the wooden huts would have thought the structures in the Novodaiveètsa monastery a sign of degeneracy, as they certainly would the substitution of the dish of rice for the old feasting and carousing, is a speculation. But there is a wide difference, indeed. Many of the houses cost from 10,000 to 15,000 rubles, and the finest one in the cemetery cost 30,000 rubles.

Our guide explained further that one of the smaller sources of the convent's revenue was the furnishing of samovars of hot water to relatives who come to drink tea with the dead in these houses. Many of the houses were occupied every day in the year for a few hours by one or another of the relatives, it being looked upon as a special mark of love to the departed to visit and drink tea with them every day. These visitors bring tea and sugar, but find it more convenient to obtain samovars of hot water from the nuns.

On saints' days, name days, etc., candles are burned, and tapers in cups of holy oil are always burning. The nuns are paid from ten rubles a year upward for watering the flowers and keeping each grave trim.

The shafts over such graves as had no house were often quite as interesting. A photograph or crayon portrait of the deceased is usually set in the monument and covered with glass. Or there is a bust or small statuette, the latter being used chiefly in the case of infants. The monument of a celebrated actress was pointed out, whose life-size bust in bronze rested on the top, together with a bronze mask and harp—heathenism again, and a relic of the days when the arms and horse of the dead warrior were buried with him, and domestic implements were interred with his wife or daughter.

The weirdest thing in the cemetery was a grave that is simply a glass house, containing a vault or cellar with a trap-door and steps leading down into it. The Sister told us its story. After twenty years of married life, during which their prayers for offspring had been unanswered, a couple were finally presented with a daughter in 1873. Three years later the new-comer died. The unhappy parents had the body embalmed and placed in a coffin with a glass opening above the face. The tomb in question was built and the coffin deposited in the crypt. Every day for fourteen years past the mother had visited the house, descended through the trap-door, and spent some time looking into the face of the little one through the glass. No change had taken place in its appearance. This last item was told us with a ring of honest pride in her voice, as indicating the peculiar fitness of the convent cemetery as a place of burial.

Afterward we went to the convent, following our guide and chaperon along a dim corridor, that betrayed a number of little doors in the walls. Before one of these doors we halted, while it was unlocked.

"Domois pazhalt gospodin," said the guide, after my friend had entered, and accepting the invitation we found ourselves in a nun's cell. It was a cellar-like room, about eight paces by four, divided into two compartments by a screen. Small grated windows were on a level with the ground without, and the sills contained pots of flowers. The floor was innocent of carpet, but was polished as if with wax.

The sitting-room contained a plain chest of drawers, chairs, table, and a little clock. A small brass samovar, which we were told was thirty years old, stood on the table, and on the wall hung small photographs of the Mother Abbotess, a couple of priests, and relatives of the outer world, besides the inevitable ikons and holy prints. A hospitable offer to steam up the samovar was declined on the score of time and trouble. The smaller compartment contained a narrow bed, with snowy sheets and a thick, comfortable mattress, stuffed with hemp, a chair, and a few other necessaries. The whole was a snug enough retreat.

We next visited the department where the convent kwass is brewed. This was in charge of a lively old nun who, in the outer world had been a countess, and showed good breeding in every movement. She wore a working suit of rusty black and devoted her time to brewing kwass for the rest of the nuns. The room was full of big iron pots, tubs and sacks of rye flour, and was partly occupied by a big oven for baking and drying the bread used in the process of kwass-making. Kwass and sugar for sweetening it were brought for us, and excellent black bread.   The erstwhile Countess was so pleased at the praise bestowed on her rye bread that she insisted on wrapping several slices of it up in a paper for us to take home.

Everything consumed by the nuns is, as far as possible, the work of their own hands.   They aim to provide for all their own wants as well as to make things for sale.   We visited the shoemaking room, where several Sisters were busy as bees with lasts, hammers, awls, wax, and thread ; and they brought out for our inspection several pairs of gaiters which had just been finished.   Shoemaking is as much beyond a woman as sharpening a pencil is, and I must confess that my admiration of these elastic sides was the grossest flattery.

We were soon in woman's true sphere, however, and there was no flattery in praising the gorgeous vestments of silk and gold which the nuns were making to sell to priests.   Nor was it flattery, in the ikon room, which led us to praise the work of twenty or thirty demure-looking Sisters who were engaged in stamping out the most intricate patterns and mosaics on metal surfaces.   Here they could work from patterns and tracings and were equal or superior to men.

There was also a department or studio where about fifty nuns were painting holy pictures, with ancient ikons for their models; and another room where other nuns ground and prepared the paint.

From these very interesting scenes of life and activity we once more sought the acquaintance of the dead,

in the burial vaults beneath the convent. Only the very wealthy are buried here.   Here was a burial-place, indeed. The cool, silent vaults were railed off with iron into squares, in which people were buried. There were marble angels, and paintings of the Saviour by eminent artists. Stained-glass windows flooded the scene with soft light. Here, too, were chairs, tables, etc., for the use of relatives. On one of the chairs in a family inclosure, sat a big tabby cat, fat and sleepy.

"Da-dah," said the Sister, laughing, ' she is keeping watch over the dead."

CHAPTER XII.

ON Saturday noon, July 26, just four weeks out from Moscow, we drew rein a moment to inquire of some moujiks the distance to Ekaterinoslav, which we could see ahead of us, spread over the slope leading up from the southern bank of the Dneiper to the steppe beyond.

A few versts through the sandy, fly-plagued bottom lands of the Dneiper, and we were crossing the river over one of the finest iron bridges in Russia. There was a railway track, and a road for ordinary traffic, above. The broad, though shallow river, far below, presented a scene that was made up of slowly floating rafts and small river steamers, carrying passengers, or towing curious round-roofed barges. Small boats, of the pointed half-moon pattern affected by the Cossacks of the Dneiper, were also moving languidly hither and thither. A small toll was collected from teams and horsemen crossing the bridge. Foot-passengers paid no toll.

Ekaterinoslav, which from a distance made a favorable impression on our minds, seemed to mock at our delusion as we sought a closer acquaintance. Russian cities, like the Russian character and nearly all Russian institutions, are seen to the best advantage when not too closely inspected. A city where all the roofs of

the houses are painted green and red, among which
are a half dozen enormous churches with golden domes,
or domes painted blue and spangled with golden stars,
in imitation of the sky, presents a pretty enough picture spread over a gentle slope, with a broad river for
a foreground.

Vast quantities of paint are used in Russia. Everything is daubed with paint—houses, roofs, railway stations, prisons—nearly everything in the cities. The
colors most in vogue are red, blue, green, and yellow.

The colors of the roofs and houses in the cities, and
the equally gay hues of the clothes worn by the peasants in the country, are the salvation of Russia from an
artistic point of view. Without the red shirts of the
moujiks the Russian villages would present not a single feature pleasing to the eye of the passing traveler;
and without the brightening paint the provincial cities
would be equally depressing.

Ekaterinoslav consists of one long, broad street, or
boulevard, and several short streets, crossing it at right
angles. It is a provincial capital, and contains about
40,000 inhabitants, with a large proportion of Hebrews
and sectarians of many creeds. It was founded by
Catharine II, on her memorable and fantastic journey of
triumph through her dominions, from St. Petersburg to
the Crimea, under the management of her gorgeous
favorite, Potemkin.

That shrewd and gallant courtier of the great Catharine, having discovered in advance that much of the
territory through which his Imperial mistress would pass
was uninhabited steppe, conceived and carried out the
truly Oriental project of building sham villages all

along the route.   Log villages, brightly painted, sprang up like mushrooms at his bidding, and thousands of peasants were compelled, *nolens volens*, to take up their residence in them and to turn out in their Sunday clothes when the Imperial party drove through.   From Kiev the Empress sailed in barges down the Dneiper, and taking a fancy to the spot on which Ekaterinoslav now stands, ordered a city to be built.   Her statue is perched on the highest spot of ground at the east end of the boulevard.

This boulevard consists of three parallel roads.   The center track is divided from the others by an avenue of trees and sidewalks, and is paved after the usual manner of provincial Russia, in other words, so abominably rough that the drosky drivers keep off it altogether, except in wet weather, when the side roads are sloughs of sticky mud.   These side roads were several inches deep in dust as we rode down the street in search of a hotel, and droskies and squeaking telegas plowing through it filled the air to suffocation.

Dusty policemen eyed us suspiciously, and news was immediately conveyed to the Chief of Police that a couple of strange horsemen had arrived in the city. Ekaterinoslav is full of latent sedition, both civil and religious, and the authorities are offensively suspicious of anything that strikes them as being a trifle out of the ordinary.   That we were dangerous characters to be at large seemed the opinion of every policeman who cast his eye on us as we rode down the street, and at the hotel our passports were at once declared " irregular."

In short, we were to be detained on some pretext or other until the police authorities had time to revolve

in their exceedingly suspicious minds all known circumstances connected with us. Of course, we were not
told this in a straightforward manner, blunt honesty
in such matters being entirely foreign to the police
authorities of Russia, except those at the top of the
tree in St. Petersburg, who have nothing to fear in case
of making a mistake. The provincial tchinovnik, when
called upon to take action upon anything outside his
ordinary routine, is prone to lose his senses and commit some remarkable piece of folly. His logic is sur-
prisingly eccentric to begin with, and he is always painfully aware of being between the Scylla of underzeal,
which may cost him his official head, and the Charyb-
dis of "putting his foot in it" through meddling with
what he does not understand.

The officials of Ekaterinoslav could not believe that
two horsemen might ride through the country and be
neither spies of some foreign government, secret missionaries bent on corrupting the allegiance of the Orthodox moujiks, political propagandists disseminating the
seeds of sedition, nor Nihilists inciting them to rebellion against the Czar. All these possibilities and a
hundred variations of these, occurred to the inscrutable
minds of the tchinovniks of Ekaterinoslav in connection with our appearance.

They could not understand my American passport.
"It should have been written in Russian." Sascha's
document was no passport at all—a fact that we had had
very good reason to know without further enlightenment here. "Why hadn't I a special passport granting the right to travel through Russia in this most extraordinary manner?"

This was indeed the rub—we were a little different from the mortals about them, a thing that never fails to arouse the suspicions of the Russian officials to abnormal activity.   A foreigner on horseback with a strange Russian for an interpreter, the one with no document except an American passport which they were unable to make anything of, the other with an "irregular" paper!   No wonder that officials, whose first qualification for the faithful discharge of their duties is to be suspicious of everything and everybody, were more than suspicious of us.

In Russia everybody is considered a criminal of some kidney or other, unless he has papers in his pocket proving him to be otherwise.   Since, to the tchinovnik mind, we were without such papers, we must therefore be "something," though they were sorely puzzled for a definite reply to their suspicions.

Arrest us?   Oh, dear, no! not yet.   No telling who or what this American might turn out to be.

Detain us, then, on suspicion?   No, not even that on direct police responsibility; this American might have friends in high places in St. Petersburg; who could tell?   Still, for all this, we must be detained on some pretext or other, and, however fantastic in his logic, the Russian tchinovnik is never at a loss for a pretext.

When we returned to the hotel, after a visit to the post-office and to the railway station, where it had taken us a couple of hours to unravel sufficient red tape to dispatch a valise to Sevastopol, the hostler informed us that a gentleman in a black coat and derby hat had been in the stable critically examining our horses. By and by we received notice from the Chief of Police that the Society for Prevention of Cruelty to Animals had pronounced Sascha's horse unfit to travel, owing to a saddle-sore on its back, and, therefore, though very reluctant to detain us, he would have to beg us to postpone our departure until further notice.

This was really a clever move, thoroughly Russian, not to say Oriental ; worthy of Mahmoud Yusuf Khan, the Afghan chief, who once obstructed the author's road through Afghanistan, not because he wished to do so, but " for your own good "; worthy indeed of the wiliest of diplomats.

It seemed odd, though, that there should be in Ekaterinoslav, the head-center of Russian Jew-baiting and sectarian persecution, a Society for the Prevention of Cruelty to Animals. There was one, however—a society of emotional old ladies, so far as we could learn. They were certainly handy for the Chief of Police to turn to in a case like ours, and the tchinovnik who thought of them, and reasoned that horses that had been ridden through the midsummer heat from Moscow might perhaps not be in first-class form, deserved promotion then and there.

We proceeded to the police station on Sunday morning, and spent an hour or so waiting for the arrival of the chief. To the under police officers an American was a *rara avis*, and his demeanor a positive enigma. The spectacle of a human being in civilian's clothes, and somewhat travel-worn clothes to boot, presuming to conduct himself in a self-reliant, independent manner in a room full of tchinovniks, filled them with amazement.

In provincial Russia the ordinary civilian is expected to cringe and cower like a whipped cur before every petty officer of police, and the constitutional attitude of the latter is one of overbearing insolence. Ekaterinoslav is one of the worst police-ridden holes in Russia, owing to the mixed character of the population, and the fact that the city aspires to the distinction of being the chief intellectual center of South Russia. "Intellectual centers" being, in the opinion of the Czar's government, synonymous with treason, political intrigue, and the like, the good people of Ekaterinoslav have to put up with a more than ordinarily troublesome dose of police officers as an offset to their human vanity in the indulgence of intellectual aspirations.

The writer flatters himself that he very likely gave the police officers of Ekaterinoslav the first faint conception which had ever entered their queer minds that a person in private clothes might, after all, possess a few abstract rights, even in the presence of minions of autocracy in uniform.

Since none of them offered me a seat, I simply took the nearest empty one.

Such a remarkable occurrence as this had probably never happened before in all the eventful history of the police station of Ekaterinoslav. A civilian so independent in the presence of police officers as to take a seat! This action produced a mild sensation among the officers, and was rewarded with side looks of consternation from half a dozen civilians who stood huddled up near the door, hats in hand, the very picture of sheepish submission.

This was decidedly amusing, and, leaning back comfortably in the chair, I now cocked my feet up on a wooden bench about two feet high. This, though a popular American attitude, was, of course, under the circumstances, wrong. But I was now merely acting a part for the purpose of giving these gentlemen an exaggerated idea of the relative positions of policemen and civilians in America, which I wanted them to understand to be opposite to their relations in Ekaterinoslav.

The last attitude caused them to redden up to the very roots of their hair, and there really seemed a danger that one or two of them might even go off into apoplectic fits. To them I was as much of a phenomenon as a sheep who should venture among wolves without exhibiting fear. Had I suddenly thrown off my civilian garb, and in familiar Russian revealed myself to them as Gen. Rusezki, of the Petersburg Division of the Third Section Secret Police, who had dropped in on them in the guise of an American traveler, they would have comprehended me at once, independent attitude and all. But since nothing of the sort took place, one of the officers summoned Sascha into an adjoining room and proceeded to question him in regard to my extremely queer behavior.

Was this gentleman aware that he was in the presence of police officers?

" Yes," said Sascha, " he knows you are police officers, but he is an American, and in America it is the police who humble themselves before the people, and not the people before the police."

This was Sascha's exaggerated interpretation of what had been told him some days before as to the relations between police and people in England and America. The officer probably did not believe him, since a Russian seldom believes what is told him, unless it agrees in some measure with his own knowledge and conceptions ; and nothing in all the wide range of human affairs could seem so wildly improbable to this man as the explanation that had been vouchsafed by my companion.

Still there must be something in it, for on no other grounds could my extraordinary bearing be explained. And so, after considerable consultation together, they decided to compromise matters by simply asking me to assume an upright position in the chair instead of the free-and-easy American loll.

Sascha explained afterward their talk among themselves, which is worth mentioning as an evidence of the Russian idea of Americans. They were more puzzled than affronted at my independent bearing. They had always had a friendly feeling toward Americans, though they knew very little about them, they agreed among themselves and with Sascha. But my conduct was decidedly different from anything they had ever thought of in connection with us.

"Tell them that the police officers are the servants and not the masters of the people in America," I said to Sascha, not, however, without mental reservations that would, if expressed, have made my case rather foggy and difficult to be understood.

"But this is Russia," replied one of the officers. " Here the Czar is master and the police represent his power among the people. Here the people not only have to obey the police, but they also have to come to the police and beg and pray to be allowed to do what they wish." And this was said in a tone of exultation: "It is we who have the whip hand in Russia, and we mean to keep it, too!"

The police stations are the busiest places in Russia. Through the instrumentality of the police the government of the Czar attempts to regulate the goings in and the comings out, and well-nigh every move, motive, and concern of the whole vast population of this broad empire, which extends from the German frontier to the Pacific, and contains 120,000,000 souls. This great organization of belted, booted, and sabered policemen are the hands, eyes, and ears of the paternal government of the White Czar. This paternal government assumes that the people are children, who are not to be permitted to take the initiative in anything beyond the mere animal acts of eating, drinking, sleeping, and working in the fields.

By means of the elaborate passport system the police are enabled to keep their hands on all this numerous family, and to require them to apply at the police stations whenever they wish to do anything or go anywhere, much as children apply to their parents. Hence it comes that in the Russian police stations there is a stream of people constantly coming and going. The people are mulcted in fees on every imaginable pretext, and the amount of money that flows into the treasury through the sluices of the police stations, in the form of petty exactions, must be enormous. Half as much more, probably, finds its way into the pockets of the police officers in the form of bribes.

Bribery is carried on in the Russian police offices in

a comically open manner.   We were in the Ekaterinoslav office probably an hour, and during that time observed three separate cases that took place under our
very noses with hardly an effort at secrecy.   The man
who seemed to come in for the lion's share of the
bribes was a little bald-headed fellow who wore a remarkably high collar.

He was the secretary, who had to fill out passports,
prepare petitions, and the like.   When seated at his
desk his back was turned to my point of observation,
and when he was bent over, writing, his enormous
collar concealed all but the baldest and shiniest part of
his head.   And when he looked up and exposed the
remnants of hair that still clung to the sides, it was as
though a young chicken had just succeeded in pecking
a hole in its shell, sufficiently large to peep out and
take a curious inventory of its surroundings.

The head did, in fact, take very frequent inventories,
not exactly of its surroundings, but of the group of
civilians who stood huddled up in a humbly submissive
attitude, hats in hand, near the door.

Russian officials who occupy situations where bribes
are offered in the presence of other people always wear
short office jackets with pockets ready to hand at the
sides.   The little man with the high collar wore one
of these jackets, as a matter of course, and the dex-
terity with which he could transfer paper money from
the hand of a petitioner to the pockets in it was beautiful to see.   There was nothing particularly rapid about
the movement, nothing of legerdemain, in which the
quickness of the hand is relied on to deceive the eye,
but there was an elegant gracefulness in the act that

stamped it at once as an accomplishment acquired by long and daily practice.

The givers of bribes seemed to be mostly ignorant moujiks from the country. Among the applicants of the morning was a moujik who had neglected to renew his passport at the proper time. Passports have to be renewed at regular intervals, and a person who absents himself for any length of time beyond brings down on himself the suspicions of the authorities in addition to penalties and fines. The " children " of the Czar, like any other children, are forever doing some foolish thing or other that would get them into trouble should it come to the paternal knowledge. Anyhow, it is extremely uncomfortable to come under the ban of suspicion, and above all things else the moujik dreads anything that will bring him conspicuously to the notice of the police.

The moujik in question stood, apparently, perilously near the precipice of police suspicion, as the bald head of the little secretary protruded once again above the white collar and scrutinized the group against the door, and slightly nodded. The moujik stepped forward, and, touching his top-knot with the hand that held his cap, handed the secretary a tattered document. It was his passport, that should have been renewed some time before.

The secretary whirled round in his chair, and, looking the delinquent full in the face, shot from the depths of his big, lack-luster eyes a look that spoke plainer than printed words. The moujik very likely could not have read print, but he readily understood the secretary's look, and, in fact, had been expecting it.

Crumbled up in his horny fist were several greasy ruble notes, part of which were to pay for the new passport and the others were to be his salvation from the dreaded suspicion of the police.

The notes were handed over, covertly slipped from one half-closed hand to another, and, presto! part of them fell into the handy pocket just below the little secretary's extended hand, and the rest were smoothed out leisurely on his desk and laid away in the drawer where they belonged. The little secretary was, in effect, a flesh-and-blood automaton : his pocket was the slot in which the moujik put the rubles, and the prize drawn was a passport, dated a month or two back—in substance, a certificate of immunity from further annoyance and suspicion for several months to come.

It is their salvation from a peck of trouble that the common people of Russia know that an automaton of this character is to be found in every police station, not necessarily with a bald head and high collar, but always with a slot for ruble notes, by means of which a surprising variety of prizes may be drawn. When not too outrageously exacting, these tchinovniks, with ready hands and pockets, are consequently to be regarded as friends rather than enemies of the people.

In Russia anything a man does, or anything he says, or even anything he does not do or say, may get him into trouble. Everything depends on how he manages to stand in the estimation of the police. The offenses of omission are as numerous as those of commission. There is a story popular among the peasants that a moujik was once found dead in the forest. The priest refused to grant him burial in the grave-yard for fear he had committed suicide, and the police refused to let him be buried outside for fear he had not committed suicide. To settle the question an autopsy was held on the corpse, and when it was cut open a police certificate was found inscribed on the heart stating his age, his name, his sex, the color of his hair, beard, and eyes, his native village, and the number of his house, etc.

In Russia almost every conceivable thing a man might do is regulated by the written law. The Russian idea of governing the people is in direct opposition to the conceptions of the West. With us everything that the law does not expressly forbid is permitted; in Russia everything is forbidden that the law does not expressly grant, which means next to nothing at all. And when the whole matter is removed from the realm of theory to every-day practice, Russia, though there is a code of between twenty and thirty huge folio volumes of about 2000 pages apiece, is a country as lawless as an African chieftain's domain. A man with neither money to bribe, nor influence in high places to protect, is at the mercy of any petty police officer or secret government spy, who, out of sheer personal spite, may get him shipped off to the mines of Siberia and ruined for life, though he be the most innocent and harmless person in all Russia.

The second man, who greased the palm and found his way to the good offices of the little bald-headed secretary by means of rubles, seemed to be a burlak or city workman. The exact nature of the transaction we couldn't make out. This time when the secretary examined the document that was handed to him he discovered the rubles neatly placed between the folds.

He didn't seem in the least surprised or disconcerted; didn't even give expression to an apologetic little cough, nor bestow a single glance of acknowledgment on the burlak, but just simply lowered the document and the rubles a trifle below the level of his desk, and when the document was spread out a moment later on the desk the rubles were gone. Only this, and nothing more.

My heart began to warm toward this worthy gentleman, as to a doctor engaged in alleviating the sufferings of the halt, the sick, and the blind, for which he refuses to charge more than they are able and willing to give. Bribery, as an abstract thing, may be detestable, but so long as the present form of government obtains in Russia, by all means multiply the number of baldheaded little tchinovniks with high collars and large pockets.

The petitioners who came to the police station while we were in the office were a curious crowd. There was an isvoshchic who came to complain that a man had ridden in his drosky without having the money to pay his fare. There was a poor old woman who was waiting when we arrived and was still waiting, without anybody paying attention to her, when we left; and there was a plump, good-looking young creature, who sailed in, was received with polite attention, shown into a private office, and bowed out again, all inside of ten minutes.

But the most interesting character of any was a loutish young moujik, of about twenty-five summers, in a sheepskin overcoat warm enough for the north pole, though he was in South Russia and it was July. This typical young Orthodox came blubbering into the police office with wet eyes, which he had rubbed with a pair of huge, greasy fists until they were redder than his hair, and between pitiful "boo-hoos!" and heart-broken snuffles, told the officers that he had been playing cards and lost eight rubles.

His chum, another moujik in a sheepskin, came with him to confirm his story. There was no complaint of being cheated. He had simply come to the police as a child, who had let an apple fall out of the window, would go weeping to tell its mother.

"Nitchevo!" said the officers, stroking his shaggy red head in mock affection and patting him gently on the sheepskin overcoat. "Nitchevo!" and they sent him off to tell his tale of woe to some official at the other end of the city. This officer would likewise reply tenderly, "Nitchevo!" and send him to some one else; and this one again to yet another distant quarter of Ekaterinoslav, to tell some one else. By the end of the day the unfortunate moujik and his chum would become weary of being sent hither and thither to no purpose, and so give it up. What they expected to gain by informing the police had probably never occurred to them.

At length the Chief of Police arrived. Behind him came a couple of policemen, bringing a wretched looking Jew, whom they said had set, or had tried to set, fire to a building. The Chief ordered him to be shut up three days in a dark cell without food or water. Sascha interpreted the sentence to me, and added that it served him right. The three days' sentence was, I suppose, preliminary to his trial.

The Chief was an intelligent, energetic man. He took us into his private office and, understanding that I knew nothing of Russian, proceeded to question Sascha.

" Why was I traveling through Russia in this strange manner? How came it that a Russian and an American were journeying together on horseback? What was our motive? Who had given us permission? Did I take notes and send off letters? Who and what was I? etc."

But the questions and answers were such a curious study of the multiformity of the suspicions that can be brought to bear on any given subject by a Russian police officer that they deserve a separate chapter. They read like one of those catechetical productions that once went the round of the American newspapers under the title of " Mullkittle's Kid."

CHAPTER XIII.

A SEARCHING CROSS-EXAMINATION.

WHEN we returned to our hotel, after the visit to the Ekaterinoslav police station, Sascha declared himself "out of mind with trouble." From the way the Chief had questioned him no end of trouble was to be expected, and all the Police Master had said in regard to letting us proceed on our way was to advise us to see the Governor of the province. Sascha's spirits, like those in a barometer in stormy weather, were much given to rising and falling, carrying him into Himalayan heights of bliss, and plunging him into abysmal depths of despair, many times during a day· Though he flung himself on the lounge in our room with the abandon of a person utterly undone, when we returned from the police station, dinner, with a bottle of his favorite cordial, brought him around at once to a rosier view of the situation. The Chief, he thought, had asked him at least two hundred questions, many of which were ridiculous. The catechetical examination, as near as he could recall it, was as follows:

" Who is this man, your companion ? "

" He is an American, Mr. Stevens."

" How do you know he's an American ? "

" He has an American passport and he speaks English. I believe he's an American."

" The passport doesn't prove anything. He might

have obtained that from some one else. How do you
know who he is? How are we to know?"

"I believe there is no doubt about his being an
American. He sends his letters to America."

"Ha, he sends letters, then?"

"Yes, to America."

"What does he say in his letters, and where does he
send them to?"

"I don't know what he says. He sends them to
New York."

"How often does he send away letters; are they
big letters?"

"Yes, big letters, and he sends them whenever we
reach a city."

"But what does he find to write about? what's his
business? is he a correspondent?"

"He sends letters to America and he will write a
book about Russia. This is what he is riding through
the country on horseback for."

"But you. What are you with him for? How's this?"

"I am traveling with him to interpret for him and
because I wish to see the country."

"But I can't understand it. A Russian and an
American traveling together in this extraordinary
manner. Who gave you leave to do this thing?"

"My brother and my mother both gave their consent. My certificate of communion and college certificate were both lost with my passport. You have seen
my passport, obtained at Orel."

"That is not a passport! You have nothing to prove
who you are! You look more like an Italian than a
Russian!" (Sascha was dark.)

CRIMEAN SHEPHERDS.

"I am a Russian Orthodox. I am well known in Moscow, where my brother is in business."

"What's your brother's name? How old is he? What business is he in? How do we know all this?"

"His name is Nicolai Critsch. All I tell you is true."

"Did you ask the Governor of Moscow to let you make this journey?"

"No, we didn't think it would be necessary."

"Did people in Moscow know you were going to start?"

"It was announced in the newspapers there."

"What newspapers?"

"The *Moskovski Listok*, the *Novosti*, and others."

"Where did you get the money to make this journey?"

"Mr. Stevens pays the expenses for both of us."

"Where does he get it?"

"I don't know. From America, I suppose."

"Has he got much?"

"I don't know."

"But there must be some motive for such a journey. People don't spend money and undergo the fatigues of such undertakings for nothing."

"I have told you—he wished to write a book about Russia."

"Ah! Has he written books before?"

"Yes; two, I believe."

"About Russia?"

"No; about Africa, and about a bicycle journey around the world."

"Is he a celebrated man? Is he the American who

was once a cowboy and has now become famous?" (A confused idea of Stanley, and Carver's "Wild America"—that had been performing in Moscow—cropped out here.)

"I don't know."

"Is he writing good things or bad about Russia?"

"I don't know. I don't think he is writing bad things, however."

"How do you know he isn't?"

"I don't know."

"Where's his writing? Where does he keep it?"

"He has sent it away, I have said."

"Sent all of it away?"

"He makes notes in a book every day—short notes."

"What about?"

"About the things we see along the road."

"What do you mean? What things has he seen?"

"He writes about the moujiks, the traktirs, the uriadniks, and the country."

"What does he say about the moujiks?"

"He tells about the way they live, what they eat, and how they cultivate the land."

"Does he have anything to say to them?"

"No; he doesn't speak Russian."

"Are you sure that he doesn't speak Russian?"

"I have never heard him speak Russian."

"Perhaps he only pretends that he doesn't. How do you know?"

"I don't believe he speaks any Russian. He asks me about everything."

"What things does he ask you?"

"About the people ; all sorts of questions."

"Does he ever go about among the moujiks without you ?"

"We are together all the time."

"He is always with you ; never alone ?"

"We have traveled together from Moscow."

"Does he sleep where you do ? "

"Yes ; we always stop at the same place at night."

"How do you know he doesn't get up when you're asleep and go about among the people ?"

"I don't believe he does."

"But do you know this positively ?"

"I should know if he did ; I know he does not."

"How would you know if you were asleep ?"

"I don't believe he does."

"What things has he got with him in his saddle-bags ? "

"A few clothes and two or three books."

"What are the books about ? Are they in Russian ? "

"No, they are in English. One is an American magazine."

"Has he got any printed matter in Russian ? "

"No."

"How do you know ? "

"I know that he has not."

"No little books, pamphlets, or printed sheets ? "

"No ; he has nothing of the kind in Russian."

"Are you sure he doesn't give the moujiks any papers ? "

"I have never seen him give them any papers."

"But in the night, when you're asleep ? "

" I believe he doesn't give them anything."

" You're a young man and have much to learn from experience. What things does he ask you about ? "

" I have said,—about the people and the country."

" You must not show him any bad things. Do you know this ? "

" He sees everything with his own eyes. I only explain them if he doesn't understand. I cannot help what he sees as we ride along."

" What else has he got ? "

" He has a Kamaret."

" What's a Kamaret ? "

" A new kind of camera."

" Who gave him permission to carry a camera ? "

" I don't know. He has no permission."

" What did they say about this at Tula, Kharkoff, and Kurskh ? "

" Nobody asked him about a camera at these places."

" How does he carry it ? "

" On his horse."

" Has he taken any pictures with it ? "

" Yes."

" Where are they ? We must see them."

" You cannot see them. They are to be taken to America to be developed."

" What pictures has he taken ? "

" Moujiks, uriadniks, houses, all sorts of things."

" What is his idea in taking pictures? What will he do with them ? "

" He wishes to show them to people in America, I suppose."

" Doesn't he know he has no right to take pictures without permission ? "

" He knows he must not photograph prisons and fortresses."

" How do you know he hasn't photographed these as well ? "

" I don't believe he has.   He knows that it is against the law."

" When did you first make his acquaintance ? "

" A month ago, in Moscow."

" How did you come to know him ? "

" I learned that he was going to ride on horseback to the Crimea, and volunteered to go with him and interpret for him."

" You didn't know him before he came to Moscow ? "

" No."

" How did you know what kind of a man he was ? "

" I and my brother went and saw him.   He is an American, and a good man."

" Did he want you to go with him first, or only after you asked him ? "

" We talked it over.   He then said he would be glad to have my company."

" Well, you must see the Governor to-morrow.   He wishes to see you.   You must not leave town or take any photographs.   Now, in God's name, go."

In addition to this catechetical examination, other ingenious arguments were forthcoming to convince us that we had no business to travel through Russia on horseback without the special permission of the Governors of the various provinces.   And these arguments are worth reproducing, because they illustrate better than whole volumes of pedantic scribbling the Russian idea of government.

"Now," said the police officer, when we called again to see about our passports, very politely and in the manner of a man who had no doubt but that he had at length discovered a thoroughly invincible argument, "a Governor is master in his province just as a man is master in his own home. Is it right that you should go into a man's house without obtaining his permission, and go to taking photographs of his pictures, his statues, his ikons, his carpets, and furniture, and take notes and write letters and books about what you have seen? Tell the American gospodin this."

And as Sascha proceeded to explain, the officer made a French-like gesture, pantomiming: "There you are; now you see who is in the wrong!"

"Tell him," I said to Sascha, in reply, "that it is true we are here without the Governor's permission, but we come into the province and go out again without stealing anything or killing anybody, and leave everything exactly as we found it. What harm is there in photographing moujiks and moujiks' houses?"

My argument, however, was American, and his uncompromisingly Russian. My position was as illogical to him as his was impossible for me. Yet this man, and several millions like him, are living under the remarkable delusion that they and the Americans are very much alike! If there is any real attraction between Americans and Russians it seemed to me that it must be of that character which sometimes draws toward each other two persons of strangely opposite natures.

The officer, of course, shook his head in disapproval.

"You have no right to enter a man's house," he pursued, "without his permission, even if you harm nothing in it."

In the name of Uncle Sam, I thereupon invited him to America, where, if he pleased, he might photograph the entire country and write anything he chose without troubling himself to inquire whether anybody liked it or not. And I pointed out that, from his standard, a man who proposed to do anything in Russia would have to get leave from the Czar, then from the Governors, then from the starostas of the villages, and from the owners of the houses ; and in order to photograph a moujik's cottage, one would have to reckon with the Czar, Governor, starosta, and moujik. How could a moujik's wretched hovel belong to four different people ?

This latter proposition, however, Sascha declined to interpret, on the grounds that we might get three or four days in jail for " making an insolent reply."

At nine o'clock on Monday morning we called on the Governor. At the door of his mansion we came in contact with an interesting individual popularly known as the "Little Governor." Russians with a sense of humor sometimes refer to the doorkeeper of a Governor's mansion as the " Big Little Governor," since this personage is in one way of even more importance than his master.

The secret of the Little Governor's power and importance lies in the fact that anybody who wishes to see the Big Governor had best first "see" him. In fact, since the Little Governor is invariably an Orthodox, it is hardly necessary to add that this plan is not only the easiest but very often the only possible way. Though the salary is only about 200 rubles a year, the position of Little Governor is said to be one of the most coveted offices in Russia. Certainly, the average Russian, below a certain rank, would ask for no better paradise than to be autocrat of the hallway of a Provincial Governor's mansion.

This particular Little Governor looked as if he were the depository of all the secrets of Ekaterinoslav; and it was as good as going to the theater to see a new comedy, to sit in his little domain an hour and observe his fine play of airs and condescension toward applicants for admission to the Governor.

His Excellency the Governor turned out to be a bland, amiable, and sensibly diplomatic gentleman. His words were honey and his smile as bewitching and irresistible as the blandishments of a lovely woman. He inquired after our health and assured us that we were to him as if we were his own sons. He had heard, he said, that an agent of the Society for the Prevention of Cruelty to Animals had examined our horses and had found one of them with a saddle sore, but hoped that this would not delay us very long.

Sascha was so thoroughly overcome by the witchery of the great man's blandishments that he seemed to rise off the very floor with electric expansion.

"I pray Your Excellency," said he, "to give us a letter saying that you have no suspicions of us; that you have seen us and believe us to be good men."

"I have seen you," said the Governor, "and have pleasure to admire you," (yubovatsa) and his Excel-

lency beamed on Sascha even more sweetly, more irre-
sistibly than ever.

In the same smooth and fascinating tone of voice,
accompanied by the same irresistible, confidence-in-
spiring smile, he then kindly asked Sascha a few questions, similar to those that had been put to us at the
police station. None but a very skeptic, however,
would have found it in his heart to have suspected
the Governor of asking those questions because he had
any suspicions of us, or of taking anything but the
most paternal and kindly interest in our case.

He also hoped that Sascha had not shown me anything bad in the country, as the Chief of Police had
hoped ; but so fatherly and benevolent a friend to us
as the Governor would never be guilty of expressing
himself in the form of a command.

It was all very sweet and bewitching, this interview
with His Excellency, and when we were graciously
dismissed, one of us, at least, was in the seventh heaven
of bliss and walked down and out of the Gubernatorial
presence with a flutter of delicious excitement.

We had been received in the Gubernatorial ball
room, a large apartment, with mirrors, gilt chairs, and a
pretty little balcony for the orchestra. We had been
shown to seats just beneath this balcony to wait until
the Governor came out to receive us, and it was under
the balcony, with backs turned to it, that we had stood
all the time that His Excellency smiled on us and
questioned us.

My somewhat varied experience of the Oriental
world led me to suspect that seats had been thought-
fully set for us under this pretty little balcony previous

to our arrival, and that all the time the Governor was interviewing us that genial gentleman's official stenographer had been ensconced therein, kindly noting down all that was said. Sascha wouldn't believe, however, that such a paragon of affability and tenderness as His Excellency could be guilty of so ungenerous a proceeding, and so the slight noise that I fancied I had heard in the pretty little balcony behind us was probably the Gubernatorial cat in quest of mice.

Had not His Excellency, forsooth, during the interview intimated that "everything would be all right?" And from this had not our sanguine souls drawn the inference that our passports were to be returned to us immediately and that the Governor would, as Sascha had requested, give us additional documents, stating that he had seen us and believed us to be good men?

So, returning to the hotel to make preparations for our departure, I left Sascha at the Gubernatorial mansion to bring on the papers.

One, two, three hours I waited, and then, wondering what could be detaining him, returned and sought him out. Sascha was discovered seated in an office deep in despair. The reason being that, although he gathered from the Governor's intimations that we were to receive our papers and be permitted to go on our way, none of the Governor's secretaries and subordinates would assume the responsibility of taking any chance in the matter of securing them for him.

After appealing in vain to the secretaries, he had even permitted himself to become indignant, that these underlings should callously ignore the wishes of so gracious a gentleman as their master, and had rushed down-stairs and appealed to our very important friend the Little Governor. To his further astonishment, however, even the Little Governor seemed all at once to have grown callous and indifferent, and confined himself to merely stating that His Excellency was a very busy man, and that Gen. So-and-so, a very important person, had once waited a whole week before he was granted an audience.

Russian officials are past-masters in the noble Oriental art of humbugging and procrastinating, and becoming alarmed at the Little Governor's hint about Gen. So-and-so, who had waited a week, I then and there determined on a somewhat heroic expedient.

The most effective weapon against Eastern humbug is Western bounce. Interpreting literally, according to my instructions, Sascha now informed the chief of the bureaucratic staff in the office that if the necessary papers to allow us to continue on our way were not forthcoming by three o'clock, I intended to "telegraph to the American government that an American citizen was illegally detained by the officials of Ekaterinoslav. That the American government would then telegraph to St. Petersburg, and then whatever happened, the responsibility would lie on their own heads." (!)

The tchinovniks didn't exactly curl up and die at this threat of communicating with Uncle Sam, but they changed color and exhibited various other unmistakable signs of having been touched on a very sensitive spot. Having delivered this home thrust, I went back to the hotel.

By and by Sascha turned up, once again in high

feather. " It's all right now," he said ; "they only want money to pay for stamps to put on the documents the Governor will give us." I gave him the money for the stamps. In an hour he turned up again, slightly crestfallen.

More money for more stamps.

This time I returned with him, and the upshot of it all was that after paying twice over for the stamps—three rubles and twenty kopecks—we received a couple of papers without any stamps on them at all and an order that I would not be allowed to proceed unless I sent my Kamaret back to Moscow. I took a firm stand, however, on the question of the camera, and told the Governor I should take it with me and he could do as he pleased about stopping me and taking it away on his own responsibility.

Responsibility is a capital word to conjure with in any trouble with Russian officers, for they dread the assumption of it worse than anything else on earth. As for telegraphing to America, the gentlemanly Governor begged that I would not do him the injustice to suppose that such a thing were necessary in connection with our visit to *his* province ; he was only too delighted to facilitate my movements, though he would prefer that I send away my camera. The Governor of the Crimea, however, he felt sure, would refuse to let us proceed, and there it might be necessary to telegraph.

During our visits to the Gubernatorial offices we were once unwittingly left in a room by ourselves, on the table of which lay a number of documents. They were reports that had been brought in that morning by secret agents of the Third Section of His Imperial Majesty's police.

We were left in that room only ten or fifteen minutes, and during that brief period a flood of light was let in on my soul, in regard to the methods of the rulers of the Russian people, as brilliant as the light that smote with blindness Saul of Tarsus. There was, however, this difference, that whereas the light that fell upon Saul came from heaven, that which came to me seemed to glare up from the opposite direction; and while he was temporarily blinded, the partial blindness with which I had hitherto been regarding the affairs of Russia was instantly removed. One of these reports read thus:

JULY 16 (our date 28), 1890.

I was invited by the priest Ivanovski to be present at his house in the assumed character of a relation of the popadya (the priest's wife) *from Novomoskovski, when the moujik Nicolai Nicolaivitch would come to talk about religion. The moujik's wife came with him and took part in the discussion. During the talk this woman spoke disrespectfully of the Czar.*   A. K.

Another one bearing the same date, but a different signature, read:

I was one of a party in the traktir of Petro Paulovitsch, drinking tea. The party consisted of myself (here came several names which we couldn't remember); *the conversation was about the badness of the harvest in the province. Alexander Petrovitsch* (or Petrovski) *expressed the belief that the Czar would not allow any grain to be exported ; whereupon Ivan Ivanovitsch spoke badly of the Czar.*   I. P.

Another paper seemed to be a description of our own case, since it spoke of a " Russian and a foreigner traveling together ; " but before anything further could be secured we were interrupted. Under the circumstances, expecting some one to appear on the scene at any moment, it was impossible to copy the reports verbatim, so that the names in them will not be identical ; but for all practical purposes these are authentic copies.

Comment on them is almost superfluous. Two hours later we were once more riding over the free steppe, and it seemed to me that our horses were carrying us away from purgatory.

All along the route from Moscow I had been impressed by the loyalty of the moujiks to the Czar. The village priests, though a thoroughly drunken and dissolute set, I had regarded chiefly as " small rogues," bent on making as much as they could out of the ignorance and credulity of the peasants, and cutting, on the whole, a comical rather than a harshly disreputable figure in the country. To come suddenly and unexpectedly on one seriously plotting with the secret police, inviting one of them to come to his house and pose as a relative of his wife on a visit, in order to play the spy on the parishioner who was coming to have a talk with him about religion, was like stumbling on a ghastly corpse.

As for the wretched moujiks, their fatal delusion, based on their impenetrable ignorance, can only be called pitiable.

No comment is necessary in regard to the Czar. Everybody who knows him personally agrees that he is an amiable man and a model husband.

In the post-offices and all public rooms of the provinces of South Russia hangs a picture of the Czar. One day we called in the post-office of Ekaterinoslav to inquire for letters. No ikons were visible, so I did not remove my hat, as I was accustomed to do, in deference to the religious customs of the people, where there were ikons.

In a moment an official stepped up to me and demanded in an overbearing tone, "Please remove your hat!"

"But there are no ikons in the room," I said, looking around.

"Ah, but there is an ikon," he returned.

"Where is it, then?"

"There it is; that's an ikon!" he half shouted, officiously. *And he pointed to a chromo of his most amiable Majesty the Czar.*

Not caring to jeopardize the success of my ride to the Crimea, I removed my hat.

But one could not help wondering whether the Czar knows how utterly ridiculous this attempt to deify his chromos appears in the eyes of foreigners.

CHAPTER XIV

MY INTERPRETER RETURNS.

WE were now in a country where a large share of the population were secretly and openly dissenters from the Orthodox Greek Church, and by no means so loyal to the Russian government as the people of the provinces we had traversed on the way from Moscow. The steppes of Southern Russia are dotted over with the villages of colonists from Germany, who have settled there at various periods of the past two centuries. These people have stubbornly clung to their Protestantism, and have infused a spirit of restless skepticism in regard to the efficacy of the dead ceremonials of the Orthodox Church, in the minds of a large share of the Russian and Cossack population. Moreover, their attitude toward the Czar and his government differs from the blind infatuation of the Orthodox moujiks, in that they are intelligent, reasoning beings, who have brought from Germany or inherited from their German-born parents the logic and philosophy of Teuton civilization.

They have also imported into the country the Teuton's methodical and thrifty habits of life; and on the road beyond Ekaterinoslav we began to meet prosperous looking farmers, driving fat teams of horses in strong, gayly-painted wagons, the like of which my companion from the old Muscovite capital had never set eyes on before, and which the improvident moujiks of the north and central provinces had never yet dreamed of. Sascha regarded these German colonists, dressed in decent clothes and driving to town in wagons as good as the wagon of an American farmer, with astonishment. Here were peasants of a status that were to him, on this, his first acquaintance with them, a positive enigma. While he could not but agree with me, when I suggested that if all the peasants of the Russian Empire were as thrifty and prosperous as these it would be a tremendous improvement on the present state of affairs, his agreement was a very reluctant, half-hearted admission.

"These people," said he, "are better than our moujiks for earning money and cultivating the soil, but they are not warm-hearted like the moujiks."

Ninety-nine Russians out of a hundred would have given this same answer. It is the stock excuse that the, educated Russian always has ready at the end of his tongue when a question of comparison is raised between the moujiks and the more thrifty and enterprising peasantry of other nationalities,—"Our moujiks are warm-hearted."

There certainly is something to be said on this score, not only of the moujiks, but of all classes of Russians who remain true to their Slav nature, and unaffected by contact with the pride and individualism of the West. One must almost necessarily be a Slav himself, however, to fully appreciate the advantages and beauty of that maudlin warmth of heart that leads big-whiskered cavalry officers to kiss one another in the public streets, and bear-like moujiks to slobber over and hug each other when in their cups. Few Americans but would much rather be kicked than kissed by a man ; and the better educated Russians are nowadays getting to be more reserved in the matter of public osculatory greetings between man and man.

We put up at a post-station, the first night out from Ekaterinoslav, twenty-five versts from the scene of our late detention and worrying by the police. A young Pole, in the uniform of an infantry regiment, here weighed the hay and measured the oats for our horses. His regiment was stationed at Ekaterinoslav, and, like most of the soldiers who comprised its rank and file, was endeavoring to augment his fat pay of two rubles and seventy-five kopecks (one and a half dollars) a year, by working in the harvest fields. He was permitted to work out, he said, twenty-five days a month. During harvest he could earn three rubles a fortnight, for which he had to work about sixteen hours a day ; at other times from three to four rubles a month when he could get anything to do. This youth, buried in a Russian regiment, a thousand miles from home, was still at heart every inch a Pole, as every Pole continues to be wherever you happen across one. " I'm not a Russian," he said, the first chance he had of speaking about himself, " I'm a Pole."

From this station we made a detour of about twenty versts off the main road to visit the historic grounds of the Zaparozhian Cossacks, on the Dneiper. Our way was over the rolling steppe, which was here and there distinguished by a mound about twenty feet high and fifty in diameter, surmounted by a wooden cross. These were the graves of the old

Cossack hetmans of the Zaparozhian military republic, the headquarters of which were on a group of islands in the Dneiper, and which we have been made familiar with in " Taras Bulba," and other works relating to the Cossacks. The Cossacks have disappeared, and the wild, free steppe, which we read of in connection with them in the heydey of the Zaparozhian *sech*, is mostly under cultivation. Nothing remains to distinguish the spot, as historically significant in connection with them and their period, but the lone crosses on the mound graves of their hetmans, and names rudely scratched on the rocks on the islands in the Dneiper.

They were a fighting, carousing, turbulent set of horsemen, who were always at war with the Turks, Poles, and Russians. Under their famous hetman Mazeppa, they joined Charles XII, of Sweden, against Peter the Great, on the battle-field of Poltava in 1709; and the punishment inflicted on them by the Czar for joining his enemies was the beginning of their end as a semi-independent people. They were afterward concerned in the great Cossack rebellion, under Pugachev, in the reign of Catherine II; in revenge for which Catherine broke up their establishment on the Dneiper entirely.

On the banks of the Dneiper, opposite the islands on which were the Zaparozhian permanent military camps, called the *sech*, is now to be found as meek and unpretentious a village of grain-growers as are to be found in all Russia. A peculiarity of the villages hereabout was the remarkably small size of the horses. Compared to the wagons and huge wagon-loads of rye and wheat which they were hauling in from the fields, they seemed ridiculously undersized. On the uncultivated parts of the steppe now also began to appear big flocks of merino sheep, and the rude day-shelters of the shepherds.

Finding nothing to justify a halt at Zaparozhia, we rode on, and for the night regained the main road and the post-station of Kanseropol. The sun was melting hot, the way was dusty, and the bare, drouth-deadened steppe insufferably dreary to the eye. The heat, the dust, the hard fare of the villages, and the dreary monotony of the southern steppes, had, ever since leaving Kharkoff, been particularly rough on Sascha. His sanguine idea of a "two month's picnic on horseback" had, of course, vanished like a shadow ere we had been on the road a week. Though a pleasant companion enough, and a very useful one in my case, his moral stamina was not equal to the prolonged hardships and discomforts of the ride. For two weeks past he had been a good deal of a drag, wavering daily between the ambition to finish what he had set out to do, and a hankering after the comforts of his home-life in Moscow.

By appealing to his pride, and reminding him of the sorry figure he would cut in the eyes of his sweetheart, who had decorated him with roses at Tula ; and of his brother and friends in Moscow, should he return without having finished the ride, I had managed to persuade him along as far as Kanseropol. Here, however, finding the sun growing hotter and the discomforts of the road increasing rather than diminishing, he decided to return to Ekaterinoslav, sell his horse,

TARTARS OF THE CRIMEA.

and go back home.   More than two thirds of our journey were accomplished ; twelve or fourteen days' ride
would bring us to Sevastopol, but Sascha was thoroughly demoralized.

"I am like Hamlet," said he, as he lay on his back
in the stable, mentally balancing the ignominy of a
retreat, and the hard experiences of the road to success.   "I am like Hamlet ; I don't know *what* to do."
He at length decided to return.

I had been so well satisfied with his intelligence and
readiness to give information that it was no more than
just to treat him very liberally in the matter of funds,
so that he might enjoy himself for a time in Moscow
by way of compensation for the discomforts he had
experienced on the ride.   In some respects, however,
I was not sorry at the prospect of finishing the trip
without him.   He was possessed of many traits that
were endurable enough and even valuable, so long as
I was interested in them as an exposition of the Russian character; such as a curious sort of suspicion as
to the motives of well-nigh everything I said or did
from day to day, and an equally Russian shortcom-
ing in the matter of reliability ; but which had become
by this time very annoying.   His virtues, however, it
is but fair to say, outweighed his faults, and the latter
were such as seem to be inherent in well-nigh every
Russian.

Though riding on horseback day after day had
turned out to be more of a fatiguing task than a picnic,
and his native country had been a revelation to him in
the matter of heat and dreariness, the ride had nevertheless been profitable in many ways, he said, during

our parting conversation at Kanseropol.   Among other things, he had been quietly studying the Americans— with me for his model.   Now, he thought, he might say he knew them thoroughly.   Among their most conspicuous traits was a peculiar fondness for dogs, horses, and little children.   They never said what they didn't mean, and always did what they said they were going to do.   (To the Russian mind the latter traits must have seemed, indeed, remarkable.)

But the most peculiar thing he had learned about them, was that they never made a big fuss about little things.   This latter important characteristic was discovered by him, it appeared, from an incident that occurred between us somewhere on the road between Kurskh and Kharkoff.   I remembered the occasion as he recalled it.   The whimsical idea had occurred to him to give his horse a feed of white bread for its midday meal.   Replying to his request, I simply answered "very well."   This laconic reply to so extraordinary a proposition as feeding his horse white bread, struck him as being so very remarkable that he had remembered it and treasured it up as peculiarly American. Two Russians, he said, would have discussed the subject pro and con for an hour, and have made observations about it for days afterward.

And so it came about that after Kanseropol, Texas and I were thrown upon our own resources and society. He and Sascha's horse had, of course, grown attached to each other; but just how strong this attachment had become was not apparent until the hour of their forcible separation.   Though mine was the hand that fed him, and Sascha's horse was an atrocious pilferer who was forever trying to get at his oats, and often bit him into the bargain, when it came to choosing between us, Texas, inconsistent as Polly Ann, who jilted her policeman lover in favor of the thief he had captured making off with her purse, went back on his human friend and protector without a moment's hesitation.

Texas's strongest points, next to his timidity, were his appetite for oats and barley, and his extremely sociable disposition. His big, sociable heart rebelled energetically against the forcible sundering of two companions, who had for a month past fed out of the same trough, drank out of the same bucket, shared the same stable, yearned for one another's oats, took snap bites at each other's ribs, fought flies together, and shoulder to shoulder had safely passed through the ordeal of inspection at the hands of the old ladies, S. P. C. A., of Ekaterinoslav. He rebelled as I led him alone out of the postayali dvor; and as though realizing all at once the dismal significance of this new departure, uttered a whinnying neigh of deep and fearful yearning.

This musical evidence of a broken heart was repeated at brief intervals for several miles along his lonely way; and when, the day getting hot, and his anxiety about his chum producing moisture under the saddle, I essayed to walk and lead him awhile, Texas bluntly refused to lead. All efforts to reason with him and to win him over by stroking him on his white nose proved abortive. His only response would be a look of melting reproach, and an effort to wheedle me into turning back.

For three days this sort of struggle went on ; the

only three days on the entire journey when I remained
in the saddle for the whole forty to fifty versts a day.
This would never do. Saddle-sores would inevitably
result ; for only by watching him with never-flagging
solicitude had I kept him in good condition through
the long, weary drag in the sweltering heat and dust of
the Russian midsummer. Even on the morning of the
fourth day he refused to lead, except toward the North.

But that morning, as I rode along, there flashed into
my mind a cartoon I had once seen of a donkey race,
in which the victory had been won by an ingenious
jockey who held a carrot on the end of a stick a foot
or two in front of his ass's nose. In its eagerness to
reach the carrot, the donkey put on such a tremendous
burst of speed that it immediately outstripped its
competitors and won the race.

There were no carrot-gardens on the steppe ; but
there were occasional patches of Indian corn, the sight
of which always aroused in Texas the criminal cov-
etousness of a born kleptomaniac. A handful of the
green succulent blades, or a half-ripe nubbin covertly
stolen from a way-side patch, would excite in him such
gastronomic felicity that the juice would run out of
his mouth ; and he was humbly thankful even for the
small privilege of being allowed to dip down his head
and secure a half-dry husk or cob which some Kiev
pilgrim or harvest tramp had dropped in the road after
gnawing off the grain. By diplomatically playing off
this inordinate love of green maize against his stubborn
sorrow at the departure of his chum, I eventually succeeded in first getting him to lead, and at length even
to following meekly at my heels.

At first it was necessary to carry a bunch of blades and permit him to get a nibble at tolerably regular intervals of time, as I walked before him rein in hand, and for a day or two he seemed to be in a state of mental bewilderment, as though unable to decide between the old love of his friend and the new love of Indian corn. By the third day of the new experiment, however, and the sixth day after the parting at Kanseropol, Indian corn had completely won him over, and now that he had forgotten his old companion he seemed to have resolved on making up to the only friend he now had to turn to, the owner of the hand that fed him blades of maize.

The road I was now traversing led to the considerable town of Nicopol on the Dneiper. Villages and habitation were farther apart than on any portion of the way thus far traversed; the population here averaging but about fifteen to the square verst. For much of the way, however, the land was under cultivation, being farmed in large tracts by capitalists and speculators.

On the road crowds of people were met on foot, in holiday costumes, wending their way from Nicopol and adjacent villages to Ekaterinoslav. All carried bottles, and their mission was to attend some religious ceremony, where a priest would bless water and make it holy; the bottles were for the purpose of carrying back some of this holy water to their homes. The pilgrims were mostly women of the peasant class, and their faces were a remarkable study. They were nearly all strong, square-jawed faces, reminding me of Indian squaws, and eloquent of great powers of physical endurance. When I met these gangs of female pilgrims, it was one of the hottest days of the entire ride. The sun seemed as fierce as in India. Yet these hardy females trudged along, some with no covering, save that provided by nature, on their heads; others with but a kerchief, and all apparently indifferent to its rays. Many of them I met whilst halting at a post-station; and so indifferent were they to the fierce glare of the sun, that had produced so demoralizing an effect on my Moscow-bred companion, that when they stopped at the station to regale themselves with the bread and hard-boiled eggs they carried, they didn't even trouble to sit in the shade. Moreover, the station-keeper, when two or three of them did take shelter in front of his house in the only shady spot, ordered them away on the grounds that he wasn't keeping a traktir.

Here, in the sturdy powers of endurance and the great patience of these peasant wives and mothers, one seemed to be in intimate touch with the real secret of Russia's strength and formidableness as a military power. Patience under difficulties and hardships and the power to endure extreme heat and cold, and to live on and be contented with the coarsest fare, were traits that were written in every lineament of these women's faces. Such women breed good material for soldiers — soldiers capable of campaigning without tents, and with the rudest of commissary departments. It is on these negative virtues of her people that Russia will have to depend, for many a year to come, to sustain her in case of conflict with any of the great Western powers. Here, as I sat on the shady side of the post-station, watching these women seated on the ground partaking of their coarse fare, stoically happy under conditions that I, who had roughed it in India, Africa, Afghanistan, and China, would have regarded as the height of indiscretion, the homely boast of the Russians, that, "what is death to the foreigner is life to a Russian," came home to me in its full significance.

Here, too, was fanaticism, that other quality which the military authorities of Russia turn to good account on the field of battle. The Russian soldier always fights in a holy as well as a national cause, and, no less than the Turk, believes that death on the field of battle is a passport to paradise. And these, their wives, mothers, and sisters, were tramping a hundred versts through the heat and dust, in preference to riding by rail or boat, because they believed there was virtue in undergoing toil to get the holy water.

The population of Nicopol, or the business part of it, seemed to consist largely of Jews and Germans. The hotel was kept by a German family, and was a tremendous improvement on the native-managed caravanserai. "English spraken?" said the worthy and fairly energetic hostess. "Ah, beefsteak!" And fifteen minutes later I was doing ample justice to a smoking steak and a bottle of lager beer.

My road from Nicopol was down the eastern bank of the Dneiper, whose waters came into view near by, to the left, many times a day. The people of the little villages I passed through were inordinately suspicious. Each contained a sort of policeman in ordinary peasant garb, and whose only badge of authority seemed to be a disk of tin as large as a blacking-box, stamped with a number, and which was suspended from the neck with a yellow cord.

Ettabozaluk was the name of the hamlet where the first sample of this particular brand of traveler-worriers came into the theater of my Russian road experiences. Drawing rein at the village traktir, in the middle of the forenoon, in quest of something to drink, the uncouth crowd of villagers and moujiks that are always loafing about these places were instantly attracted by the appearance of an evidently foreign horseman. Comments, as usual, were indulged in of the most *naïve* and unreserved character. The more officious demanded to see my " billet," as a passport is called in Southern Russia.

Seeing that there was no officer among them, I refused to gratify a curiosity that was nine-tenths suspicion, and merely answered that I was an American. Instead of allaying their suspicions, this immediately increased them. One old wiseacre declared triumphantly that it was quite impossible that a man on horseback should come from America, because he had heard that between that country and Russland there was water. A second took quite an indignant fit of suspicion on the grounds that my saddle was not American but Circassian, a positive proof to his comprehensive brain that I was trying to deceive them. These two subtle discoveries convinced the whole assembly that I was grossly deceiving them in saying that I was an American, and consequently must be a spy.

" What was I doing in Russland ? "

" Oh, admiring it ! " (*smahtrait ;* literally, to look). The crowd shook their heads. What kind of blockheads did I suppose them to be to believe that a foreigner would ride on horseback through Russia merely to see it? To these poor wretches, born and bred in an atmosphere of low, crafty suspicion; nourished on it; educated to it in the school of daily experience; growing old in its baleful shadow; and by the time they reach middle age hardened in it to a degree that disfigures their very faces, it seemed altogether ridiculous that a foreigner should turn up in this strange manner and not be engaged on some sinister mission.

I refused to truckle to their impertinent suspicions, however, seeing no one among them who had any police authority to demand one's passport, and was about riding off, when they seized Texas by the bridle. An individual then stepped forward and demanded in a tone of authority to see my passport. There was nothing of the policeman about his appearance, however, and I demanded to know if he was the uriadnik. Fumbling under his moujik's coat, he then produced the disk of numbered tin and the yellow cord that proclaimed him an official of some peculiarly humble degree, but nevertheless an official.

Fit companions, indeed, to these suspicious villagers, seemed another class of inhabitants that now began to make themselves conspicuous on the steppe. These were tremendous flocks of geese, which were encountered feeding about the fields and grassland, miles away from any human habitation, and as many miles from water. They belonged to villages on the banks of the Dneiper, and flew daily back and forth between these distant foraging grounds and the river.

Beyond Novo Veronsofka the country became more and more thinly inhabited. Uncultivated steppe characterized the greater part of the way, and big herds of horses and cattle, and flocks of sheep, began to be the most prominent feature of the day's ride. The only habitations seen in a day's ride would be the post-stations, from twelve to twenty-five versts apart; and across the steppe, off the road, the stone-walled houses of the ranchmen. These ranch-houses, the headquarters of the herds and flocks, were more like big stone barns, and attached to them were square-walled kraals for the cattle. Now and then, however, where a wealthy landlord and cattle owner lived on his own estate, some pretense to embellishment would be seen in the form of ornamental gateways, or a porch to the house.

On wheat-growing estates were now seen threshing-machines and steam engines, denoting that the land of moujiks with small holdings had given place to large proprietors who could afford expensive machinery. The straw was often built into big hollow squares for sheltering cattle in winter; and, in the shimmering heat of the day, mirages would convert such as were a couple of miles away, across the level steppe, into cities and fortifications.

An amusing, though often very annoying feature of the day's experiences, would now be a curious spirit of hostility, displayed by the incumbents of the post-stations. These gentlemen seemed to think that I was setting a dangerous example to the traveling community by riding my own horse instead of hiring them to convey me from one station to another, as had been

the custom from time immemorial in that part of the
country. Some treated me with brusque inhospitality;
others endeavored to convince me of the superior advantages of traveling by post. With my own horse I
could only ride forty or fifty versts a day, whilst by
changing horses at every stanitza I might make more
than a hundred, etc.

It was with the utmost difficulty that hay or oats
were to be procured, except by bribery in the form of
exorbitant prices. Texas and I were true soldiers of
fortune these memorable days, and on down through
the Crimea. To-day a feast, to-morrow a famine, forsooth, though feasts came to him oftener than to his
rider, since oats were nearly always to be obtained by
means of extra money, whilst decent human food was
out of the question except in a city. There were times
when Texas had to dine the best he could off the
scanty tufts of wire-grass on the droughty Crimean
steppe, whilst his master, because he also was not
herbivorous, came in for no dinner at all.

The post-boys or yemchiks, at the station-houses,
were an improvement on their employers, the " Ka-
zans," in their demeanor, regarding a person riding
his own horse, as a curiosity rather than a dangerous
innovation. The chief concern of the yemchicks was
largess for looking after Texas. One evening a yem-
chick looked after him so well that he, in conjunction
with a nest of outraged wasps, created something of
a circus in the yard. The yemchik tied him to a
sleigh that had been standing in a corner untouched
since the previous winter. On the under side of the
sleigh, unknown to the yemchik, a colony of wasps

had built their house. Before he had been tied up five minutes, one of the wasps, regarding Texas as an intruder, sallied out and stung him on the nose; and the commotion that followed brought the entire swarm about his ears. Texas started across the yard with the sleigh in no ceremonious fashion, and would probably have injured himself seriously had the sleigh been equal to the knocking about. Luckily it was rotten, however, and breaking away from it, he, after considerable rolling and kicking, came running to me.

A day's rest was indulged in at Berislav, where the Dnciper was crossed on a pontoon bridge. Berislav is a dead-and-alive town with one roughly paved street that the people use for a promenade in the evening. The whole town apparently went to sleep about ten o'clock in the morning, and woke up again at four in the afternoon for the purpose of drinking tea. Business must have been transacted, I suppose, if there was any to transact, before ten and after four. The symptoms of the afternoon awakening were boys coming from every shop in town, to the apology for a hotel at which I was staying, with blue enameled kettles for hot water to make tea. The hotel-keeper did a roaring trade in hot water at two kopecks a kettle, but he was not overburdened with guests. The only patrons that haunted his establishment whilst I was there were moujiks from the country, who provided their own food, tea, and sugar, as well as feed for their horses. The amount one of these customers would contribute to the income of the establishment would be about twenty kopecks during the day, paid for hot water, and the privilege of yard-room for his team and wagon.

The proprietor of this lively concern was an amiable, and, for a Russian, fairly honest young man, who kindly informed me that serfage was abolished throughout the Czar's dominions; speaking as though he were communicating a piece of news that I, being a foreigner, had perhaps not heard of, though the emancipation must have taken place soon after he came into the world.

Shortly after crossing the Dneiper I happened on an old acquaintance that I had last seen in Persia, in the form of the neat iron posts and triple wires of the Indo-European Telegraph Line.

From London to Calcutta, overland, by the most direct practicable route is somewhere near 8000 miles. Stationed here and there at intervals of a few hundred miles all along this distance are little groups, or solitary British subjects, the links of an active chain of political and commercial sympathy connecting two widely separated capitals of the British Empire, the home capital and the metropolis of India. The links of this great Anglo-Indian chain are strung out through Belgium, Germany, and European Russia to Odessa; thence through the Crimean Peninsula to Kertch; down through Circassia and Georgia to Tiflis; across Transcaucasia and the Persia frontier to Tabreez. From Tabreez they continue on eastward to Tcheran. At the Persian capital the Indo-European line connects with the line owned and operated by the Indian government. Practically one is but a continuation of the other, however, and from Tcheran the little groups of Englishmen extend on south to Bushire, passing through the cities of Ispahan and Shiraz. From

Bushire they follow along the Mekran coast through Beloochistan into India north of Karachi, where the chain, which has been on foreign soil from the west coast of Belgium, debouches upon British territory.

These numerous groups and isolated subjects of Victoria, Queen of England, Empress of India, are simply the working force of the largest and finest-equipped telegraph line in the world. From the Belgian coast to distant India, there stretches one continuous long row of splendid iron poles, climbing over rugged mountains in the Caucasus; stretched out across the level Persian deserts in long, straight reaches; protruding like black, tapering stems from the white, glaring sand-waves of Beloochistan. My first acquaintance with this remarkable telegraph line was made at Tabreez, during my bicycle ride around the world. In riding from Constantinople, through Anatolia and Koordistan, I had been accompanied from time to time by stretches of dilapidated Turkish line, usually one wire mounted on rough poles, twice as far apart as they ought to be and leaning toward all points of the compass. At Erzeroum I seemed to have got beyond the territory covered by the Turkish system, and had ridden several days' journey into Persia.

It was a wild, barbarous country about the Turko-Persian border, inhabited chiefly by nomad Koords, and I missed even the occasional welcome company of the Turkish telegraph line. Its disappearance seemed like casting off the last strand of Western civilization.

At that time I hardly expected to see another telegraph line until I should reach Japan, my intention being to reach the Pacific through Turkestan and China.

Suddenly one day, when nearing Tabreez, I saw away off on the desert a sight that made me blink and rub my eyes to make sure that it was not a mere optical illusion I was looking at. The deserts of Persia are famous for producing bogus objects—mirages of lakes and waving palms; of lovely castles, and similar fascinating scenes; but this time it was none of these. Miles away to the north, seemingly suspended in mid-air, was a league-long row of telegraph poles, straight as a die, even as the pickets of a garden fence.

As I drew nearer, the line assumed more definite form. Its marvelous symmetry, I then discovered, was not the enchantment of distance, but a solid reality in English iron, with the name of the contracting firm stamped on the poles. Every pole tapering from a circumference of twenty inches at the bottom to six or eight at the top, and, across the dead-level wastes of the Persian plains, set up as evenly and perpendicularly as they might have been in Hyde Park. It is worth noting, perhaps, by the way, that the English always take particular pains to have everything of this kind very superior in the East; it is a perpetual source of wonder and admiration to the natives; a standing advertisement of England's wealth, power, and ability to the multitude who have no other way of learning.

From Tabreez I was able to follow this infallible guide into Teheran. Often I could see it stretching ahead of me mile after mile, the poles so even that they seemed not to vary an inch, and disappearing in the

heavens at the farther end by the curious legerdemain
of the desert.   The æolian music of its triple wires, as
the desert breezes played through them, and the mes-
sages flashed past from India to England, from England
to India—how companionable it was, that bit of civilization in a barbarous country, only those who have been
similarly placed know.

CHAPTER XV.

ON THE CRIMEAN STEPPES.

THE country between the crossing of the Dneiper and the narrow entrance to the Crimean Peninsula, at Perekop, is a dead-level, treeless steppe. Broad areas are devoted to the production of wheat, and long bullock trains were met, hauling the newly harvested crop to Berislav for transportation down the Dneiper to Odessa. Bullocks, wagons, and drivers looked like animated shapes of dust ; the drivers either liked it or were too indifferent and lazy to care about keeping out of the dense clouds that the oxen kicked up as they crawled along.

Near the river bottom were melon gardens, and it seemed to me that there was about one watcher to every dozen vines, from which the reader is at liberty to draw his or her own most charitable inferences as to the character of the passers-by.

On the wild steppe were numerous flocks of merino sheep in charge of Tartar shepherds ; and there now began to appear wells for watering them, operated by bullocks hauling a rope wound round an enormous drum.

These wells on the Southern steppes are different from anything the writer had ever seen before. They are the places of rendezvous on the steppe for all sorts and conditions of people, who collect about them for water and to rest during the heat of the summer's day. To the wayfarer, they are the oasis of the steppe ; and the stages of his journey are from one well to another.

At noon on a hot summer's day there may be as many as fifty people about one of these wells, not one of whom will be there at sundown. There may be ten thousand merino sheep and a dozen Tartar shepherds, who will be snoozing the hot hours away inside their curious tent-carts, standing in the midst of their respective flocks. They have shepherd dogs that have more wool on them than the wooliest sheep in the flock. Some of these odd-looking canines are so loaded down with wool, which grows particularly heavy on the legs, that they almost seem incapable of waddling along. Wool-growing is one of the principal industries of the southern steppes, and the favorite sheep seems to be the merino.

On Wednesday morning, August 6, I reached the town of Perekop, and was gratified by a glimpse of the Black Sea—a welcome enough sight after the monotony of the drouthy steppe. Perekop was an abominably hot and dusty hole, containing not one redeeming feature beyond its nearness to the sea. A few wooden shops and vodka-drinking dens, houses, government buildings, and a postayali dvor were scattered over an area of gray, verdureless soil, in size out of all proportion to the number of inhabitants dwelling on it—this was Perekop. Situated on the narrowest part of the isthmus that connects the Crimean Peninsula with the body of Russia, one may stand on the roof of one of its houses and see the Black Sea on one side and the Azov on the other.

The keeper of the postayali dvor was a son of Israel, who, instead of receiving me with the traditional cordiality of the boniface in dealing with a traveler who desires to become his guest, regarded me with such a panic of suspicion that he immediately shuffled off across the street and reported my arrival and foreign appearance to the pristav. Thus it happened that, ten minutes after reaching Perekop, a police officer walked into the stable, and before I had fairly relieved Texas of his saddle, demanded my passport and took possession of my saddle-bags.

Books and papers, even private letters, were critically examined by the pristav, who, however, not being equal to English, could make nothing of them.

The only thing he understood was the paper I had obtained from the Governor of Ekaterinoslav. He hesitated some little time over this, probably suspicious that it was a forgery, but finally contented himself with making a copy of it ; and after worrying his brain for half an hour about my camera, reluctantly allowed me to proceed.

I was now in the Crimea ; and among the experiences of the first day's ride in it was the refusal of a landed nobleman to grant me the most trifling expression of courtesy or hospitality for the night. I arrived at this place at dark. He was superintending the watering of live stock at the well, and by way of a hint I rode Texas up to the trough and watered him. Seeing that the gentleman made no offer of hospitality, I requested the privilege of tying Texas up in his yard, and sleeping there myself for the night.

" This is not a postayali dvor," said the nobleman.

I explained that I had not mistaken him for a station-keeper, but that it was now dark, my horse was tired, the road unfamiliar to me, and the post-station a long way off.

"This is not a house for travelers," he reiterated, and turned on his heel by way of bringing the matter to an end.

The night came on very dark, and so, within a couple of versts of this gentleman's place, I was compelled to tie Texas, supperless, to a telegraph pole, and spreading my rug on the ground beside him, also supperless, wait till morning.

Nearly all travelers who have spent any length of time in Russia agree that the Russians are hospitable. The lavish hospitality of the country houses of wealthy Russians, and the ostentatious plenty of the Russian merchant's table when guests are in his house, have been attested by more than one English and American traveler. Wallace tells of being the guest in a merchant's house, where it was difficult to obtain anything simpler than sturgeon and champagne; and the same authority, treating this time more particularly of noblemen's houses, says: "Of all the foreign countries in which I have traveled, Russia certainly bears off the palm in all that regards hospitality. Every spring I found myself in possession of a large number of invitations from landed proprietors in different parts of the country, and a great part of the summer was generally spent in wandering about from one country house to another."

In spite of my own experiences, then, the Russians are hospitable. There is no doubt that a foreigner who

ORTHODOX VILLAGE PRIEST.

goes to Russia and takes the trouble to make himself conspicuous and agreeable in St. Petersburg drawing-rooms in the winter, will, like the gentleman I have just quoted, receive many invitations to country houses, and in them meet with most hospitable receptions.

This is hospitality, of a truth ; but there is a higher form of hospitality than this ; and it is to this higher interpretation of the word and its meaning that my own experiences must be applied.

Primal hospitality, as the writer understands it, is not so much the readiness to receive into your house a gentleman who has made a favorable impression on you at a social gathering, as a willingness to entertain the passing stranger, in need of assistance, whom you never saw before, and never expect to see again. This is the test that is applicable to a country where distances are great and the traveler liable to find himself fatigued or benighted where public accommodation is not to be found.

Possibly this sort of hospitality prevails in Russia, as well as the secondary stage ; which might be termed its European, or civilized expression, as against its Asiatic interpretation. I can only say that if so, it was my misfortune to see absolutely nothing of it, until, during the last two or three days' ride, I came in contact with the Crimean Tartars. We were hospitably entertained by Count Tolstoï ; and near Kharkoff, as earlier pages explain, we stumbled upon the family of a Rostoff shipping agent, who were summering there, and who likewise showed us hospitality.

But apart from these two cases of exceptional circumstances, we received not so much as a solitary glass of milk from one end of Russia to the other without buying it.   This, among the poverty-hardened moujiks was, of course, not be expected, nor desired.   But in the middle of a scorching hot day, I have ridden up to a nobleman's house in Southern Russia, and with a voice husky from thirst inquired for milk, where there was evidently no lack of an abundance of that article, and received a negative answer, embittered with a stare of mingled curiosity and suspicion.

Mayhap it was all owing to their miserable suspicions of me that their reception was so inhospitable and boorish ; but, whatever the cause, it upset completely all my preconceived ideas, as well as the preconceived ideas of their Moscow compatriot, my companion, who likewise was disappointed in this same manner north of Ekaterinoslav.

The day after being turned away from the big land-owner's door to pass the night supperless on the steppe, I reached a wayside traktir.   The principal article of consumption there was vodka, and the customers were a mixed company of Russian and Tartar shepherds.   Besides vodka were black bread and the inevitable barrel of cucumbers in brine.   These precious commodities were kept in a corner of the room which was railed off from the rest by means of perpendicular wooden bars.   Behind these bars, looking through, like a prisoner in a cell, was the proprietor, a black-whisk-ered Semitic-looking gentleman, with a nose as purple and ripe-looking as a luscious plum : a nose that must have cost him barrels of vodka to bring to such a state of perfection ; and which was seen to singular advantage when he thrust it through the wooden bars.

The Russians and Tartars sat carousing around rude wooden tables, their feast consisting of the above-mentioned epicurean ingredients. Now and then the purple-nosed proprietor would pass out through the bars a refilled bottle of vodka, a handful of squashy cucumbers, with the brine streaming through his fingers, or a piece of bread. These Tartar shepherds have yielded to the influence of their Russian surroundings, and, though still nominally Mohammedans, drink vodka as freely as the moujiks. While I was there, an ancient Tartar dame drove up in a ramshackle one-horse telega, bringing a sack of newly threshed wheat to swap for vodka. She was as shriveled as a mummy, and must have been eighty years old.

In the eyes of the Tartars it was a recommendation to their good will that I had been to Stamboul and knew a few words of Turkish.

Even here, in this rude company, the difference in the two races was oddly conspicuous to the casual looker-on. The vodka was paid for chiefly by the Tartars and consumed chiefly by the Russians. A boozer of the latter nationality, be he never so fuddled, always took care to pour down his throat about two glasses to his Tartar comrade's one, out of the bottle that had been ordered through the bars by the Tartar. These Crim Tartars, indeed, seemed to be a particularly generous-souled set of people so far as my passing experience of them enabled me to judge.

Another hot, dreary day across the level steppe, on which, however, was seen at one point the agreeable oasis of a German colonist settlement,—a village of neat white houses, with red tiles, and an avenue of trees along the streets ; and on the following morning there appeared on the southern horizon the irregular out-lines of the Yaila Mountains. It was the landmark indicating the end of my ride on horseback.

Though there is nothing in the shape of a mountain all the way from the frozen limits of the Russian Empire to the north, on the longitudinal line of my journey, my last two days' ride would be over moun-tain roads. The Yaila Mountains fringe the southern shore of the Crimean Peninsula, which in all other parts was as monotonous as any other part of the ride. The mountains were as welcome a sight as land after a long sea voyage ; so welcome, indeed, that a sense of depression, born of the monotony of the steppe, im-mediately gave way to something akin to the enthusi-asm of a new discovery. " Hail ! blessed mountains !" was the mental greeting called forth by their first revelation ; the truism, that our appreciation of a thing is in direct proportion to its scarcity, applies no less to mountains than to any other object.

In these mountains, at Yalta, is an Imperial palace, where members of the Imperial family sometimes reside, coming all the way from St. Petersburg to enjoy the luxury of mountain scenery and air.

They seemed yet more to be appreciated as I drew near them in the evening, and found that they had conjured into existence, rows of stately poplar trees, orchards of luscious fruit, and acres of productive melon gardens by the roadside, where one could halt and obtain from the Tartar melon gardeners the choicest of "karpooses."

Here it was, too, that I once again experienced, at

the hands of the Tartars, that simple, spontaneous hospitality which had charmed me, years before, among the Turks of Asia Minor. The day before, I was among a grasping, overcharging set of Crimean Jews, who had charged me for the privilege of watering Texas at their well; now I was invited to halt, and help myself to melons, by a Tartar who refused money when I offered to pay.

The remainder of the ride to Sevastopol was over mountainous, stony roads, for the most part a government military *chaussée*. This *chaussée* connects Sevastopol with Simferopol, the governmental capital of the Crimea, and is in slow process of extension to the north. The idea is to eventually connect it with the road I had followed from Moscow to Kharkoff.

Though hilly and frightfully hot, the novelty of the change was keenly appreciated, though probably less so by Texas than his rider. His compensation for the hills he had to climb was the novel luxury of slices of watermelon, and the rinds of the same, which he seemed to relish as keenly as the green maize with which, a few days before, I had cajoled him into forgetting Sascha's horse and warming toward his master. By this time the remarkably social disposition which had formerly distinguished him in his demeanor toward his equine associate had developed into something more than mere sociability toward the only companion he now had to claim his attentions.

Whether it was the magic influence of green maize and slices of watermelon, or because I had, during the past few days, fed him chiefly on barley, which he liked better than oats, was past finding out; but he had now become so affectionate that he would follow me about like a dog—always excepting when I attempted to lead the way across a bridge or toward a stream of water when he wasn't thirsty. The horror of wetting his feet and of crossing bridges, which he had exhibited the first day out from Moscow, was at the end of the journey as much of a quarrel between us as at the beginning.

Occasionally the road led through charming little valleys, with gurgling streams, devoted to the cultivation of pears, plums, and grapes. Vineyards were surrounded with stone walls, the handiwork of Greek proprietors, of which there were a fair sprinkling among the population. Nicopol, Melitopol, Simferopol, and the many other ——'opols of this part of Russia told the story of the old Byzantium Empire.

Beside the Greeks and Tartars, gypsies were now encountered, camps of basket-makers by the wayside underneath the trees. The women were importunate to sell me a basket or tell my fortune; the men to buy, sell, or swap a horse. The children ran alongside Texas begging for kopecks; the very doubles of those who, four years before, had raced beside my bicycle in Hungary begging for kreutzers, and again in India, for pice. All were alike, save that those encountered in India had darker skins, teeth of more dazzling whiteness, and eyes even more black and flashing than their relatives of Hungary and the Crimea.

Nor was the muse forgotten by the good genii of these magic mountains. Wherever there are mountains, Greeks, and grapes, the wandering minstrel appears on the scene as a necessary part of the local coloring of the picture. The noontide halt of the last day but one of the ride was made in the old Tartar town of Bekchiserai, where the population is now chiefly Greek and Tartar. Here a band of itinerant Greek musicians regaled my ears with the only music, save of military bands, that had been heard on the journey.

All through Malo Russia, the land of the balalaika, not a solitary twang of that instrument had been heard; the dead level of the eternal steppes seemed to have found an echo in the monotony of the people's pursuits, which were the gratification of their animal wants. After harvest, possibly, the Little Russian picture might have brightened somewhat; but the absorbing concern of the population, as they came under my observation was, monotonously,—work, food, and money.

But the mountains introduced the pleasure-loving Greeks; and so here at Bekchiserai were musicians at mid-day, and the little girls dancing graceful Hellenic measures to the playing. There was an element of doubt as to whether this was altogether an improvement, however, on the Little Russians, from their own standpoint, so much as it was from mine; unless, indeed, the main object of life is the seeking of butterfly pleasures. As compared with the children of the Russian villages, the little Greek girls were amusingly precocious. Small misses of eight and ten danced and posed in rivalry for the applause of the lookers-on, as soubrettes on the stage; and some of them smoked cigarettes, producing paper and tobacco from their pockets to roll them.

At Bekchiserai, and other neighboring places, were old Tartar tombs and mosques. Both Perekop and Simferopol have Tartar quarters, with mosques and minarets. The latter are neither tall nor conspicuous, however, being completely overshadowed by the splendid Russian churches. It seemed rather rough on the Tartars, too, as showing scant consideration for the religious susceptibilities of a subject people, to find some of the domes of the Orthodox churches ornamented with devices proclaiming the triumph of the Cross over the Crescent. This sort of thing is flaunted in the face of any Tartar who looks at a Russian church throughout Russia south of Kharkoff. A favorite device is a Cross towering above a Crescent, with Gabriel perched on the top of the Cross blowing his trumpet.

But there seems to be no friction whatever between the two races, on account of their religious differences; probably owing to the fact that no proselyting is attempted on either side. In many villages of the Crimea, as well as in the provinces of Samara and Kazan on the Volga, one side of the street is Tartar, the other Russian; and the two rub along together in perfect harmony without actually mixing any more than is necessary for the transaction of business.

It was in such a village as this that I passed the last night on the ride; a place called Baalbek, about twenty-five versts from Sevastopol. I had been loitering at a Tartar melon garden during the afternoon, and reached Baalbek at dark. The place contained no public accommodation for man and beast traveling in an independent manner, though there was a post-station, where travelers by the regular Russian post might stay. Here the proprietor, a Russian, either from suspicion of what I might be, or from prejudice because I was riding my own horse, or from sheer inhospitality and indifference, refused either to sell me any feed or stable room for Texas for the night.

On the opposite side of the street, some young Tartars, who were drinking coffee in front of a little coffee shop, seeing the dilemma of a passing stranger, came over to the rescue at once. They had neither horse-feed nor stable; but one of them led Texas away to water, then tied him up in a little private yard on their side of the village; and another skirmished around and obtained a bunch of hay. Bread, a boiled sheepshead, and coffee were obtained for supper, and I was provided with a rude divan in the coffee shop for a bed. I had at length, after six weeks in the saddle, arrived among a people who neither regarded me with suspicion, nor as a windfall to be overcharged and financially made the most of.

From Bekchiserai I was riding over historically interesting ground. Between Simferopol and Baalbek I watered Texas in the Alma, a small stream from which the well-known battle of the Crimean War derived its name; and an hour or two from Baalbek the evidences of the struggle of 1854 were on every hand. Dismantled batteries still frowned from the heights of Inkerman, as though the ghosts of war still haunted the fields of carnage, reluctant to depart.

Leaving the main road, I picked a way toward Sevastopol over the rocky heights on which the batteries and trenches of the allied armies had invested

the city, and between the pits in which the soldiers
had been buried.

There was little of interest to arrest the attention
here, only the remains of the trenches and half-moon
mounds of the batteries, and everywhere the sunken
pits of rocks and bowlders which had once been piled
into mounds above the soldiers' graves.

By ten o'clock, Monday, August 11, I was in Sevastopol, and by two o'clock of the same day had
parted—not without a pang of regret—with Texas.
Here were good hotels, steamships, people who spoke
English, tourists, and all the comforts of a civilized
city. I was no longer in Russia, but only on that surface of it which tourists glide smoothly over by means
of rail and steamer; the Russia known to the visitors
who get their impressions of it by a trip to St. Petersburg and Moscow; or by making the " grand tour " by
rail and by steamer, up the Volga.

CHAPTER XVI.

UP THE DON AND VOLGA.

SMOTHERING, as best we may, a sense of remorse and ingratitude at the necessity of leaving in the hands of a Sevastopol horse dealer, the gallant little horse that had carried me more than a thousand miles across the Russian steppes, in the hottest part of the year, in six weeks,—June 20 to August 11,—the reader is invited to glide with us over the surface of Russia, eastward and northward, to take a peep at the great fair of Nijni Novgorod. It seems good to get off the dreary road, to get away from the heat and fatigue and the meager food of the Russian road, to find one's self aboard a Black Sea steamer, eating good dinners, and sleeping in a fairly comfortable bed. All things go by comparison, and though the little Sevastopol steamer was by no means an Atlantic grayhound in the matter of size, accommodation, or speed, the change to its breezy deck from a Cossack saddle and a tired mustang, was a jump over a hundred years of progress in the path of civilization.

We touched at Yalta and Kertch, and in three days and a half landed at Taganrog. I stayed at Taganrog over night, and carried away one vivid impression. It was the sign of a barber's shop, opposite my hotel, Englished, and it read: " Room for shaving cutting hairs and bleed." Our way to Nijni is up the winding

Don to Kalatch, thence by a short railroad to the Volga, and up that Russian Mississippi to our destination.

Our starting point is Rostoff, a city near the mouth of the Don. The boat is a paddle-wheel steamer of about two hundred tons burden, and, like the spinster in the story, of uncertain age. Fresh paint gives it, again like the spinster in the story, the bloom of youth, but in the dining-saloon you discover that it was doing service on the Don twenty-one years ago, and probably several years before. In 1869 the Emperor, Alexander III, then Czarevitch, ascended the Don in this steamer, and his autograph, commemorative of the event, written with a lead-pencil on a plaster of Paris ground, hangs in the dining-saloon.

Above it depends a big steel portrait of the Czar, and beside it, but in a corner, and curiously inconspicuous, is a tiny ikon. The size and prominence of pictures of the Czar and the smallness and unobtrusive position of the ikons—those two features of every Russian public hall and most private rooms, representing " God and the Czar "—were among the writer's most vivid impressions of South Russia.

In a former chapter something was said of the emotional display on the platforms of Russian railways at the departure of a train. A new revelation broke over my astonished senses upon the departure of our steamer from Rostoff. Every passenger must have had at least twenty friends at the landing to see him or her off. And the flood of tears, kisses, laughter, injunctions, admonitions, and all-around emotion—how can mere words depict it? One would think these people were parting for all eternity. At every warning of the steamer's whistle the departing one was spasmodically seized by first one, then from six to twenty others, and kissed as though he or she were the only person in the world any of them had ever loved. And after it seemed to be all over, and the roustabouts were about to remove the gangway, one young woman rushed frantically off the boat, and, in defiance of the captain, who stamped his foot, and the bell that continued to ring, kissed again everybody who had come down to see her off, from the red-eyed old grandmother to the blinking and unresponsive infant in its nurse's arms.

The Don is not a large river, though its volume of water is considerably larger in the spring than in August and September. In August, 1890, the traveler could shy a stone across it at most points, and even this is apt to convey a false idea regarding its volume. Its bed is a tortuous depression in a flat and somewhat sandy country, and its shallowness in proportion to its width, as well as the scenery, or absence of scenery, on its banks, reminds one of the Platte River in Nebraska. It differs from the Platte, however, in having much less current. To this, and to the fact that it traverses a lower and somewhat heavier country, it owes its value as a navigable river.

Before we were well away from Rostoff the steamer had to begin whistling and tooting at big lumber-rafts that were floating down, with exasperating placidity and indifference to up-coming craft, in the only channel deep enough to let us pass. These rafts occupy two months in descending the river from Kalatch.

They contain shipbuilding timber for the Black Sea, telegraph poles, railway ties, logs, and firewood. Two or three huts, in which the navigators live, are built on each, and besides the navigators they sometimes carry wood-choppers, who convert logs into firewood on the voyage down.

In reply to our tootings and the threatening gyrations of our irascible little captain's arms, the red-shirted raftsmen lazily worked huge sweeps that are attached to the fore and rear ends of the raft and slowly and grudgingly gave us the channel. The captain shook his fist at them as we steamed laboriously by, and removed his eternal cigarette-holder from his mouth, as if to annihilate them with a volley of invectives. Mindful of the lady passengers at his elbow, however, he thought better of it, and blowing the remnant of the last cigarette away with an impatient puff, he lit a new one and sent his orders down the speaking-tube to put on full speed.

Our steamer was thoroughly Russian in its disposition to make a tremendous fuss about nothing. In response to the captain's orders for full speed its engines throbbed and pulsated at a feverish rate, and its paddles set up such a prodigious splashing that one might easily be deceived into thinking it was making fifteen knots an hour, if our surroundings would only assist in the delusion.

Neither the Cossack urchin on the right bank (who was amusing himself by keeping up with us) however, nor the herd of horses swimming and wading across the river ahead of us were to be humbugged by our fussy outlay of noise and steam. The youngster easily kept abreast of us at a dog trot, and the horses refused to accept us as a thing to avoid till we took to tooting and whistling at them, as we did at the raft.

The country was monotonous, and life on the banks of the river might easily have been more picturesque and stirring. Our steamer was winding and twisting about through the heart of the country of the Don Cossacks. We saw these Cossacks on the banks in charge of big herds of horses and cattle, and we had them, passengers and deck hands, on the boat. On shore the passengers saw them galloping about, throwing the lasso with the expertness of Texas cowboys, and as fishermen, in little half-moon boats, they were an ever-present feature of the river. But the passengers looked in vain for the realization of the figure the Cossack cuts in romance.

Where were the picturesque horsemen of the stirring tales of Count Tolstoï, and Gogol, of " The Cossacks," and " Taras Bulba," the descendants of Mazeppa; the wild borderers and free-lances of the steppe? The men on horseback looked like ordinary mortals. They were neither richly armed nor gorgeously caparisoned. In fact, they were armed only with whip and lasso, and caparisoned with very sorry-looking saddles and bridles. Their only striking feature was a red-banded cap and red-striped trousers, which gave them a semi-military appearance. Both horsemen and fishermen wore these red evidences of their allegiance to the Czar. All Cossacks are soldiers. Every able-bodied man is under obligation to serve in the army. They hold their lands and are exempt from every form of Imperial taxation, on the condition of always being ready-equipped with horse and accoutrements to take the field. They provide their own horses and saddles and the Government supplies them with rifles.

These ordinary-looking mortals, who squat in their cockle-shell craft and spend their days and nights in mending fishing-nets and baiting hooks, are the descendants of the bold buccaneers who used to descend the Don in big fleets of these same boats and pounce on Turkish galleys in the Sea of Azov, and who, after the Crimean War, boasted that they would in the same way have captured the British fleets before Sevastopol, had the Czar given them permission.

At times the sinuosities of the way were aggravated by a bewildering number of white and red pyramidal buoys, and the necessity of obeying their directions to prevent running aground. So tortuous was our course, half the time, that the passengers of the upper deck, under a scant awning, were kept in good exercise moving from one side to the other to keep in the shade.

In spite of buoys, and all other precautions, however, we found ourselves aground about once every two hours, day and night.

Among the third-class passengers were several sturdy raftsmen, who received a free passage back to Kalatch on condition that they lend a hand when the steamer runs aground. They assisted her over shallow places by means of a crude anchor and a cable. The "anchor" consisted of a beam about thirty feet long, peaked at one end, and with an iron cross-bar near the sharpened end. Wading ahead a hundred yards or so with this beam and the noosed end of the cable, they placed the noose over the cross-bar and dipped the sharp end of the beam in the sand. All hands then bore down on the long end of the beam, while the steamer was hauled forward by working the capstan.

This process was slow and not always sure. Sometimes, when the free passengers were complacently perched along the beam holding it down, something slipped and all were precipitated into the water. Passengers are expected to take an interest in overcoming the difficulties at these shallow places. The sounding-pole betrays the fact that the water is three inches deeper on one side of the boat than the other. All passengers are then required to crowd over to the deep water side to help ease her off.

Sometimes a station consisted of a housed hulk, and sometimes the steamer merely thrust her nose up against the bank to let passengers on or off. In the latter case a plank was run ashore and a hand-rail improvised by means of a sounding-pole and the shoulders of a couple of roustabouts, one on deck, the other ashore.

The passengers were the most interesting, and often the most amusing, not to say instructive, objects seen on the trip. There was a light-haired, light-eyed lady with a shrill voice, who flirted all the way with the captain and wanted to give orders for him down the speaking-tube. Some of these orders are given in English on Russian boats, the choicest one of them all being " shtop-a-leetle." To hear this lady shout shrilly in the speaking-tube " shtop-a-leetle," was one of the diversions of the journey, and will always be associated with my reminiscences of the Don.

There was a gray-whiskered army officer who tried

to cut out the captain in the esteem of the light-haired lady, but failed. This officer looked a general, at least, and when talking you felt certain that he was discussing the movements of monster armies and the manner of conducting big campaigns. Since the pale-haired lady refused to give up the captain and the speaking-tube on his account, however, it is safe to say that he was nothing but a senior lieutenant and gave utterance to nothing in particular.

There was an Armenian lady, with three children and three nurses, who took as much trouble looking after the lot as if they were all children and all in her charge.

There were merchants who talked rubles and kopecks all day long, and a couple of seedy-looking popes or priests—gentlemen of the cloth.

The martial element of the company was increased at one of the stations by a very much booted, spurred, sworded and whiskered Cossack officer, who spoke to nobody and smoked cigarettes without a break for an hour at a stretch. He looked the very incarnation of war. Higher up the river, on a bank that did service as a landing-place, was seen, as the steamer turned her nose to the shore, another officer who seemed to be a counterpart of our fellow-passenger. He, too, looked an understudy of Mars. Surely the captain was never going to commit the folly of bringing together these two martial atoms? Nothing less than a duel could be expected from a contact between these two. Come together, however, they did, on the bank, in sight of all. And the catastrophe that we witnessed was such as happens when a couple of school-girls meet after vacation. Like a pair of amiable misses these whiskered

Cossacks threw their arms about each other's necks and kissed.

Kalatch is three days' journey by steamboat up the Don from Rostoff. The time occupied in reaching it, however, conveys to the American altogether a misleading idea regarding the distance between the two places, until he understands the sinuous and shallow nature of the river and the extraordinary methods that have to be resorted to at times to help the steamer along.

The prominent features of Kalatch were lumber, vodka shops, red-shirted lumbermen, and a boat hotel for the accommodation of travelers. On the upper deck of this floating caravansary, at a near table, were a party of Russian travelers. Noticing that I was a foreigner, they ceased talking their mother tongue and began chattering in French. In a few minutes they dropped French and took a turn at German.

This peculiarity of the traveling Russian had come under the observation of the writer many times, and I have yet to come to a satisfactory solution of their motive. The airing of their linguistic accomplishments was, on the whole, too modest in its manifestations to justify a verdict of ostentation. Their talk was to one another and not at the foreigner, whose presence, nevertheless, undoubtedly had stimulated their tongues to the international exercise.

The explanation that occurs to me as being the most probable is this, nearly all Russians of education and noble birth learn several languages in their youth. English governesses, French teachers, German nurses, instructed them in their tender youth, and made these

languages as easy to them as their own.   The number
of Russians one meets who once knew these languages,
and for want of opportunities to speak them have forgotten one or all of them, is surprising.   When, therefore, a party of educated Russians suddenly discover
the proximity of a foreigner, the circumstance reminds
them of their lingual abilities, which they immediately
proceed to exercise.

Shortly after the Crimean war had brought home to
the Russian government the necessity of improving
communications, a short line of railroad was built between Tzaritzin and Kalatch, connecting the Volga
and the Don.   The railroad was built as a temporary
expedient and forerunner of a canal, by means of which
steamers could pass from one river to the other, and it
early gained the reputation of being the worst piece of
railway traveling in the world.   Two trains a week
used to start in a venturesome way over it, and the
chances of running off the rails, or breaking down,
raised the odds against the travelers to such a level as
induced many of them to prefer the old way of horses
and tarantasses.

August, 1890, the canal had not been dug, but the
railway had improved with age, for the author found
nothing disreputable about it save the indifference of
its management to the flight of time.   It now has a
daily train, and by means of petroleum-refuse fuel, and
plenty of axle-grease the fifty miles are overcome in
the brief space of four hours.   We should have done
it in three hours and fifty minutes had not the conductor lingered at one of the stations, for about ten
minutes, haggling over the price of a young sturgeon,

which a Cossack fisherman had brought to try to sell. The conductor succeeded in cheapening the fish twenty kopecks (twelve cents), and from the tremendous interest taken in the transaction by the passengers it is fair to presume not one of them had any objection to the brief delay of the train. To many of them, no doubt, a railway ride was one of those rare pleasures that are all the better appreciated for being long drawn out.

The chief feature at every station were women and girls with heaps of watermelons, and the heart's desire of about every passenger on the train seemed to be to obtain a melon at each stopping-place for half the price the venders appeared willing to take. The number of melons was so ridiculously out of proportion to the possible number of purchasers that it seemed a veritable case of commercial suicide on the part of the women to refuse anything that might be offered. This glaring evidence of an over-stocked market was not by any means lost on the passengers, who would not have been Russians if it had been, and just before the departure of the train every bargainer would secure a melon at reduced rates and hasten aboard. Between one station and another the journey was a picnic of melon-eaters, who added one day's contribution to an already well-defined streak of melon rinds on either side of the track.

Trees and gardens at the pleasant little station houses relieved the monotony of the otherwise treeless steppe, and a leather medal should be awarded to one of the station-masters who, about midway of the line, had produced a flower garden that would be a credit to any country.

We started at eight o'clock, and in the broad glare of the August noon there came into view from the windows of the train a dusty-looking town and a river broad as the Mississippi, a section of which was half hidden by a multitude of rafts and shipping. The dusty town was Tzaritzin, and the broad river the Volga.

After a few weeks of experience in knocking about Russia, and of the inevitable disillusion of its provincial towns, one comes to dread, rather than rejoice at the prospect of making the acquaintance of a new city.

The first glimpse of Tzaritzin was peculiarly ominous and depressing, and a closer acquaintance with it amply confirmed one's worse presentiments. People, horses, droskies, drivers, houses—everything in it was yellow with dust. Dust was ankle deep, even on the best parts of the streets; everywhere else the spaces that answer the purpose of streets offered the most villainous succession of holes and humps that ever disgraced a town. On the way from the station to the hotel one had to cling to the ramshackle drosky with both hands to escape being pitched out, and the performance of the dusty jehu in keeping his narrow seat was a masterpiece of equipoise. The character of horses and droskies was in keeping with the streets, as in other places, which in Tzaritzin means that the former were the scum of the herds on the adjacent steppes, and that the latter were calculated to inspire in the mind of the passenger visions of broken bones.

Happily, my acquaintance with this dust-hole of a city, as well as its hotel, was destined to be brief. The caravansary in question was a combination of hotel and variety theater. In it the guests could take their choice between eating their meals in bed-rooms, as cheerless as prison cells, or dining to the accompaniment of squeaking fiddles and shrill-voiced young women, who held forth as song-and-dance artists on a stage at one end of the dining-room.

Wondering the while which of these two evils is likely to be the worst, you turn your attention to the toilet arrangements in your room. There is neither soap, towel, nor water. Your spirits revive, however, at discovering something resembling a washstand in one corner, and in answer to a few rings of the bell a melancholy woman brings a pitcher of water which she pours into a tin receptacle above the stand. This receptacle you have made the acquaintance of in other Russian hotels, and have learned that if you press a treadle with your foot it squirts a jet of water that is understood by the natives, but which will very likely strike an unsophisticated foreigner in the face.

Here, however, you discover that there is no treadle and no visible way of getting at the water. A careful search at length discloses a loose brass spigot, with the thick end inside, in the bottom of the vessel. If this spigot could be removed altogether, a stream of water would trickle out with which you could dally in comfort. But a knob at the small end forbids this liberty, and requires you to hold the wretched stopper in with one hand in order that sufficient water to wet the other may escape. A more ingenuous arrangement to thwart the efforts of a person to wash the hands and face could scarcely have been invented.

There was to be a boat for Nijni Novgorod at nine

o'clock next morning. Kamaret in hand, I sallied
forth in the glare and dust to see if there was anything worth photographing. Some Turcoman teamsters, with a string of camel carts, filed past, an Asiatic
spectacle that I had not before seen in European Russia. Tzaritzin, however, is in easy touch with Asia by
an all-water route down the Volga to Astrakhan and
across the Caspian.

A rude bench on the edge of the bluff on which the
town is built attracted me by reason of the good view
to be obtained from it of the Volga, and the multitude
of busy workers among the rafts and shipping.

About five o'clock there appeared on the southern
horizon of the river a white speck that grew larger
apace, and finally assumed the shape and dimensions of
a magnificent steamboat, patterned after the floating
palaces of the Mississippi. As it steamed majestically
up to the landing, there could be no manner of doubt
that the steamer owed its existence to American enterprise, which must have either placed it on the Volga or
furnished the pattern for those who did.

My chief interest in it, however, was as to the time
of its departure up stream, and I at once repaired to
the office on the floating dock, to which it was shortly
moored. By dint of insistence with the ticket agent,
who persisted in replying " sei tchas," which means
any length of time, from a minute to a year, I at
length discovered that it would start in half an hour,
and would take me to Nijni Novgorod. At the hotel
I was advised by the proprietor to remain and witness
the performances at the theatrical end of the dining-
room in the evening, the character of the entertain-

ment being indicated by the sawing of an imaginary violin.

Not to be tempted, however, by the blandishments of resin and catgut, as manipulated by the talent of the Lower Volga, I hastened aboard the steamer. I got aboard in time to shut the window of my cabin against a hurricane of dust that sprang up and obscured everything at the distance of a hundred yards. As we paddled away nothing was to be seen of Tzaritzin but the dust of its streets, which had been converted into a dense cloud, and which completely hid the city from our view.

The cabins were spacious and left nothing to be desired, save sheets and a pillow. Since every traveler in Russia is supposed to carry these articles with him, the steamboat people consider they have made ample provision for the comfort of their first-class passengers by providing broad, soft lounges for them to lie down on at night. The steamboats carry no bed linen, though the trips occupy several days. In every other respect the cabins are superior even to those on the Fall River Line and other crack American steamers.

The cuisine is very good. You can dine *à la carte* on sturgeon and champagne, or you can get a four-course *table d'hôte* dinner with a half bottle of drinkable Crimean claret for a couple of rubles. Or, if you are economical, and care to do in Russia as plenty of the Russians do, you can forage for yourself whenever the steamer calls at a town, and obtain from the steamer nothing but hot water to make your tea.

The arrangements are better than on the Don steamers, where at dinner-time every window of the saloon is apt to frame the unkempt head of one of the third-class passengers, who regards with wolfish interest the contents of your plate and speculates vaguely as to the probable sensation on the palate of the various dishes as they come in.

Every Russian passenger carries tea and sugar, usually in a little calico bag. Bread and lemons are bought at the stopping places, and every steamer keeps a lubberly, unwilling sort of youth, whose duty is to provide plenty of hot water. Teapot and glasses are obtained from the steward, and the Russian family by means of these ingredients manage to pass no small share of their time drinking tea and sweetened water. The Russian would probably rebel against the insinuation of sweetened water, but the straw-colored fluid that is yielded by the overtaxed leaves after the teapot has been replenished over and over again with hot water is not to be converted into tea by a mere politeness of the tongue.

Life on the boat was dull. The men played cards and the women read novels. There was a spacious promenade deck, but no promenaders to speak of, though the nights were moonlight and the weather all that could be desired. By walking round the deck a few times one made himself conspicuous. If, perchance, one of the Russian travelers took to strutting up and down, it was some vain young peacock of an officer who had nothing to recommend him but a new uniform, or some giddy member of the opposite sex posing for the admiration of the men. Russians rarely walk for exercise, they being in this respect thoroughly Oriental.

In the third-class section of the boat life was somewhat more interesting. Here the moujik in his red shirt and unkempt hair was in his element with an accordion and plenty of weak tea and melons. As on the railway, melons formed a prominent feature of all the landings, as well as of the traffic on the river. They went past by boat-loads, and at the stations they were built up in pyramids by the thousand, like cannon-balls in a fortress. In season the common people almost seem to live on bread and melons.

The river life consisted of tugs towing monster rafts and strings of huge barges. The bigness of the rafts and the number of barges hooked on to one tiny tug seemed to curiously illustrate the Russian disposition to overreach and get the best of a bargain. You meet undersized tugs struggling along with no less than six barges, each one of which is several times larger than itself, and though you may be mistaken, you cannot help thinking that the owner of the barges has somehow defrauded the owner of the tug.

All steamers burn refuse petroleum, which is brought from the Baku refineries on the Caspian and moored in tank hulks at various points along the river. It is stored in tanks over the fire-boxes, into which it is fed by means of taps. As it leaves the taps, jets of steam convert it into fine spray and scatter it over the fire-box, where it is consumed by instantaneous combustion. The interior of the fire-box presents to the eye nothing but a mass of yellow flame.

The scenery of the Volga is tame, but not devoid of beauty ; and in places, to one coming from a journey over the monotonous steppes, seems really beautiful. It is not to be classed with the Rhine or the Hudson; rather does it belong to the class of the Danube, the Mississippi, the Yangtsi-Kiang, and other principal rivers of the world. Though shallower than any of these, it compares favorably with them in size and length.

In the internal economy of Russia it plays as important a part as the Mississippi did in that of the United States before the development of the railroads. The railroad system of Russia is (1890) as yet in its infancy, and the great artery of commerce between the lumber regions of the North and the grain-producing steppes of the Southeast is the Volga. Years ago the huge barges used to be laboriously towed by teams of men, as are the big freight sampans on the Chinese rivers ; and the burlaki, as they were called, and their exhausting labors, have been the theme for the inspiration of Riepin's brush. Later they used to haul them upstream by means of anchors and capstans. These primitive methods were relegated to the past by the defeats of the Crimean War, which did Russia much more good than harm, by teaching her that national greatness could only be achieved by progress in the arts and sciences. Now there are several lines of good steamboats, which leave little to be desired, unless it be an increase in speed. The distance from Tzaritzin to Nijni Novgorod is but 1685 versts, yet the journey occupied six and a half days.

At Samara, Simbirskh, and Kazan the passenger list assumed a more polyglot aspect from the addition of Tartars, many thousands of whom reside in the provinces of the Middle Volga. They retain their Mohammedan religion, and the small minarets of their mosques in Kazan are visible from the deck of the steamer. In the evening they retired to the stern of the boat, and kneeling toward Mecca, performed their devotions. The zigzag course of the river befooled them sorely as to the direction of the holy city. Sometimes they commenced their prayers by kneeling and bobbing their heads in the direction of Mecca and ended by addressing themselves, unwittingly, to a wellnigh opposite direction, from the steamer having passed, during their pious meditations, a bend in the river.

These scenes were varied at times by a diversion of some kind ashore. One night all the people of a village congregated on the bank near a station. The moonlight, the broad river and the majestic steamer inspired the female part of the crowd to song. For some distance after we had left the vicinity we could hear this vocal tribute to a moonlight night on the Volga, sung by the wives and daughters of an entire village.

CHAPTER XVII.

IN a previous chapter I said, among other things, that the journey up the Volga occupied six and a half days, which I condemned as an indication of Russian indifference to the flight of time.

On the Volga steamers the ticket is for passage only; food is obtained and paid for as at the Russian hotels, where rooms are under one management and dining arrangements under another. Just before landing at Nijni Novgorod, when the obsequious young man in swallow-tail coat and semi-immaculate shirt-bosom, who had been so devoted and disinterested in his attention to my wants, presented my bill for dinners, etc., I made a fairly startling discovery. We had been, not six days and a half on the journey, but eight and a half! In humble imitation of Rip Van Winkle I had, at some part of the voyage, laid down and slept for two days without suspecting it!

It is surprising how rapidly and unconsciously the traveler becomes cynical and suspicious under the benign influence of the paternal rule of the Russian Tchin. Yet how could one suspect the young gentleman in the swallow-tail coat? For did he not instantly summon a brother swallow-tail to decide between us, whether we had been six days or eight coming from Tzaritzin? And how could the author, with an extremely limited stock of Russian words at command, hope to withstand the torrent of convincing consonants that rolled from the tongues, and acquired new force from the pantomime of these two practical knights of an honorable profession?

The contest was most unequal; and then, when it occurred to me that these two trusted servants of a steamboat company, who should naturally take pride in promoting the interests of their employers, would be most unlikely to attempt to reduce the record of speed one fourth, I succumbed. It is true that if I had slept for two days without eating anything, there still remained the inconsistency of charging for eight dinners when I had ordered only six. I was, however, so delighted at having gone through so remarkable a performance, that I not only paid the bill without further dispute, but gave the swallow-tails a ruble *douceur* apiece as a slight recompense for having at first suspected them of duplicity. Unfortunately I was never able to recall any extraordinary visions or dreams in connection with my forty-eight hours' sleep; nor was I able to discover, by comparing it with an almanac, any two days' jump in my diary.

Fast or slow, however, I felt grateful to the steamer for having landed me in Nijni Novgorod at the full tide of the great annual fair. This feature of Nijni Novgorod, to which the city is indebted for its world-renown, was in full swing. The hum and bustle of the fair were suggestive of a hive of very busy bees, in which the workers, however, were not bees, but men and women, and the queen bee a woman with scales, like Justice, only not blind, and weighing, instead of equity, products of human industry from every quarter of the globe.

There is an impression abroad that, owing to the development of the Russian railway system, the great fair of Nijni Novgorod is no longer what it was. This is true in one sense, but not in the sense that people commonly accept the information. To the astonishment of the Moscow merchants themselves, who fully. expected that the railways, by distributing merchandise to all parts of the country, would reduce the Nijni fair to an historical curiosity, merchants flock to the place from every town in Russia and Siberia in numbers as great as ever. The volume of business was, in 1890, as large as it ever was.

In Russia, as elsewhere, conservatism is apt to predict all manner of evil consequences to established institutions by radical economic changes. The conservative merchants of Moscow and St. Petersburg saw the collapse of the great institution of the Nijni fair in Russian railway extension. But these conservative merchants, in no way abashed by the discovery of their own false reasoning, continue to come to Nijni as of yore and to dispose of about the same quantity of goods.

The lesson they learned from the experience is that improved transportation facilities, by cheapening goods and placing them within easier reach of the people, have simply brought about an increase in consumption and demand. The merchant's *pro rata* profits have been reduced in favor of the consumers by the new order of things, but since he sells twice as many goods as formerly, the results to him are in the end the same or better than before.   He now not only sells as many goods as ever at the Nijni Novgorod fair, but, by reason of the railways, ships an equal quantity off to a ever widening circle of new customers elsewhere.

The old order of things, the smaller trade and the exorbitant profits, were of course more congenial to the conservative Moscow merchant, who, like any other fossil, dislikes to be stirred up by the unceremonious pole of modern progress.   But the consumers have benefited immensely, while the only result to him has been the necessity of waking up to a juster and livelier sense of commercial competition.

In the shop of a Moscow merchant I met traders from widely remote parts of the Russian Empire. One from far Irkutsk, in Eastern Siberia, informed me that it cost him three and a half rubles freight on every pood of goods from Nijni to Irkutsk.   At the then rate of exchange, this is equivalent to $120 a ton, American weight.   I asked him why he didn't obtain his goods by way of the Pacific and the Amoor River. He replied that the paternal Russian government had placed the lock of prohibitive customs duties on that door, and so compelled him and his brother merchants of those remote regions to come to European Russia to buy goods, and to pay the enormous addition to their cost in getting them home.

My merchant friend, who had attended the Nijni Novgorod Fair for twenty years past, gave me some particulars of the trade.

The fair opens officially on July 15, and ends on August 25.   Merchants begin to arrive and do business, however, before July 15, and the fair drags along into

September. Altogether it may be said to last two months. At the opening ceremonies, flags are hoisted all over the city, and processions of priests with crosses and ikons pass through the streets. Squads of police arrive from Moscow and St. Petersburg, and from July 1 to September, the Governor of the province is invested with full powers, even of life and death, as in military government.

For ten months in the year, the long rows of substantial stone and brick shops, the cobbled streets, the numerous hotels and palatial restaurants of the modern fair-city of Nijni Novgorod are deserted, save by a few watchmen. During the seasons of high water, at the melting of the winter snows in the northern forests, the lower stories of the houses are often under water, and in order to get about the streets a visitor would require a boat.

At the thawing of the Siberian rivers, in April and May, the movement of goods and merchants toward this rendezvous begins. Down the rivers, in barges and in steamers, wool, hides, tallow, pelts, and other bulky produce from Siberia gravitate toward this common center, and, during the fair, occupy the " Siberisky priestin " in huge stacks, covered with canvas, or long sheds roofed with tin. As fair time draws near, a similar movement of the goods for which this raw material is to be exchanged begins from the West. Goods are packed up and shipped to Nijni from every city in Europe, and, indirectly, through Russian and German houses, from America also. It would be difficult to mention an article that one could not buy in the streets offhand, and quite impossible to mention anything that could not be obtained through agents.

The variety of goods is bewildering; and I was informed that there is an exchange in the two months of about 300,000,000 rubles, or $175,000,000. Most business is transacted on a year's credit. Goods are sold to be paid for at the next fair. On the whole, bad debts are rare, and, while the system of long credit survives, the exorbitant profits that in the past history of the fair have justified the risk, no longer obtain, owing to increased competition.

When the Russian, Persian, Bokhariot, Siberian, or other merchant who trades at Nijni pays his last year's obligations, he expects a present. If a wine merchant, after settling his bill, he looks over the wholesaler's stock, and selecting a bottle of high-priced champagne, jokingly walks off with it. If the transaction has been in saddlery, he appropriates a fancy bridle. While I was in my friend's magazine, a repository of hardware, a Samarkandian merchant who called to settle for a couple of American cotton gins, commenced to examine critically a cross-cut saw. My friend, who had just been explaining this peculiarity of the trade of the Nijni fair, gave me the wink. The Samarkandian stepped to the door, and summoning a youth, quietly made off with the saw, hardly giving the owner of it a smile as he went out.

In many little ways customers have to be indulgently humored, to meet the peculiar ways and ideas of the East. The Asiatic customers have a habit of dropping in about zakuski time, when, of course they are politely invited to partake of the tempting spread of caviare, cheese, sardines, etc., that is set out in the little rear room.

Everything counts. Shrewd Moscow and St. Petersburg merchants make a point of sending with the goods and staff of clerks to Nijni, one or two of their handsomest young women clerks, who are expected to "look their prettiest" and attract custom. There is said to be no sentiment in commerce. Perhaps not, in a world-wide sense. But one has only to attend the Nijni fair and watch one of these lady saleswomen from Moscow selling a bill of goods to a rough, half-civilized merchant from Central Asia, to shatter his faith in the maxim. How can this rude denizen of a distant mud-built town, inhabited by unwashed men and bedraggled women, bargain on fair terms with this dainty young saleslady, gotten up for the express purpose of wheedling such as he into making purchases?

Rent is higher in Nijni Novgorod than in any other city in the world. Persons who invest capital in buildings to be rented must get a reasonable return on the outlay, whether it be in Nijni Novgorod or in New York. And since in the former city the shops, hotels, theaters, restaurants, etc., are unoccupied for ten months in the year, twelve months' rent has to be charged for the other two. In other words, the merchant who rents premises in Nijni for the two months of the fair has to pay as much rent as if he remained for a year.

The utmost precautions are taken against fire. The electric light had about driven from the streets and shops the old system of petroleum lamps, and in another season or two will probably be the only illumination permitted by the authorities. The regulations in regard to fire are amusingly rough on the cigarette smoker, whose habitat is, above all other places, Russia. A person caught smoking in the streets is arrested and ingloriously marched off to the police-station, where he is fined fifty rubles. At the hotels a couple of lynx-eyed lackeys in the employ of the proprietor are stationed at the entrance to warn the outgoing guests of this regulation, and to bar the way of the uninitiated, who would otherwise step jauntily into the street and into the arms of the nearest policeman. These dvorniks reap a rich harvest of tips from the guests of the hotels, who naturally feel under obligations to them from saving them fifty ruble fines.

The wisdom of these precautions against fire come to be understood as the traveler walks about the city and realizes the enormous value of the merchandise that it contains. Every hole and corner is literally crammed with goods. The shops and warehouses are as prolific of goods as the streets, cafés, and hotels are of people, and both goods and people are of a polyglot character not to be seen anywhere else in the world.

To a person who has never traveled in Asia, a trip to Nijni Novgorod during the fair would more than repay the trouble. Merchants from distant parts of Asia bring their manners and customs with them to Nijni. The Persian may be seen in turban or tall lamb-skin hat squatting in his little bazaar, complacently stroking his beard and smoking his kalian, precisely as he is to be seen in Teheran or Ispahan. Young Tartars are seen by the score strolling about the streets peddling bunches of Astrakhan lamb-skins so beautifully dressed as to tempt almost anybody to buy.

There is a hide and peltry section, where Tartar furriers may be seen currying Siberian sables, bear-skins, and all manner of costly furs. There is a part devoted to the sale of nuts, the trade of which seems to be in the hands of the Persians, who can fill your order from stock in hand, whether it be for ten kopecks' worth of walnuts to crack and eat, or for twenty tons of a dozen varieties.

There is a quarter occupied by temporary booths and stalls, where crowds of Russian peasants, the men in red shirts and the women in red dresses and red 'kerchiefs, are purchasing or cheapening red calico, and all manner of red and other bright colored wearing apparel.

And close by is the show quarter, where twenty rival showmen and an extremely loud-mouthed crowd of assistants are hooting, whistling, beating gongs, drums, tins, and extracting from all manner of wind instruments a very Bedlam of noises. Here may be witnessed to the best advantage, perhaps, the childlike innocence and gullibility of the moujik, his wife and daughters. These simple folk are to be seen in the densest throngs, gazing in mute wonder at the cheap paintings on the booth fronts of the showmen who succeed in kicking up the greatest and most unearthly racket. This is very likely their first experience of city and fair life, and the tremendous difference between the outside and inside of these places is as yet unsuspected. A curious feature of this place to the foreigner is that soldiers in uniform are employed by the showmen to attract the crowd. As mentioned in a previous chapter, Russian soldiers are permitted to work twenty-five days a month.

There is a Chinese quarter without any Chinamen in it, and nothing to justify the name beyond the fact that tea is sold there, and that a rude attempt at pagoda architecture has been made, with a few figures of exceedingly doubtful mandarins on the roofs.

A few minutes' walk from these reminders of Asian and Russian interior life brings the visitor to the finest building, apart from cathedrals—of which there are two—in Nijni. On the way you have traversed a neat boulevard, shaded by an avenue of trees and lined with shops, whose windows are as attractive as any row in Paris, London, or New York. The building you have reached is a magnificent arcade, three stories high, the upper floors being occupied as government offices and banks, and the lower by dealers in fancy goods. Here are electric lights, tubs filled with tropical plants, and a military band in the evenings. Can it be possible, you think, that all this is only an affair of a few weeks, and that for ten months out of every twelve solitude and the high waters of the Oka and the Volga are in possession of this city? Still stranger does it seem that cathedrals and churches should be abandoned to the owls and the Evil One, and the Stock Exchange to the twittering of the birds.

The curious incongruity of the Bokhariot and the electric light, and the feverish activity all about, remind you, however, that the surroundings are altogether too extraordinary to last long. You are also reminded of this in your hotel. The dining-rooms of

the restaurants are converted into *cafés chantants.*
Young women from all the towns of Russia, in costumes as abbreviated as the law allows, sing, or attempt
to sing, to the diners at the restaurants and hotels,
standing on raised platforms at one end of the room.

Everywhere is a feverish pressure that, in the nature
of things, cannot endure. It is commerce on a spree.
The debauch lasts a couple of months, and when it is
over, this extraordinary collection of goods and people
disappears.

Some of the merchants ship the remnant of their
stock to Irbit, on the borders of Siberia, in the province
of Perm, where there is a winter fair of which we hear
nothing, but which is the second largest fair in the
world. The Irbit fair lasts a month, from January 20
to February 20, and though small compared with Nijni,
nevertheless shows a business of 40,000,000 rubles a
year. Like the real city of Nijni Novgorod, which is
perched on a bluff, overlooking the fair-city, which occupies a peninsular at the junction of the Oka and
Volga, Irbit amounts to nothing except during the
brief life of the fair.

TARTAR FURRIERS AT NIJNI NOVGOROD.

CHAPTER XVIII.

WITH the completion of the equestrian tour from Moscow to Sevastopol, and the return to Moscow by way of the Don and Volga to Nijni Novgorod, thence by rail to the starting point, the " grand tour " through the Czar's European dominions was ended. And as we return westward by rail, halting briefly at Moscow, St. Petersburg, and Warsaw, a brief record of impressions, in addition to the observations recorded on the ride, will serve to round out and complete the object of our visit.

A foreigner visiting Russia for the first time is always deeply impressed by the outward and visible signs of religion that confront him at every turn. Long before he reaches St. Petersburg the golden domes of its splendid churches and cathedrals, twinkling brightly in the sunlight, have been visible from the deck of the steamer or from the windows of the train. He admires from afar these costly evidences of the religious character of a great nation, and they are among the first places he visits after his arrival.

St. Isaac's and the Kazan Cathedral of St. Petersburg, and St. Saviour's of Moscow, each in turn dazzles and bewilders you by the splendor and wealth of gold altars, ikons all ablaze with diamonds and every variety of precious stones, priceless paintings, columns of malachite, millions on millions lavished on marble and granite.

The isvoshchic who drives you about the city is forever removing his hat and crossing himself as the drosky passes a church or a holy picture in a shrine. The throngs of people in the streets; merchants, soldiers, sailors, peasants, clerks, truckmen, officers, gentlemen, ladies, boys, nurse-maids, the whole heterogeneous population of a city, follow your coachman's example. Passing in and out of the churches are never-ceasing streams of people going or coming on errands of devotion. Before the principal shrines on the street corners a throng is never absent.

Hung up like a picture in one corner of your room at the hotel, not always in St. Petersburg, but always in the provinces, is a holy ikon, and if you are the guest of a Russian family, uncorrupted with European influence, a little ikon very likely will be fastened to the head of your bed. In short, you have arrived in Holy Russia ; Russia, the Orthodox ; Russia, the home. and the champion and defender of the " only true Christian religion."

As for you, whatever else you may be, Catholic, Protestant, Hebrew, Moslem, or nothing in particular, you are, in the eyes of these holy people, whose government, after looking over its black list to make sure that you are not an active champion of liberty or enlightenment, has permitted you to cross the frontier, a heretic. Since nobody troubles to reproach you, however, nor to convert you from the errors of your own religion, you can easily assume the attitude of a non-belligerent, and set about fathoming, without bias or prejudice, the depth or shallowness of the sweeping claims of the Orthodox.

That the Russians are strict observers of the outward forms of religion there is no room for dispute; but are they really a religious people? The first doubt probably finds its way into your mind through the medium of the extremely pious coachman, who has been driving you about to visit the gorgeous cathedrals. Though he has removed his perky isvoshchic's hat twenty times and made twenty crosses with every mark of reverence during the hour of his engagement, when you come to pay him off he will not unlikely assure you that you engaged him not one but two hours ago, and all but literally pick your pocket. The smile of roguish enjoyment that comes into his face is in no way abashed by the sign of the Cross which he immediately makes, and if he has swindled you to his heart's satisfaction he will very likely jog along to the nearest shrine and make several signs of the Cross.

Though this happens at a very early stage of your investigations, a glimmer of light begins to break over your understanding, and awakens a suspicion that all this show of holiness springs less from fear of God than fear of evil spirits. This idea grows upon you in proportion to the length of your stay in the country, and increases with the growth of your acquaintance with the people. And if you stay long enough, and investigate the subject as thoroughly as may be, your first suspicion is very apt to be confirmed.

The educated Russians may be dismissed from the subject of religion *sans ceremonie.*. As a class they represent the extreme section of atheism, free thought,

" advanced ideas," etc., of the age ; and of those who bare heads before churches and ikons, one half do it as a matter of policy and the others because it is less trouble to drift with the stream than to stand still in it, and altogether too much of a strain to think of swimming against it.

Apart from this Voltairian fringe, the mass of the Russian people are passing through much the same moral and religious transformation that Western Europe passed through in the Middle Ages. Allowing for a difference in social conditions, the Empire of the Czar presents a similar picture of splendid religious edifices towering over the habitations of squalid poverty ; of large monasteries full of treasures of gold, silver, and jewels, rich abbots and fat monks, standing in the midst of the broadest and fairest portions of the land. The Russian moujik of to-day is about as full of superstitions and the dread of the Evil One as was the villein of the West in the fourteenth century, and his conceptions of religion are leavened, as those of the villein were, with the lingering remains of paganism.

His creed is largely composed of superstitions and · demonology. To him the holy ikon, that is never absent from his humble abode, is a mysterious, living thing, representing the saint, after whom it is patterned, not only in form, but in spirit and power.

St. Nicholas is the moujik's favorite saint, and a " Nicholai ikon " is found in nearly every peasant's house in Russia. It consists of a small picture of the saint, a figure holding in one hand a church and in the other a sword, set in a deep box-like frame, and gaudily decorated with brass, silver, tinsel, or wax flowers.

The peasants burn tapers before it, and place offerings of food, etc., before it, much as the Hindoo ryot of India does before his household idol. And the place that the ikon holds in the Russian moujik's mind seemed to me to differ very little indeed from that of the idol in the ryot's.

One day, in the province of Kurskh, while drinking kwass in a peasant's house, I asked the housewife why she kept a taper burning before the Nicholai ikon.

She immediately made the sign of the Cross. The ikon had been very good to them that summer, she said ; the crops were good, and the eldest son, who had been away several years in the army, had returned and brought home thirty rubles. I asked her if the ikon was a living thing, capable of influencing the affairs of the family. She seemed almost frightened at the question, as some good old soul in America, who from infancy had lived and prayed in simple faith, would if suddenly challenged to prove the existence of God. Again she rapidly made the sign of the Cross, but gave no answer. I asked her the question in another form. She shook her head.

"Such things are not for ignorant people like me to say," she replied. Determined to corner her if possible, I then asked her how many rubles she had paid for it, and where she had bought it. But it was a family heirloom, inherited from her husband's people.

Although Christianity has been the religion of Russia for more than eight centuries, the customs and superstitions of old pagan times continue to exercise

considerable influence on the every-day life and surroundings of the peasantry. With all their church
ceremonies and outward observance of the official
religion, and their self-denomination of "the Orthodox," the superstitious moujik is only a half-converted
heathen. So much is this the case that it is sometimes
difficult to define where paganism ends and Christianity begins in his creed.

For instance, not only does he regard the Christian
ikons much as his ancestors of the old pagan days did
their idols, but he enthrones them in precisely the
same place in his house that they used to occupy. In
the home of the pagan Slavs the household idols used
to stand on a bench or shelf in what was and is still
known, as the "Upper Corner," the farther right-hand
corner from the door, and facing the big stove which
occupies the central part of the house and around
which the rooms are built. Then, as now, this was
the sacred corner of the house, and the holy ikons of
the present day have merely dethroned the pagan
images and occupy the same shelf in the same corner.

This corner is also referred to as the "Great Corner,"
or the "Beautiful Corner," and no member of the
family thinks of crossing the threshold to enter the
room without making toward it the sign of the Cross.

Near this corner is set the family dinner-table,
another custom that connects the present with the
past, when the heathen Slavs used to transfer the idols
from the shelves to the table during meal times. The
moujik of to-day does not place the ikons on his dinner-
table, but he believes the souls of his ancestors, and of
any members of the family who have died, are hiding

behind the ikons, and bread or little saucers of food are often placed on the shelf where the holy pictures stand. Small loaves of holy bread, made of fine white flower, purchased from the monks in the monasteries, are favorite articles of food to keep on the ikon shelves. To make those loaves more acceptable to the departed, inscriptions are sometimes written on the smooth white crust with pen and ink by the monks or the village priest.

In religious matters the more ignorant of the Russian peasants still waver, so to speak, between the devil and the deep sea. They are afraid to make themselves too familiar with the village priest lest they give mortal offense to the old pagan gods, which have now taken the form of various mischievous and malignant spirits ; and, on the other hand, to protect themselves from the evil designs of these they are eternally making the sign of the Cross, and spending their scant earnings on candles to burn before the shrines of protecting saints.

Though centuries of time have naturally modified this fear, it would seem to be a matter of doubtful credit to the " only true Church " that its children and chief supporters, the very Orthodox, on whose patient shoulders it rests, still shy at its priests lest the agents of the Evil One be offended. In many instances the peasants have transferred, in a foggy way, the attributes and functions of their ancient gods to the saints of the Christian Church, or to reverse the transformation, have simply bestowed the names of the saints on their old pagan deities. In transferring their allegiance from the old faith to the new, they have not always escaped getting matters curiously muddled. Thus the Prophet Elias has succeeded to the office of Perun, the ancient god of thunder. St. Elias is now the Russian peasants' "clerk of the weather." He it is who gives or withholds the rain necessary to the growing of their crops. And when it thunders and lightens, it is St. Elias driving in his chariot across the heavens.

A Russian peasant will not harm a pigeon, nor would he think of eating one, even if suffering from want of food. All through Russia, and particularly in the lower forest zone south of Moscow, the country is full of pigeons, that enjoy complete immunity from molestation. In the country they are as tame as the semi-domestic pigeons owned by breeders in American cities.

The pigeon has always been a sacred bird in Russia. In the old pagan times it was consecrated to Perun, the god of thunder, just mentioned. When the missionaries of the Cross invaded the country and prevailed against Perun and his associates, the lucky pigeon lost nothing of its sacred character by the new order of things. The converts, by some occult process of reasoning, came to associate it with their idea of the Third Person of the Trinity. The sacred character of the pigeon, like the office of "weather clerk," has been brought over from the old religion to the new and consecrated to the Third Person of the Trinity, which the majority of the peasants think to be St. Nicholas.

Readers will remember stories that have occasionally reached us from Russia of atrocities committed by fanatical peasants in the villages of the interior. On one occasion the burning of a poor old woman startled the Western World and taxed the credulity of the newspaper-reading public. Then a man or woman was buried alive ; and we heard of a woman severely mangled by a wolf while rescuing a child from attack, left to perish in an out-house because no moujik would admit her into his house. On this horseback ride, which put me for several weeks in contact with the peasantry, I managed to pick up more or less information concerning their peculiar superstitions.

Although the peasants have certainly advanced a step or two in knowledge and understanding during the thirty years since their emancipation, the powers of darkness still hold well-nigh undisputed sway over the minds of a majority of the rural population of Russia. Ignorance links arms with superstition, and the two revel in the interior villages whenever the normal apathy of the moujik brain is disturbed by fear or suspicion. Though he is sitting on the threshold of the twentieth century, and the humblest tillers of the soil in lands not far from him learned years ago that the world they live in is a planet revolving around the sun, the moujik still thinks that it rests on the backs of three whales, or monster turtles, in the ocean.

No limit exists to the absurdities that find expression in the beliefs and superstitions of such a people. The women and girls, of course, are the most superstitious. Unreasoning faith makes them tenaciously loyal to their old pagan traditions. In Little Russia it was the rather uncomplimentary lot of myself and companion to come daily under the suspicion of being the Evil One, Antichrist, the "Cattle Plague," or other malignant spirit in disguise.

In many of the postayali dvors of Little Russia

a young peasant woman performs the functions of hostler. One of the small diversions of the day's ride would be to speculate on the form these manifestations of fear would assume in the next girl hostler. There was nothing fantastic about our appearance; we were simply strange horsemen in a country where strangers are rare, and were dressed differently from anybody they had ever seen.

The consternation of the girl on opening the tall gate in response to our summons, and suddenly finding herself in the presence of a pair of the supernatural beings of the popular witchcraft, often caused us to laugh outright, and always provoked a smile. A wild sort of fear came into her eyes, and she would shrink behind the gate. The first impulse would be to make the sign of the Cross, but fearful lest we, being Antichrists, might take offense at this, she would wait until we had passed in, when, fancying herself unnoticed, the holy symbol would be furtively and rapidly made.

This sort of girl would be rooted to the spot with fear. Other girls, of more robust intellects, occasionally took to their heels, scampering away into the house like wild creatures. During our stay these superstitious damsels would be in an exceedingly uncomfortable frame of mind. Fearful of coming near us, they were equally fearful lest their all too evident reluctance to serve us might give offense and cause us maliciously to "wither their souls," or bring them other evil fortune. As an occasional phenomenon, we would find a girl who would be neither afraid of us nor of submitting to the camera.

The Russian peasants still believe in the agency of witchcraft and sorcery, and when visited by an epidemic, such as the smallpox, cholera, or cattle plague, a stranger appearing in their midst alone is sure to be regarded with suspicion. And if the stranger happens to be a " tall, shaggy old man " or a " withered old woman with flashing eyes," or otherwise resembles the creatures of the popular superstition who are associated with these malignant maladies, the fanatical peasants would not hesitate to bury the unfortunate wretch alive.

On the base of a memorial to Czar Nicholas, in St. Petersburg, is portrayed a scene in which the Czar quells a tumult among the peasants by raising his arm in anger. It depicts an actual occurrence of his reign in the streets of St. Petersburg, at the time of the cholera, when the moujiks rose in tumult against the police because they refused to arrest persons who had been seen "carrying cholera powder into a house " for the purpose of spreading the disease.

Certain curious rites are still faithfully practiced in many Russian villages to ward off the " cattle plague," which the moujiks believe to wander about the country in human form. Among the Malo Russians the cattle plague is an old woman who wears red boots, and can walk on the water. Hence an old hag-like woman who should turn up in a Russian village in red boots would, especially in time of an epidemic, be in danger of her life. Stories are current among the people of moujiks who unwittingly gave a night's lodging to this weird creature, and in the morning every member of the family was dead.

In some districts remedial measures are periodically taken against a visitation of the murrain. The cattle are all driven into the village, and a big circle is made around it with a plow, which is dragged by the oldest woman in the community. All the female villagers follow in procession behind the plow, carrying ikons, chanting weird incantations, and beating tin pans and cooking vessels. One old woman bestrides a broom *à la* witch, and a widow, wearing nothing but a horse-collar around her neck, keeps pace with the one who is dragging the plow. If a dog or a cat, frightened by the noise, rushes out, it is immediately seized and killed, on the supposition that it is the cattle plague in disguise, trying to escape.

In other districts casting a black cock alive into a bonfire at the end of certain ceremonies is believed to be efficacious in warding off many contagious diseases. Bonfires are built in the village, and young women in night-dresses drag a plow and carry a holy picture, with much unearthly screeching, after which the unfortunate rooster is cast into the flames. In some villages, when a visit of the cattle plague is to be dreaded, if a stray cow happens to be found among the herd, it is burned alive, as the peasants believe that the "cattle death" has thus assumed the form of a cow to escape detection.

One of the most curious and widespread beliefs of the peasants is that every house contains a domovoi or house-spirit. Russian peasants catch glimpses of the domovoi about as often as Americans see ghosts, but they all believe in his existence. The domovoi is described as a little old man, no bigger than a five-year-old boy. Sometimes he is seen wearing a red shirt, with a blue girdle, like a moujik on holidays. At other times he sports a suit of blue. He has a white beard and yellow hair and glowing eyes.

Though mostly invisible, the peasants firmly believe that he is always about the premises and busying himself in their affairs. His usual hiding-place is understood to be behind the big brick stove that forms the chief feature of a Russian cottage. When the people are asleep he issues forth and conducts himself amicably or otherwise, according to the humor he happens to be in. The domovoi is mischievous as a monkey, and like that animal is inclined to fly into a passion at very short notice if he is not satisfied with his surroundings and treatment. Many peasant families after eating supper always leave a portion of food on the table for the domovoi, who would otherwise consider himself ill-treated and disturb their sleep by pounding on the table with his fist.

In some of the peasants' stables are little glasses or saucers of oil, the use of which is a mystery to the uninitiated stranger. They are found in villages where the domovois are believed to be fond of horses and cattle and of visiting the stables at night. As the domovoi likes oil the saucers are put in the stables to keep him in good humor and to induce him to be kind to the horses and cattle. If angry, he has been known to take a horse out and ride it nearly to death; the peasant finding it panting and covered with foam in the morning.

Though troublesome if not well treated, the domovoi usually takes the kindliest interest in the affairs of the

family with whom he has found shelter. He keeps
count over the poultry to see that nothing is stolen,
and many moujiks, when they kill a chicken for the
table, hang its head up in the back yard that the domovoi may understand what has become of it. When a
death occurs in the family the domovoi is inconsolable
for many days, and may be heard at times wailing behind the stove.

In the province of Orel, through which my road lay,
many of the peasants endeavor to have all their live-
stock as nearly as possible of one color. This applies
even to the poultry, the dog, and the cat. This is because the domovoi of their house is believed to like that
color best, and will be pleased at this deference to his
taste. The manner of finding out what color the domovoi likes best is one of the ceremonies of Easter
Sunday. On that day the peasants hang up in the
stable something perishable in a piece of rag. When
maggots appear they judge from their color what is
most likely to be the preference of the domovoi.

If ill luck seems to attend the rearing of their domestic animals, it is believed that a strange domovoi
of a malignant disposition has appeared in the household. A shovel or other household implement is then
dipped in tar. During the night the strange domovoi
will rub himself against it, and, taking offense at the
insult, will leave the premises.

On certain nights of the year the kindest of domovois will become malicious, and special precautions
have to be taken to appease them. In some districts
little cakes, baked expressly for the domovoi, are placed
near his retreat, on the stove, on the eve of the Epiph-

any. January 28 is another date on which the household domovois of certain parts of Russia are believed to get into tantrums. When angry, they sometimes stop the breath of the sleeping members of the household and produce nightmare. On January 28, therefore, a pot of mush or stewed millet, to which he is very partial, is set on the table for the domovoi before the family retire.

Wizards and witches still flourish in rural Russia in great numbers. They interfere in all manner of ways with the moujik's prosperity and peace of mind—almost as much so, in fact, as his other and more tangible enemies, the priest and the policeman.

When a milch cow dries up sooner than the peasant thinks she ought to, he has no doubt whatever that she is being milked by the witches. To keep the witches out of the cow-shed crosses are chalked or painted on the doors. If the witches brave the crosses, indicated by a lack of improvement in the milk-giving capacity of the cow, the moujik will try the experiment of a church candle, such as are burned before the shrines and ikons of the saints.

As a matter of fact, the visitor sees these crosses everywhere in rural Russia. A cross is erected on the framework of a house in process of building, and crosses are seen on the ceilings of inns, houses, sheds, stables—everywhere. The first impression of all naturally is that you have stumbled upon an extremely God-fearing, reverential set of people. This impression is intensified by the spectacle of the people themselves making the sign of the Cross at well-nigh every turn, and at every act performed.

There is reverence in all this symbolism of the Holy Cross. But you awaken to a clearer conception of the religious ideas of the peasantry of Russia when you finally come to understand that the cross is painted on the stable door to keep out witches, and that the crosses on the ceiling are to prevent these same malicious sprites from entering the house.

Amulets are still worn, attached to pieces of thread, about the neck by many moujiks, in addition to the little pectoral cross. The old spell used by the peasant's pagan ancestors is very likely tied to the same neck-thread as the cross. Both are to preserve him from sickness and disaster. As between the two he has more faith in the cross nowadays, but he still clings, with the stubborn conservatism of ignorance, to the symbols of ancient heathen faith, nor does it ever occur to him that to tie a bat's-wing amulet obtained from the village sorcerer to the little cross obtained from the priest, and hang them both about his neck is an insult to his religion. When he bathes in the river he makes the sign of the Cross to keep the water-witches from strangling him.

CHAPTER XIX.

ORTHODOX CHURCH AND PRIESTS.

ON the streets of every city, every town, and in every
village, from one end of Russia to another, the
foreign traveler passes men whose habit is sufficiently
distinct from others to attract attention. The habit in
question consists of a long cloth gown that reaches to
the ankles, a soft felt billycock hat, and heavy top
boots. The gown usually is black, but is sometimes
blue, and is girdled snugly about the waist. Whether
you meet one of these odd figures on the most fashionable street in St. Petersburg, or in a remote village of
a distant province, the dress, figure, and deportment
are identically the same.

These gentlemen are the popes, or "white clergy" of
Holy Russia. The long gown and severely simple at-
tire are supposed to be in imitation of the Saviour
when on earth, and the likeness is increased by wearing long hair.

From the standpoint of an outsider the Russian
pope cuts a comical, not to say contemptible, figure on
the world's stage. Viewing him from a plane beyond
his sphere of influence you feel like laughing him off
the boards, but install yourself among the people who
are forced to have dealings with him and he changes
from a comical to a serious character, whose deserts
would be hootings and carrots rather than merriment.

But because the pope is born into his position and in-
herits his characteristics from many generations of
sires and grandsires, every one of whom was as incongruous and out of place in the garb of Christ as he, it
behooves us not to be too uncharitable in our judgment.

The Russian priest occupies a unique and unenviable position in the society of his own country as well
as among the spiritual representatives of the earth.
The Romish priest and the Protestant pastor, who take
the initiative in works of charity and keep a sharp eye
on the morals of their parishioners, would find in the
heart and the deeds of the Russian pope no chord of
sympathy. The pope rarely preaches sermons and he
takes no part in charitable works nor bothers himself
about the moral welfare of the people. His interest
in the benefice to which he has been assigned on ordi-
nation, probably begins and ends with the amount of
money he is able to squeeze out of his parishioners.
As he neither pretends, nor is expected to make any
pretense, to a life of morality, his methods of adding
to his income are often strangely at variance with our
ideas of what pertains to the office and functions of a
priest.

In some districts the popes receive small salaries
from the government and in others grants of land, off
which, with the addition of baptismal, marriage, burial,
and other fees, they are required to make their living.
Short of stealing and robbery with violence, the more
unscrupulous of the clergy resort to any method of
extortion and money-getting. Their most notorious
methods are to act in their parishes as agents for the

sale of certain brands of vodka, and by their own example and all manner of insinuating measures promote its consumption among the peasants.

The Imperial Government looks with indulgent eye on the drunkenness of its subjects, and resents temperance agitation with almost as much jealousy as political, the reason being that the greater part of its revenue comes from the tax on liquor. The priests, who in other countries are ever foremost in checking the growth of intemperance, in Russia promote it by every means short of pouring vodka down the people's throats. With a view to commissions on its sale, the popes excuse its consumption by the too willing moujik on the most specious pretenses. They will even quote Scripture to them to prove that there is no harm in getting drunk, their favorite quotation being: " Not that which goeth into the mouth of a man defileth him ; but that which cometh out."

The size of the pope's income depends as much on the ignorance, superstition, and credulity of his parishioners, coupled with his own shrewdness, as on the size and population of the parish. His legitimate fees among the peasantry are three rubles for officiating at a funeral, one ruble at christenings, and one ruble for a private morning mass. At weddings he receives anything up to ten rubles, and at betrothals a bottle of red wine. In addition to these, however, he manages in one way or another to lay the moujiks under contribution to the extent of cultivating his land.

A pope deems it no disgrace to get drunk, nor does he, by loose living, lose caste in the estimation of his parishioners, so long as his looseness affects nobody's pocket but his own. In fact, in Russia as elsewhere, and among popes no less than among other people, the man of convivial habits is apt to be at the bottom a generous soul.

As a class the popes are cordially despised by the Russian people. The peasantry regards them not as spiritual fathers, but as corrupt agents of the Church, just as the police and the hordes of officials who prey upon them are corrupt agents of the government. One set are disreputable tools of the Church, the others of the Czar. Both Church and Czar they reverence, but they expect nothing but extortion and corrupt practices from the minions of either. Among the peasants the worst-hated minions of the civil government are our friends of a previous chapter, the uriadniks, a horde of nearly 6000 rural police, who, in 1878, were let loose among them with almost unbridled powers of petty persecution. The uriadnik has become a byword among the people, and on a par with him, in the estimation of the moujiks, is what is known among them as the "merchant pope."

For a drunken, dissolute clergyman, the moujiks have no special aversion, because in their eyes drunkenness, even in a priest, is no sin, and as before stated they trouble themselves little about what does not affect their own pockets. It is because the practices of the "merchant pope" do affect their pockets that they hold him in special abhorrence above others of the cloth.

The "merchant pope" is a priest who is forever scheming to extort money from his parishioners. His ways of reaching their pockets are multifarious, and his

ingenuity is exercised in preying on the credulity, the fanaticism, and the superstition of the wooden-headed moujik. The " merchant pope " not only acts as agent for the sale of vodka, for the greater consumption of which he multiplies the holidays and merry-makings in his district, but he also concerns himself in the sale of ikons, and by granting bogus certificates of communion.

Every Orthodox Russian is required by law to provide himself with a certificate, showing that he has partaken of the holy communion within the year. To backslide from the church is a penal offense, for which thousands of Russians have been transported to Siberia, and a subject of the Czar known to have been born in the Orthodox faith, found by the police without a eucharistical certificate from his priest, would find himself in trouble. Under the surface, dissent is rife ; and it is in districts where dissatisfaction with the senseless rituals of the established Church abounds that the commercial pope flourishes and grows rich the fastest. For the heretics who come to him, rubles in hand, he makes out bogus certificates of communion, and those who think to escape notice he ferrets out and levies upon.

The commercial pope bargains and chaffers over the fees for baptisms, weddings, and burials, and every religious service required of him by his people is a financial speculation. For rubles he will officially condone all offenses, and grant absolution for all manner of evil-doing. Without pay he will neither pray for rain to revive the moujiks' withering crops nor burn candles before the ikon of St. Nicholas, the moujiks' favorite saint. Much as they despise him, the moujiks believe him to be the medium through which the blessings or the curses of the Church and the saints affect them and their interests, and of this belief the commercial pope takes every advantage to transfer from their lean pockets to his own their hard-earned kopecks. Perhaps it was studying, at close range, the ungodly transactions of the commercial pope that brought Count Tolstoï to the conclusion that the primary duty of every minister of the gospel is to earn his own living as a husbandman.

To the foreigner who has been accustomed to regard the wearers of the cloth with something akin to the same reverence that he feels for the Church, the Russian pope, and the place he occupies in the minds of the people, is something of an enigma. In the Russian mind the pope seems to have no connection with the Church beyond a financial interest in its forms and ceremonies. The government has appointed him official purveyor of baptismal forms, marriage rites, holy water, and masses, for which he receives fees, and by means of which he makes capital out of the superstition and ignorance of the peasantry.

The Church they reverence; but the pope who stands between it and the people and acts the middleman in dispensing or withholding its blessings, is the butt of the national satire and figures largely in popular songs and stories as a charlatan and a despicable fellow generally. The Russian who has committed some grievous sin, and is prepared to go to any ruinous length in regaining the favor of the saint, approaches the pope on the subject of special masses for the purpose in much the same spirit as he would approach a rascally dealer in spavined and broken-winded horses. He broaches the subject cautiously and in a round-about manner, lest by appearing too eager he betray to the pope the fact that his services are urgently required; a piece of indiscretion which he knows only too well would result in an immediate inflation of that gentleman's fees.

On his part, the pope, by means of long practice and an hereditary insight into the workings of the Russian conscience, has acquired such an expertness in detecting the very things that these would-be cheapeners of the holy functions try to conceal that he invariably gets the better of the bargain. It is this prostitution of the holy office to a bargaining and haggling over rubles and kopecks that is the secret of the pope's unenviable position. All business in Russia is transacted on a low moral basis. Every Russian merchant cheats and overreaches, as a matter of course, nor do customers expect anything better of them. The moujik feels no resentment against the man who tries to overreach him in a bargain for a red shirt; because if he fails in his bargaining with one merchant he goes to another. But with the dealer in masses and sacraments he is deprived of this freedom by the government, which has practically given the pope of his parish a monopoly. If the mass merchant refuses to chant and burn candles for him, save at extortionate rates, which he very often does, the extortionate rates have to be paid.

Russians will tell you that cases are common in the villages of popes refusing to bury the dead and administer the sacrament to the dying until the prices they demanded were forthcoming. Thus it has come to be a common saying among the people that " the pope takes money both from the living and the dead.

From what the author saw and experienced among the Russians, however, I am far from taking a one-sided view of the matter between popes and people. Take the popes as they are, without any pretense to a higher degree of commercial morality than their parishioners, and it is a fair battle of wits between them. If the popes overreach the people in charging for their services, there are, on the other hand, few communicants among their flock who would not, if they could, bamboozle the pope into praying for him and administering the sacrament to them for nothing. There are no people in the world so intent on getting something from some one else for nothing as the average subjects of the Czar.

In addition to being despised by the people, the two orders of clergy in Russia—the black clergy or monks and the white clergy or popes—hate and despise one another. The popes hate the monks because it is from their ranks that all the higher dignitaries of the Church are chosen, and because the monastic orders attract nearly all the death-bed bequests of the wealthy, which they think might otherwise come their own way. This abhorrence is repaid with interest by the monks, who affect to despise the popes as being the " small rogues of the Church," and responsible for the scant esteem in which both orders are held by the people.

One day, during the ride from Moscow to the Crimea, we met a pope on the road. A party of moujik tramps who were ahead of us met him first, and, after they had passed him, they, without any visible motive, wheeled round and walked straight across to the opposite side of the road. In explanation of this my companion informed me that it is considered bad luck to meet a pope on the road, and, by crossing his trail at right angles, thereby forming a cross behind him, the moujiks hoped to avert any calamity that would otherwise overtake them as a consequence of having met him.

Many of the popes are men of fair education, but others are woefully ignorant, particularly of the Scriptures. Sascha told me of a village pope who knew only one passage of Scripture, and this he used to repeat over and over again as a regular order of service. The congregation used to respond with the same. The passage was, " And Christ went down to Jerusalem.'

One day the pope was thrown into consternation by hearing that a nobleman who owned an estate in the district was coming from St. Petersburg and would attend mass next Sunday. It would never do to betray to the nobleman the fact that he knew but one passage of Scripture. He consulted a brother pope in the adjoining parish. This gentleman didn't know any Scripture at all, but advised him, as the easiest plan, to substitute Bethlehem for Jerusalem for the occasion of the nobleman's visit.

This was an easy thing for a man of education like the pope, but, when it came to the responses, the thick-headed moujiks forgot their pastor's instructions about Bethlehem and bawled out the word they had, from long usage, grown accustomed to. The pope was furious.   Forgetting the presence of the nobleman, he shouted out :

"You wooden-heads! it isn't Jerusalem to-day.   I told you it was to be Bethlehem!"

Priests of this class are known to the Russians as "one-mass popes."

The Orthodox Greek Church of the Holy Russian Empire is the most gigantic monopoly that exists on the face of the earth at the present day.   It owns the exclusive right to regulate the morals, direct the consciences, and warp the souls of 100,000,000 human beings.   It has a patent, supported by the mighty power of the Russian government, granting to it the exclusive right and title to the religious exploitation of a fourteenth part of the population of the earth, and the power to punish severely the least infringement of its rights.

Monopoly may not always be a curse in commerce. Its defenders have sometimes even been able to make out, owing to peculiar and exceptional conditions, cases where it may have been a blessing in disguise. But there can be no manner of doubt as to the influence and the results of the monopoly in religion.

The blight of intolerance has smitten the priests with moral leprosy, that has left them without any resemblance to the same class in other countries. Russia is the only country in Christendom where the servants of the Church and the wearers of the cassock and gown neither exercise, nor attempt to exercise, a good moral influence on their parishioners.   Exceptions there are of course, but they are exceedingly rare.

The Russian Church is at one with the government

in that it regards the people merely as a means for its own support and aggrandizement. The two are gigantic Siamese twins, who wax fat and continue to grow in power at the expense of the toiling millions of peasantry, who live harder and enjoy less comfort than any set of people whom the writer, who has been in twenty-four countries, can call to mind, unless it be a certain class of coolies in China. One loots them by means of the tax-gatherer and the police, the other by means of the priests, and by trading on their ignorance, which it encourages, and their superstitions, which it is too lazy and indifferent to root out. And while one forbids the victim to move even out of his house into another without permission, or to escape through any channel whatever, the other has the monstrous power to imprison or send to Siberia any one who presumes to assist him out of the slough of ignorance and superstition that keeps him helpless.

To convert a Russian peasant from the Greek Church to any other branch of the Christian religion is a penal offense, punishable by a long term of hard labor in Siberia. If he is already a sectarian, the peasant may remain so, subject to various humiliating restrictions. What the Russian Greek Church demands of the people is that they " keep quiet " and do nothing. " Work and pay for masses and sacraments ; give money to enrich churches, and buy candles to burn before the ikons of the saints ; but don't think ; don't read ; and, above all, make no move toward worshiping God according to the dictates of your own conscience, or you will be punished and imprisoned."

Secured in its monopolistic power and position by the strong arm of the Government, the policy of the Church has become that of the dog in the manger. Its intolerance of propaganda is only equaled by its lethargy. It will neither bestir itself to the betterment of the people who have been given into its power nor permit others to do so. Like any other monopoly that has no fear of competition, it refuses to trouble itself about the quality of the goods it supplies, concerning itself solely with the question of warning off infringers of its prerogative.

In Southern Russia, however, notwithstanding the severe penalties enacted against apostacy, a very large proportion of the people are, either openly or covertly, dissenters. If born outside the province of the Orthodox Church, all well and good; there is no need of concealment; but if a convert from Orthodoxy, peace and security from imprisonment is usually secured by bribing the priest to make out false certificates of communion, which are, so to speak, "religious passports." This the apostate has to get renewed every year, as every peasant does his civil passport from the police. Selling false eucharistical certificates to backsliders from the established Church is said to double the income of many parish priests in Southern Russia.

All dissenting sects are known as heretics. The more numerous are the Stundists and the Molokani, or milk-eaters, so called because they drink milk on fast days. In riding across the steppes of Malo Russia and the Crimea, I used to stumble upon the villages of these dissenters, as well as of German colonists. A most curious thing to me was that you could tell a

German or a sectarian colony as far as you could see it, on account of the vast difference between its surroundings and those of an Orthodox moujik village.

Only a few miles across the steppe, on the same soil and with no advantages or favors from nature, you reach a village that seems to belong to another country or to an age centuries ahead of the one you have just left. The houses are built with some pretext to architectural beauty; they are painted white and roofed with red tiles. The windows, which in the Orthodox villages were broken, stuffed with rags, or covered with dirt, are as clean as in an American house. Each house stands in a flower-garden, neatly fenced, and avenues of trees are along the streets. Here, too, if it is harvest time, you will find the peasants owning a threshing-machine and other modern appliances for saving time and labor. Hitherto, though you have ridden on horseback all the way from Moscow, you have seen nothing but flails and rude stone rollers for threshing, and the grain has been winnowed by tossing it in the air on windy days.

The secret of this tremendous transformation is that you have reached the colonies of the sectarians, who have pulled their necks out of the yoke of the monopolistic church. When I first reached one of these clean and prosperous villages, after several weeks' experience among the Orthodox, my eyes were gladdened as at the sight of an oasis in the desert.

I was alone, a stranger and a foreigner, unable to speak the language beyond making known my wants. My companion and interpreter had returned to Moscow. As I expected, I was received with suspicion.

For all they knew I might be a secret agent of the government coming among them for sinister reasons as spy. These sectarians dread an agent of the government more than the Evil One himself.

I showed them my American passport, which puzzled them and seemed only to add to their suspicions. At length, however, I was taken in. The house was as scrupulously clean as a house in Holland. Shining brass candlesticks stood in the broad window-sills and flower-pots full of plants gladdened the eyes and added to the cheerfulness of this model interior of a cottage. Everything that could be polished was bright ; everything of linen, as white as soap and elbow-grease would make it.

For supper I had white bread, fried eggs, cold milk, and the only eatable butter I had seen since leaving Moscow. In the province of Ekaterinoslav there is a maxim applied to a careful housewife : "She is good, like a Molokani wife." At night I slept between clean, sweet sheets, a luxury that I had given up all hopes of ever enjoying in a Russian village. Though they treated me in this highly acceptable manner, the residents, however, never ceased to regard me with suspicion. They positively declined to talk about themselves, though it is fair to presume that I might have had better success in drawing them out had I been equal to a less disjointed way of asking questions. They were Russians, in no way different from their slovenly, ignorant Orthodox brethren, except in the difference that had been brought about by their emancipation from the slavery of a mediæval church. The contrast between the two was so striking and so sharply defined that the only night I spent in a sectarian village is among the most vivid impressions of the ride across Russia.

Every traveler in Russia has noticed this same difference between the sectarian communities and those of the Orthodox peasantry. It admits of only one explanation. The Orthodox moujiks of Russia are at the present day, in spite of the vaunted emancipation of the serfs, the veriest slaves that were ever chained to the earth. No negro in the United States was ever owned and exploited as is the average Orthodox peasant of Russia in 1890. He is owned jointly by a pair of hard taskmasters, of which one exploits his body and the other his soul. Of personal, political, or religious liberty, he is about as destitute as he was when he was a serf. If now and then one peasant of exceptional brains and energy manages to better his condition, thousands are materially worse off than they ever were before. The moujik has simply changed masters. The rod has been taken from the nobles and placed in the hands of the tax collector. And the latter, having no personal interest in him beyond exacting Cæsar's tribute, often spares him less than his former master did.

His spiritual master, the Orthodox Church, instead of sending him a benevolent, religious gentleman for a pastor, spiritual teacher, and guide, who would teach him temperance and morality, and cheer and encourage him in the hour of adversity, saddles him with a knavish servile, who encourages him to drink vodka, and bargains like a horse-dealer with him over the price of baptizing his children.

Ten chances to one, if he ever had a copy of the Scriptures in his hand in his life. And if he could read, and was found by his pastor with a copy in his possession, that precious gentleman would very likely cause him to be thrown into prison as a heretic and a dangerous person ; or, still more probable, would demand a bribe for omitting to do so.

If by some extraordinary freak of human nature the pastor should happen to take interest enough in his work to preach an occasional sermon, before he may deliver himself of a word of what he would say he has got to write out his sermon and submit it to the *blagotchinny*, a sort of ecclesiastical spy and censor. It is unnecessary to add that this worthy takes very good care that no light shall penetrate the darkness of the moujik's understanding by the channel that he controls.

CHAPTER XX.

"WHAT do you think of the Russian ladies?" was a question often asked me upon my return to New York. Rather a delicate question, and one not to be answered beyond recording a few observations picked up on the journey and information gleaned from residents of the country. One of my recollections is, that within a stone's toss of the balcony of my room in the Hotel Europe, Sevastopol, a score of Crimean and visiting nymphs were paddling and splashing about merrily in the blue waters of the bay, in full view of half the city. A plank fence, jutting fifty feet out into the water, separated them from three times the number of male bathers. Beyond the fence Russian propriety was observed, if the sexes mingled not too promiscuously in swimming and paddling about. Some wore bathing-dresses and others did not, according to individual preference. A boatload of soldiers passed along in front of the ladies' bath-house and every head in the boat was turned inquisitively in that direction.

One of the peculiarities of Russian women is that they appear to have no objection to this sort of scrutiny. One day my horse refused to cross a stream at a certain point. A little farther along were a group of women, bathing. Seeing my difficulty, one of the women stood on the bank and motioned to me that there was a better crossing close to them. The water proved to be shallow enough, in all conscience, where they were, and Texas crossed without further objection. As for the fair bathers, they contented themselves with dipping down in the water until I had passed through.

This, however, is only preliminary. It is as a study of character rather than form that I would endeavor to present to my readers a few brief impressions of the Russian woman.

An English governess whom I met in Moscow, who had spent twenty years in Russia as tutor in the families of the nobility, told me that Russian ladies of rank and wealth are nearly all "spoiled children." Their virtues are warm-heartedness and financial generosity, though she unwittingly qualified the latter by adding that they knew nothing of the value of money.

Russian ladies are clever and talented, but are afflicted with both mental and physical laziness. In a young ladies' conservatory there will be a very large percentage of promising pupils, but very rarely indeed does one of them get beyond that rather vague point. One of the teachers of the Moscow Conservatory, speaking to my informant on this subject, said that out of fifty bright, promising pupils who came within his especial sphere of observation, not one turned out a success. The trouble is, lack of will power to persevere to the end—a poverty of application. They learn to speak a language readily, but not to write it, the reason being that the former requires next to no mental effort in a person of ready perception, while the latter demands close application and attention to study.

Music, the languages, and dancing are the accomplishments of the Russian lady. The former is a useful accomplishment to her; but the number of Russians, both male and female, who have learned languages and forgotten them is surprising. They have learned superficially, and in a year or two forget, for the lack of some one to talk to. One meets many ladies, however, to whom the English and French tongues are as familiar as the Russian. This is not, as is generally supposed in America, because Russians learn languages more easily than other people, but simply because the children of every well-to-do Russian family of any pretension to nobility have English and French governesses.

Their vices are laziness, untruthfulness, extravagance, cigarette smoking, and deceiving their husbands. The Russian lady is a poor housekeeper and she rarely nurses her own children. A hatred of mental exertion in the matter of detail and carefulness is a fundamental trait of her character, and the keeping of accounts in the matter of household expenses is a species of intellectual slavery with which Mme. Ivanovka will have nothing to do if she can avoid it. If household economics thrust themselves upon her shoulders, whether she will or not, she gets rid of them in a slovenly, shiftless manner, and consoles herself with Zola and cigarettes.

I was assured, however, that Russian ladies of the upper class are far less addicted to the habit of smoking than they have been in the past. Among society dames it is becoming " the thing " not to smoke at all, save in the privacy of their own apartments. The habit is largely the outcome of the Oriental ideas that belong to old Russia. A state in which the women of the household are excluded from the society of the opposite sex, and are required to live the life of the harem, is favorable to the development of such habits as cigarette smoking and indulgence in opium, as in Turkey and Persia.

Oriental ideas in regard to the fair sex still prevail among the Russian mercantile class, and the merchants' wives and daughters are the most inveterate consumers of cigarettes. But the nobility and the educated section of society have wholly emerged from the Eastern conception of female seclusion, and many women of this class would nowadays be ashamed to smoke in a railway carriage or public garden. A woman who chooses to smoke in public, however, is by no means regarded as unladylike. Rather is she in danger of being looked upon by her more "advanced" country-woman as behind the times—a sort of country cousin, who is regarded with much the same scorn as if she wore unfashionable clothes.

The foreigner going to Russia would, moreover, never suspect that cigarette smoking is on the wane. Whether on train or on steamboat he is not unlikely to be approached by more than one woman, cigarette in hand, begging a light. And when he returns to his own country, among the reminiscences of his travels will be visions of both old women and young, fair and otherwise, who have engraved their images on his memory by reason of the great number of cigarettes they consumed in his presence. I have seen women on the train lay a box of ten cigarettes in their lap and make a "chain smoke" of the lot. Some women carry tobacco and paper and roll their own " papyros," but mostly they buy the ready-made Russian cigarettes with the paper mouthpieces.

The great want of the Russian lady seems to be something congenial to occupy her time. She finds no pleasure in needlework, nor in walking abroad, lawn tennis, or any active pursuit whatever. She is not permitted by the paternal government under which she happens to have been born to take any active interest in politics or to promote societies for the advocacy of women's rights. Clubs and societies of any kind are looked upon with suspicion, and it is only by special permission of the authorities that she may even form a society in her native town for the distribution of rye bread and cabbage soup in winter to the poor, or a S. P. C. A.

Novels and cigarettes and sunflower seeds are well-nigh all the legitimate occupations that come within her reach ; especially at her country residence, away from theaters and balls. She feels within her an inspiration to a wider sphere of usefulness than reading, smoking, and nibbling,—but what can she do? She would teach the poor children of the neighborhood, but the government won't allow it. She has an idea that the ritual and ceremony of the Orthodox Church is the merest mummery, and would seek information in other directions ; but the government won't grant that privilege either.

She eventually finds diversion in the attentions of a lover. By a curious coincidence, my information on this score seemed to be verified by an incident that came under my notice before I had been a week in

Russia. About three o'clock one morning, in the hotel where I was staying at St. Petersburg, I heard a loud report. It awakened me, but thinking it was the slamming of a door I paid no further heed. In the morning, however, it turned out to have been a revolver shot, fired three doors from me by a Russian countess, who attempted to commit suicide during a quarrel with a young officer.

A Swedish teacher of languages, whose acquaintance I made in St. Petersburg, confirmed the above information from his own personal knowledge. This was a gentleman on whose word I place full reliance. He had been tutor in many noble families in and about St. Petersburg, Moscow, and Kharkoff in Little Russia. His experience and observation were that, for the want of something better to occupy their minds, Russian ladies, with very few exceptions, amused themselves with intrigue.

With all this, I was asked not to judge the Russian ladies too harshly, or by the same standard that one would apply to the women of other countries. Their conduct is not immoral. This would be too harsh a term altogether. The Russian ladies simply have such large hearts that it takes more than one man to fill one of them.

The maternal instinct is a conspicuous trait of the Russian female character. Women of all classes like large families; the larger the better. In the villages nearly every woman has a baby in arms. I came upon a fine example of maternal instinct in the person of Sascha's prospective mother-in-law, with whom we took dinner at her country house near Tula. This good lady had fifteen children of her own. Yet she had adopted two orphans; and, at the time I made her acquaintance, was watching over, with motherly solicitude, a parrot that had had one eye knocked out, and a daw with a broken wing!

Ladies of quality rarely nurse their own children. The nurse, with her charge, is always a conspicuous figure on the streets of a Russian city. The fantastic garb and coronet of beads constitute one of the most picturesque costumes in Russia; and you can tell by its color whether her charge is a boy or a girl. If a boy, the prevailing color will be blue; if a girl, pink.

Vanity is not one of the Russian lady's cardinal sins. Though bad complexions are the rule, as a result of the climate, bad ventilation, irregular living, and want of exercise, no well-bred lady paints. Small feet and hands are common, and if the Russian lady takes pride in any particular part of her person it would be the smallness and shapeliness of these extremities.

Though the Russian does not, like the Sultan of Morocco, fatten his wife by forced feeding, as poulterers gorge turkeys for Christmas, his idea of womanly beauty is still somewhat Oriental. He prefers a fat wife, with a pink and white skin, and is very apt to break the second clause of the Tenth Commandments if his neighbor's wife comes nearer this ideal than his own.

Among the merchants and peasant class many old-fashioned, conservative Muscovite notions in regard to women still prevail. The Russian merchant thinks it no disgrace to knock his wife down with a blow of his huge fist, and the moujik beats his better half with a stick whenever he thinks she needs correction. The wife has no remedy in law against physical chastisement at the hands of her husband, nor thinks of resorting to the protection of the authorities. Her opportunity occurs whenever her lord and master comes home helplessly intoxicated. While he is thus powerless to defend himself, she seizes a stick and repays with interest every blow she has received from him since his last drinking bout.

One day Sascha, who belonged to the merchant class, and expected after a term of soldiering to follow the life and traditions of that caste, surprised me by a remark in respect to women. He was a young man who knew absolutely nothing about horses, and consequently was always giving me, who did know something about them, advice as to the management and care of Texas. On the occasion referred to my horse was a trifle fractious.

"You must beat him," said Sascha. "A horse is like a woman ; if you don't give him a good beating now and then he will be capricious and want to do as he pleases, and not as you wish. With women it is the same."

" Do you intend to beat your wife when you get one, if she is willful in her behavior? " I asked.

"Beat her? Of course," he returned. "I should be thought a fool if my wife acted counter to my wishes and didn't get a beating for it."

Among the middle and lower orders of Russian society the model wife is she whose good conduct and slavish obedience to the will or whims of her husband give him no excuse to lift hand or rod against her, and

who never beats her husband when he is drunk.   Wives
beating their husbands is, however, a recognized phase
of Russian social life.   Among the cheap chromos that
adorn the walls of village tea-houses and traktirs one
of the most familiar scenes is a drunken moujik on the
ground and his wife beating him in no gingerly manner.

The merchant's wife and daughters still keep out of
sight, in accordance with Oriental custom, when male
friends call on the husband; and when they go shop-
ping the husband and father goes with them, assists
them with their bargains, and pays the bills.   The
merchant's wife paints her cheeks and is fond of
bright-colored clothes.   You often see them arrayed
from head to foot in garish red.   She spends the
greater part of her time in drinking tea, smoking cigarettes, and gossiping with visiting friends.   There is a
saying that "a merchant's wife can drink a whole
samovar of tea."

Her mental abilities are held in light esteem by her
spouse and his friends, who, though keen merchants,
are, for the most part, men of scant education.   Their
ideas of women find expression in many contemptuous
axioms and sayings that have come down from father
to son.   The Russian merchant or peasant will tell you
that "a woman has long hair, but a short mind;" that
she is a child of the devil; and that when you fall in
love with her, you fall in love with the Evil One.   It
is considered bad luck to meet a woman when you are
going fishing or shooting; and plenty of Russians will
turn back and start afresh, confident that ill luck will
wait upon their rod or gun if they happen to meet a
woman upon the road.   In the churches " neither

women nor dogs " are permitted to penetrate into the inner sanctuary, though men and boys are freely ad mitted.

Marriages among this class are always marriages of convenience.   They are usually arranged by the parents or an old woman go-between, known as the *svaha*, the contracting parties having little or nothing to say in the choice of their partners.   The business of the *svaha* is to keep herself informed regarding the rising genera- tion about her, and bring about marriages between suitable persons.   Her reward is a commission on dowries, or liberal presents.   She knows the worldly prospects and the personal worth of every youth in the town, and the amount of dowry that each young lady of her acquaintance is likely to receive.

Having ascertained, by frequent business-like talks with the parents, that the prospects and personal recommendations of two young people are mutually satisfactory, she arranges a simultaneous attendance at church or theater, where the proposed bride and bride- groom may get a sly peep at each other.   If they are satisfied with their choice, preliminaries are at once entered upon, a formal betrothal takes place, and, soon after, the wedding.

Gypsy fortune-tellers are often resorted to for the purpose of finding out what sort of a husband the daughter will obtain.   Russian gypsies like Russian horse dealers, Russian merchants and Russian officials, are a good deal more tricky than the same classes in most other countries.   Well aware of the credulity of the merchants' wives and daughters, they some- times enter into partnership with a scheming *svaha* and a penniless young man to obtain possession of the hand and dowry of a wealthy young woman. The scheme is an ingenious one and, leaving out the question of dishonesty, ought to succeed and does.

It would be an inexcusable act of injustice to the Russian woman to dismiss her without pointing out that whenever the true test of womanhood is imposed upon her, she proves herself as great a heroine as any in the world.

In her hours of ease she may be " uncertain," even " coy and hard to please," but when her husband is overtaken by the exile's garb and starts on the dreary road to Siberia, perchance to a living death, lovers and all else are forsaken, and she is herself again—a woman.

CHAPTER XXI.

A NATIONAL CHARACTERISTIC.

FINALLY, if any one were to ask me what trait of character is most conspicuously developed in the Russians, based on observations during my ride through the country, I would answer—suspicion. On reflection I might perhaps hesitate a moment between suspicion and superstition, and bestow a passing thought on servility; but whichever of these three graces prevails, the Russians are, to my mind, the most suspicious people under the sun.

From this sweeping assertion I don't except even the Chinese. My acquaintance with John Chinaman, though not of long duration, was nevertheless exceedingly close while it lasted. I need only refer to my " Around the World on a Bicycle." One who has ridden a bicycle, alone, seven hundred miles through the highways and byways of a dimly known section of China, where a large part of a dense population had never set eyes on a " foreign devil," let alone a bicycle, before, is entitled to a hearing on the question of suspicion, if on no other subject.

The ride through Russia, though on a flesh and blood horse, instead of a steel one, was, so far as opportunities for observation among the people are concerned, substantially a similar performance. Coupling these equal chances of seeing to advantage, with an unprejudiced judgment between them, I have no hesitation in yielding the palm, with a considerable margin in their favor, to the subjects of His Imperial Majesty, the Czar.

Patriotic Russians will tell you that in the person of the Czar are embodied all the virtues of all the Russias. Alexander III undoubtedly possesses most of the negative virtues and some of the positive ones, and in his benevolent countenance you look in vain for the cynical suspicion supposed by many to be the inherent expression of autocratic sovereigns. The Czar possesses his full share of the passivity of the Muscovite character, which leads men to shift their burdens and responsibilities to others; and so, perhaps, he has honored his faithful Chief of Police, by handing over to him his own lawful share of the national trait in question.

In the natural order of things, from an American point of view, the Czar should be the most suspicious person in Russia. That honor, however, undoubtedly belongs to His Imperial Majesty's deputy just mentioned. He is the Czar's watchdog. And just as a householder may dismiss all worry from his mind after giving his watchful bull-dog the run of his premises, so, within the measure of human fallibility, does the Czar resign his care.

Suspicion is, so to speak, the stock in trade of a police officer in any country, and when he figures as a cog in the wheels of a thorough-going autocracy his business is fairly to bristle with it. The usefulness of the Czar's Chief of Police depends on the amount of suspicion that is concentrated in his person and his alertness in putting it to active use. So efficient is Gen. Gresser in this particular that about 15,000 persons are sent away from St. Petersburg every year; and under his drastic administration the tourist who goes and peeps at Russia through Peter's window sees a city that creates a pleasant and favorable impression on his mind, and streets through which the Czar may drive without a guard.

From the chief of the Russian police to the humble moujik of a squalid hamlet on the steppes is a long jump, but suspicion seems as inherent in one as it is the necessary qualification of the other. And through every gradation of Russian society, official and unofficial, this baneful quality of the mind, thrusting itself on the writer's notice, weigh heavily in the balance against the better side of the national character.

Russia is a land of surprising contradiction, in character as in institutions. The autocrat is obeyed by a multitude of tiny republics (mirs), and in the average Russian you find a truly paradoxical character in which a warm, impulsive frankness links arms with an ever-present suspicion.

The figure that looms most prominently in my mind, apart from the fountain-head of the whole fabric at St. Petersburg, is, strange to say, perhaps, my equestrian companion, Sascha. He, in fact, carries off the honors and distinction of first attracting my attention to this very pronounced element in the character of his countrymen. Thrown in daily contact with him for several weeks, I came to understand him thoroughly, and through him got an "inside glimpse" of many things that would have escaped the observation of a foreigner traveling alone through the country.

Sascha was warm-hearted and impulsive as a child. Full of faults and contradictions, it was yet quite impossible to entertain harsh feelings toward him. From first to last he never ceased to regard me with suspicion whenever anything happened contrary to his preconceived ideas. In one of the villages between Count Tolstoï's estate and Orel he lost his passport. Ten hours later, after I had bribed a troublesome uriadnik to let him proceed without it to the next provincial government, he confessed in a burst of confidence that he had believed I destroyed his passport in order to get rid of him. All day he had nursed this suspicion, quite unsuspected by the victim of it at his side, who, at the end of that time, unwittingly cleared himself through bribing a policeman.

In this odd manner was discovered the traces of "color" that led up to the discovery of a veritable mine of the precious commodity that forms the subject of this chapter.

Like my horse, Texas, who had such a deep-rooted repugnance to wetting his feet that it required as much persuasion to get him into the last stream of the Crimea as the first one from Moscow, so Sascha persisted in the display of this Russian peculiarity to the end of our comradeship. Between the affair of the passport and my parting company with him at Kanseropol, there were perhaps a dozen trifling instances of ordinary and extraordinary affairs on the road, where I came under his suspicion. On no single occasion was there the faintest shadow of reason in it. This he was always quick to see and ready to admit in tones of self-reproach after the cloud had rolled by; yet when, at parting, I wished him to sign a receipt for money that I gave him to pay his way back home, his ridiculous suspicions immediately came again to the surface.

Though he understood that I only wanted something to prove to his people in Moscow that I had treated him fairly and liberally, in case anything should befall him, Sascha objected. And the reason he gave was singularly Russian.

" It is quite right," he said, " that you should have such a receipt."

" Then why do you hesitate about giving it ? "

" You will promise not to be offended if I tell you ? "

" Certainly."

" Well, then, with such a paper you could make me pay the money back again in Moscow ! "

When arranging for the trip in Moscow, Sascha's elder brother, a city merchant, had asked me to give him fifteen rubles a month spending money beyond expenses. I had been so well pleased with his intelligence and readiness to talk about Russian affairs as we rode along that I had given him fully three times the amount, besides which I had gained from him both admiration and respect. Yet the strange mistrust of his fellow-men, that seems to be latent in the heart of every Russian, obscured in a moment all our pleasant relationship and transformed me into a most uncomplimentary character.

This I pointed out, and Sascha, blushing with honest contrition, gave me the receipt without a moment's further hesitation. I was always rallying him about this side of his nature, but it was not to be dislodged either by ridicule or discomfiture. In an American, an Englishman, a German, this pertinacious suspicion would have called for resentment, but with the Russian it is plain as daylight that he is no more responsible for his suspicions than a crow is for being black.

And speaking of crows, since there are supposed to be white crows, it is fair to presume that there may also be such phenomena as unsuspicious Russians, though I should say one would be as rare a bird as the other.

Though I never lost patience with my companion on account of his absurd suspicions, there was a certain malicious delight in seeing him come daily under the suspicion of others. He never grew weary of relating to his countrymen that his companion had ridden around the world on a bicycle, and, though he never succeeded in getting one of them to believe it, he returned to the unequal combat on an average of three times a day. "*Eato na mozhet buet*" (Such a thing cannot be) was the answer he nearly always got, and any further attempt to explain away his auditor's suspicions only tended to increase them. His sole reward would be their admiration of what they considered his extraordinary abilities as a disciple of Munchausen, artistic lying being regarded in Russia as a valuable accomplishment.

Among the peasants, the suspicions of the people with whom we had dealings assumed many curious forms. In a general way we were always under the ban of suspicion ; primarily because we were strangers, and secondly, because we were strangers of an uncommon sort.

The recognized tendency of the densely ignorant to regard with suspicion anything they cannot understand, operated against us in every village we entered. Curiosity might greet us with a fair measure of hospitality to begin with, but suspicion was very sure to be close in its wake and would eventually come to the fore.

By the men we were suspected of being secret agents of the government, visiting them in the artful guise of passing travelers. By the women, whose dread of the Evil One was more palpable than their dread of government spies, we were suspected of being Antichrists, wizards, or " Cow Deaths."

One poor old soul is distinctly remembered among many others because of her innocent confidences. She didn't know what we might be, she confessed; as for her, she was very old and had nothing more to live for, so could very well be indifferent as to what might happen as a result of our visit.

She remembered, however, that two strangers, "very much like us," had ridden through the village during the war with the Turks; that three boys who had followed them down the road to call them names were never seen again. We took this as a powerful hint to deal gently with her grandchildren who were playing about near by, should we be meditating a supernatural visitation of any kind on the inhabitants of the place.

Another form of suspicion was equally amusing, though very annoying.

Whether we obtained accommodation over night with a rustic inn-keeper or a moujik, it seemed to be a most natural suspicion in the mind of our host that if not watched very closely we might clear out and leave him to whistle for his money. As a general thing, our entertainer would content himself with keeping a sharp eye on our movements from the earliest streak of dawn, and with presenting himself before us at the slightest movement toward saddling our horses. But others would reassure themselves with a sly peep at us once or twice during the night. So universal was this form of suspicion that the few rare exceptions shine out very prominently in my recollections of the journey.

The same trait is to be observed to advantage in Russian hotels. The waiters and chambermaids, instead of acting after the manner of the same class in England, who manage with considerable tact to " happen along " at your departure, in Russia commence hanging about for tips, like a pack of hungry dogs at feeding time, an hour before the traveler thinks of leaving. The explanation of the difference is that the lower orders of society in England have confidence in human nature, whereas the Russians are as distrustful as monkeys.

In addition to the suspicion of being " beats," we were frequently suspected of attempting to pass counterfeit money. Whether such paper is common in Russia the writer had no means of learning, but we were, all along, in the villages, suspected of having it in our possession and of attempting to pay our bills with it.

" What makes these people so long in bringing the change ? " was a query I put to Sascha, after the first few experiences in patient waiting.

" They are afraid the note is a counterfeit," he replied, " and are taking it to various people in the village for their opinion before bringing us the change."

"Well, the change is only thirty kopecks, we will not wait any longer; the cool of the morning will be frittered away."

"That must not be either," returned my companion, "or they will conclude at once that the bill is a bad one."

A curious phase of this particular suspicion was that the length of time we were kept waiting was in proportion to the denomination of the suspected bill. If it were only a two-ruble note, our suspicious host evidently would content himself with submitting it to the verdict of two or three other capable financiers, and would keep us waiting only ten or fifteen minutes. If a five-ruble note, however, he would take extraordinary precautions, probably getting the opinion of half the experts in the village, resulting in most exasperating delay for his guests.

Of the suspicions of the provincial police it is sufficient to say here that they assumed every conceivable form that the Russian mind could invent in connection with the appearance of a couple of strangers traveling in an extrordinary manner.

In Malo Russia the suspicions of the people multiplied, owing to a more polyglot population. In the North the villagers were all Orthodox Russians; in the South there is a mixed population of Russians, German colonists, Jews, Malo Russians, Cossacks, etc. There the Orthodox would suspect me of being a Molokani, or Stundist propagandist, with whom it would be dangerous to associate, and the sectarians suspected me of being an ecclesiastical spy.

The Jews were more suspicious than any of the others, particularly as the government was then venting on them one of its periodical fits of persecution.

The women of the better orders of society are by no means free from this unlovely trait. One morning, after an all-night ride in a train, I roused up from fitful snatches of sleep, indulged in sitting up, and bade a nice old lady on the other side of the car, whom I had conversed with the evening before, good-morning.

"Some one has stolen my watch in the night," she replied, holding up ruefully the chain that dangled from her bosom. Seeing that the snap was broken, I suggested that it was only lost under the seats. She shook her head, but acted on my suggestion, and immediately found the watch.

She and a young woman had slept on the same seats, which can be pulled out and used as a mattress, and missing her watch in the morning, she had, without a moment's reflection, suspected the young woman of robbing her. The idea that it might only be lost seemed not to have entered her head.

One cannot help laying the blame for this abnormal development of one of the most unlovely traits of human character to the pernicious influence of the system of government under which they live.

Suspicion and mutual distrust are the legitimate legacy that an autocratic government, which has to be suspicious in order to exist, transmits to the people. In short, it seemed to me simply a case of "like government, like people."

Indeed, it occurs to me, as I reach the end of this record of a journey of investigation, that most of the blemishes that deform the Russian character,—the suspicion of which the last few pages treat ; the corruption of the clergy ; the intellectual degradation of the peasants; the dishonesty of the mercantile element; the poverty of the masses; the drunkenness and improvidence, are mainly chargeable to the monstrous thing we call the Russian government. The people have naturally many admirable traits, which, if they were allowed to develop and expand, would enable them to put to shame many of their lofty and self-sufficient critics. They are charmingly simple, and free from the caddish affectation of superiority that disfigures the society of Western Europe, and in which America is not the least of the offenders. The Russian is by nature a " good fellow "; and it is agreeable to believe that by and by, when he is allowed to read newspapers, educate himself properly, and develop politically and religiously—in short, to be a man, and take charge of himself, instead of a child in the crib of a paternal government,—he will in time develop the sturdy virtues of manhood's estate, and take the place he ought to occupy in the brotherhood of civilized men.

THE END.